THE VAMPIRE AND THE CASE OF THE BALEFUL BANSHEE

HEATHER G. HARRIS & JILLEEN DOLBEARE

PUBLISHED BY HELLHOUND PRESS LIMITED

Copyright © 2024 by Heather G. Harris and Jilleen Dolbeare.

All rights reserved.

No portion of this book may be reproduced in any form without written permission from the publisher or author, except as permitted by U.S. copyright law.

Published by Hellhound Press Limited.

Cover Design by Christian Bentulan.

Firstly, we want to thank you, our readers. You have taken Portlock into your hearts, and we are forever grateful that you chose to join us on this wild adventure. We hope that Bunny will have many more escapades to come! Thank you for your unending support. We cherish you.

Secondly, thank you to our editor, Karen, our proofreader, Sara and our amazing Advance Readers Teams who are worth their weight in gold. Thank you to Alyse Gibbs who brings our books to life in the most amazing way.

Finally, thank you to our Patreons, with special mention to Mel, Amanda and Beba. Thanks to Jason who helps us get all the police details right, grounding this story in reality so you can enjoy it all the more.

You do so much for us Jas, we're so grateful.

Chapter 1

I woke when the world tilted sideways. The whole house was shaking and shuddering – and so was my undead heart.

'We're under attack!' I shouted in panic to my pets. Fluffy gave a low whine, though he didn't seem to be joining me on Team Freak-the-Fuck-Out. Shadow let out a yowl and disappeared under the bed. The bed! That seemed like a good option, actually.

And that's when my brain connected the dots...

I suddenly realised that I wasn't so much under attack, rather I was going through my first earthquake. Alaska is on an active tectonic plate boundary. I'd read about it – but it was a whole different thing to *experience* it.

'Doorways!' I barked to my dog. 'We're supposed to stand in doorways!'

You didn't need to tell Fluffy twice – he is the very best boy. In seconds, the two of us were braced against the wooden beams, waiting for this fresh hell to stop. Shadow stayed under the bed, and who could blame him? The earth was supposed to gently revolve, not shake me like a magic eight-ball that's providing a dissatisfying answer.

Finally, after what seemed like hours, the tremors stopped. I was being overdramatic – the whole thing didn't last long – but it was my first freaking earthquake and it seemed like a big deal to me.

I bit my lip. I should probably verify that it *was* an earthquake and not some pissed-off witches casting spells at my house.

The metal shutters around my home were closed, but my watch told me it was late afternoon so I called Sidnee. She'd be up and she'd know what the heck was going on.

'Sidnee,' I said breathlessly when she answered, 'was that an actual earthquake?' I sounded a teensy bit excited; now that it had stopped, I could get behind a new experience. It wasn't something that was going to happen often. Was it?

'Yup,' she agreed cheerfully. 'A good-sized one too. A 5.5.'

'That's the Richter scale, right?'

'That's the one, although now we say magnitude scale,' she chirped.

'I wonder what happened to Richter to make him so interested in categorising earthquakes,' I mused aloud.

'Maybe he got dropped on his head as a baby.' Sidnee's tone suggested that was the only way someone could possibly find such things interesting.

'During an earthquake?' I joked, making her snigger.

A 5.5. I searched my memory for a frame of reference, or so I could *add* a frame of reference. I recalled that every point on the earthquake scale indicated ten times the increase in power. Shit. A 5.5 had almost given me a heart attack; the shock of a 7 would probably kill me.

Sidnee sobered. 'Hey, are you okay? Any damage or anything?'

'No, I don't think so. There was a lot of shaking but nothing wiggled off my shelves. It's just that it was my first earthquake. It was scary for a minute,' I admitted.

'Of course it was,' she said softly. 'But we have them all the time, so you'll get used to them. Before you know it, they'll seem ordinary.'

'Great,' I muttered grumpily, not encouraged by the thought.

'Most are so small you barely feel them,' she added hastily. 'We've had two since you've been here and you didn't even notice!'

'Do you remember any bigger than a 5.5?' I couldn't quite hide my nervousness.

'Yeah, there was one about six years ago. It was wild. But apart from that one...' Then she added helpfully, 'Mind you, Alaska had the second biggest earthquake ever recorded, a 9.2. Of course, that was way before my time,'.

A 9.2? Jesus, I couldn't even imagine that. I hoped the quakes stayed sub-5; that would be scary but okay.

I could cope with that. 'I didn't know that and I wish I still didn't,' I said drily.

Her tinkling laugh made me smile. 'They'll seem ordinary soon. I promise.'

'They better. Talk to you later. I need to get ready for work. Thanks for reassuring me.'

'Anytime, Bunny.'

We rang off and almost immediately my phone rang: Connor. I swiped to answer. 'Hey.' His tone was casual. 'Just ringing to see if you're okay after the shake. That was a big one.'

I realised I was smiling. 'I'm fine. It took me a moment to work out what was going on, but then I was okay. Your call is well-timed – I just got off the line with Sidnee.'

There was a pause. 'I rang a couple of times but I couldn't get through. You guys can sure chat.'

I grinned. 'How many times did you try?'

He gave a barely audible sigh. 'I'm trying to play it cool,' he complained.

'Five?' I guessed.

'Seven,' he admitted.

My grin was now ear to ear. 'That's so cute. Thank you.'

'Cute?' He sounded outraged.

I laughed. 'Sorry, what I meant to say was "that was so manly and tough of you to dial repeatedly until you knew I was okay". Very tough.'

'Is this the right time to confess I'm panic-driving to your house because I couldn't get hold of you?'

'Well turn yourself back around! I have to get ready for work and I don't have time for distractions!'

His voice dropped an octave. 'Do I distract you, Bunny?'

'More than a fake shipwreck does a goldfish,' I said, entirely too honestly.

It was his turn to laugh. 'Good to know. Okay, if you're sure you're safe, I'll head to the council chambers. Speak soon.'

'You got it!' I hung up. *You got it?* Ugh. I was the least sexy thing since assless chaps were invented for cowboys. And now I was thinking of Connor in assless chaps and re-thinking their previous un-sexy status.

Shadow crept out from under the bed, his yellow eyes studying me. 'Hey, bud,' I said softly to the frightened lynx. 'It's all over. You can come out now.' He gave a plaintive squeak, darted over and climbed on my lap. I stroked his head for a minute until he nipped my finger to let me know he was done with being affectionate. Then he barrelled off in search of a mouse, or a box to climb into.

The calls and snuggles had made me late so I got ready lightning fast. I'd bought Shadow a little animal pram and a carry cage and, after a few minutes debate with myself, I persuaded him into it. He could come with me and wreak havoc at work; I didn't want him alone and scared if another earthquake came. Gunnar would be fine with it, I told myself. He was a dog person, which meant he was an animal person. A cat was an animal, so it would be fine. Logic.

When I walked in with the pram, the lynx and the dog, Sidnee was packing up her things. She flashed me an amused look. 'Is it bring your pet to work day?'

I sighed. 'I know. I'm ridiculous. But Shadow was really scared after the quake and I worried about leaving him all day. You think Gunnar will mind?'

'Not at all. Weird things were happening tonight. The cat will be the least of his worries.' She looked away. 'Trouble is stirring.'

That was ominous. My scalp prickled. 'Something else happened besides the earthquake?' I asked tentatively.

'Yeah. There's another protest going on at the barrier, and we've had tonnes of calls about people seeing it flashing. Gunnar had to call Liv to get her witches to check on it.'

I tried to inject some humour. 'You think the barrier needs some attention? What does a mooning barrier look like?'

Sidnee rolled her eyes. 'Stick to crime. Stand-up is not your forte.'

I held a hand to my heart. 'You slay me.'

'Not yet,' she said drily, 'but I'll be tempted to if the dad jokes continue.'

She was teasing but there was a tension in her that had been there ever since her boyfriend Chris had betrayed and abandoned her. She was dealing with it, but slowly and badly; mostly she was shoving it in a box and ignoring it, like I would have done. It might not have been the healthiest coping mechanism but I didn't have another solution to offer. I was there for her; when she was ready to talk, I'd be there to listen.

'Gunnar had to call Liv? Does that mean he's in a bad mood?' I asked.

'Yes, he is,' Gunnar bellowed from his office.

I grimaced. 'Oops.'

Looking a little less strained, Sidnee grinned. 'Wanna meet for lunch later?'

We often ate out together for my lunch, which was her supper. I was pleased she'd asked because she'd shot me down the last few times I'd invited her.

'Absolutely. Garden of Eat'n?'

'Yeah, the usual.'

'See you then!' Sidnee gave Fluffy a quick kiss on his head and strolled out of the building.

I settled my dog on his bed next to my desk and smiled when Shadow curled up beside him, then I checked on what Sidnee had left for me, readying myself for the long list of phone calls the Nomo's office received. I'd had the bright idea of putting one of our numbers in the local paper as a 'hotline' number and now we got dozens of calls about stupid stuff.

The hotline had originally been for sightings of fisheye; a drug that some black-ops government agency had experimented with in our town, but now people used it to complain about keelut sightings or – apparently – flashing barriers. The fisheye tips had pretty much dried up even though the majority of the perpetrators, including Chris, were still at large.

I went to make myself a cup of tea and Gunnar a conciliatory coffee, but the phone rang before the water was even warm. Let the deluge commence.

Chapter 2

I jogged back to my desk to answer the phone. 'Nomo. This is Officer Barrington.'

'Hey, what's up, doc? It's Stan.' I let the Bugs Bunny joke slide since he carried on talking and his tone was brisk. 'I'm at the corner by the mayor's office. The barrier protestors are getting agitated. They're blocking the road and access to local businesses. It's probably time to come by.'

I looked longingly at the kitchen: no tea for me. 'Thanks. I'm on my way.'

I hung up, stuffed Shadow in his carrier so he couldn't run loose around the office and gave him an apologetic kiss that he clearly didn't accept. I retrieved the black bag from the back room and put Fluffy's K-9 vest on him; my German Shepherd would be an asset in rounding up protestors if they got out of hand.

Next I popped my head into Gunnar's office. 'The protestors are getting unruly. I'm going to go and visibly be the law.'

Gunnar had had two close calls with fisheye and was still recovering. His wife, Sig, had him parked at a desk so at the moment I was handling anything physical.

I could see he was wrestling with himself. He wanted to come with me, but if Sig heard he'd be sleeping on the sofa for a week. 'Take the megaphone. If it looks even a little violent, you call me for back-up.' His tone brooked no argument. 'Strong as you are, you can't handle twenty or thirty protestors by yourself if things get messy.'

'Will do – though Stan is there to help.' I paused. 'Oh, and the lynx cat we rescued is in the office. See you later.' I dashed out before he could reply.

I grabbed the megaphone, clipped on Fluffy's lead and headed out. It wasn't far. When we arrived, it was less of a protest and more of a mob. People were throwing insults and there was some argy-bargy going on; we were minutes from punches being thrown. I should have called Gunnar but I didn't.

'This is a mess,' I said to Fluffy. He barked agreement.

I clicked on the megaphone. 'This is the Nomo's office. You are ordered to disperse.' There was a little shriek of feedback – then a rock came soaring at my head. 'Motherfucker,' I swore as I ducked. Fluffy growled loudly.

No more Miss Nice Girl. This time, I hit the siren feature on the megaphone. After it howled for thirty seconds, I tried again. 'This is the Nomo's office. You will cease and desist or I'll start arresting people.'

A few listened and drifted off, but the majority of the protestors stayed put, determined to stick it to The Man. The citizens who were upset by the protest also remained and the yelling continued. Despite my instructions, they were neither ceasing nor desisting.

I got out my phone and took photos of the protestors. After all this was over, I could ID them if we needed to. Then I sidled up to Stan. 'Do you know who the ringleaders are?'

'Your main men are Ezra, Maverick, and Grayson.' Stan pointed to three men spread through the mob, each visibly stirring the pot and riling the crowd.

Stan and me against thirty protestors wasn't good odds. I needed backup but I didn't want Gunnar to be it, so I texted Sidnee. Hopefully she'd barely had time to get home and sit down, and she'd still be dressed for work. If she saw the message, she'd be here in minutes. She was my best option: that's what I'd say to Gunnar later when he bitched at me for not calling *him*.

'All right,' I said. 'I'll go for Ezra. You get Maverick. Whoever is free next gets Grayson. Hopefully nabbing those three will calm things down.' Or it would light a fuse to a powder keg. I handed Stan some flexi cuffs from my trusty black bag. 'I've contacted Sidnee. Hopefully between the three of us we can get this situation under control ASAP. Okay?'

'You got it.' Stan mock saluted me and waded into the crowd. I went the opposite way towards Ezra.

He was tall, muscular, blond and dressed neatly compared to a lot of the protestors; if it hadn't been for the sour expression on his face, he'd have been handsome. Fluffy stuck to me like glue and I used the microphone again to set off the siren sound. The people nearest clutched their ears and glared at me. Look at me making friends.

'You're disturbing the peace,' I said loudly to Ezra. 'Disperse, or I'll take you down.'

His eyes flicked up and down me, making my insides squirm, then he raised an eyebrow and smirked. 'You and whose army, babe?'

I moved lightning fast and had him on the ground with his hands cuffed behind his back before he could blink. Vampire speed had its advantages – that and Gunnar's hours of training. Getting someone down safely was a big deal, but after practising felling my boss, Ezra was a breeze.

His little cohort was gaping at me. 'Fanged Flopsy,' one of them whispered loudly. I glared at the ridiculous nickname then took advantage of their dismay. 'Leave!' I barked. They turned tail and scarpered, leaving me with Ezra. Lucky guy.

I hauled him to his feet. The smirk was gone and he glared at me. 'You can't do this! I have rights.'

'You have the right to protest peacefully,' I agreed. 'But you were inciting violence and there's a difference.' I tugged him towards the Nomo vehicle. He clearly intended to drag his heels but Fluffy growled sharply and he rapidly changed his mind.

I was shoving him in the SUV as Stan appeared with two other men in tow. 'Show off,' I muttered.

Stan smirked and sent me a blinding smile. Stupid sharp supernatural hearing.

With the three ringleaders taken care of, the protest died a rapid death. Sidnee rocked up looking glum. 'Looks like things are cooling down. Colour me disappointed.'

'Sorry to have hauled you out for nothing,' I apologised. 'I was worried taking these three down would stoke the fires.'

'No biggy. It could have gone the other way. For what it's worth, I'm glad it went this way.'

'You can't do this! This is still America,' a greasy-looking man objected. His white T-shirt was decorated a handwritten word, *BARRIER*, surrounded by a red circle with a slash through it. It was covered with the remnants of his last meal.

'Shut up, Grayson,' Stan rebuked him.

'You are entitled to peaceful protests, not brawling in the streets,' I told him.

I secured the three men in the back then closed the door so I could talk to Stan and Sidnee without being overheard. 'What do we do with them?' I asked. 'We could arrest them, but I think that will add more fuel to the protestors' fire.'

Stan shrugged. 'Removing them de-escalated the situation. It was the right call,' he said approvingly. 'I'd say giving them a verbal warning and letting them go is also the right call. Tension is ramping up, and a lot of it is over the expense of the barrier. This is something the council will need to address sooner rather than later. I'll raise it – but everyone has their own agenda.'

Wasn't that God's own truth? In a town full of every type of supernatural, was it any wonder that tempers were reaching boiling point? I hoped we could cool things down before the inevitable explosion came.

Chapter 3

Having let the three ringleaders go with a warning, I returned to the office. I was amused to see Shadow curled up in Gunnar's lap, his happy purr filling the office.

Yet again Sidnee cancelled our lunch date. I could hardly blame her after I'd hauled her out after hours but I couldn't deny the sting of disappointment; I'd been really looking forward to seeing my bestie. Although I knew she was dealing with a lot of crap, I missed my friend. Even though I'd only had a friend for such a short while, I'd grown accustomed to having someone to laugh and joke with. Things were a little flat without Sidnee in my life.

I showed Gunnar the photographs and he gave me a list of names for the protestors that he recognised. We made an unofficial file and I attached the photographs, ready to start to build a case if one was needed.

The phone rang yet again. I answered, feeling a hot lick of foreboding in my tummy. The caller didn't identify himself but went straight into it. That was always a bad sign. 'Someone needs to come to...' The man rattled off an address, his tone urgent and slightly panicked.

'What's the issue?' I asked, pen poised.

'We've had a break-in. Tell Gunnar that the fire gemstone has been stolen! Hurry!' He hung up. What was it with these people and hanging up after only giving the most minor details? I grumpily scrawled down the address, not because I couldn't remember it but for the official records. Contemporaneous notes were important in legal cases.

I knocked on Gunnar's door before entering. 'Someone called and said the fire gemstone has been stolen,' I announced.

All the colour drained from Gunnar's usually ruddy face. 'Fuck,' he said. I blinked; it was rare for him to swear.

'What does it mean?' I asked. 'Why is the gemstone a big deal?'

'For one, it's cursed. For two, it powers the barrier.'

'Fuck.'

'Indeed. We can talk in the truck.' He stood up. 'Get Fluffy's vest, I'll put Shadow in his carrier while we're out.' He gently cradled the sleeping kitten.

I did as I was told. The theft was definitely a big deal if Gunnar was risking Sig's wrath by going out. I secured Fluffy's K-9 vest, Gunnar put some food and water in Shadow's crate and we headed out back.

'Won't you be in trouble with Sig?' I asked nosily.

'She'll understand,' he grunted.

'You want the address?'

'Don't need it. I know where to go.' He was being laconic, a sure sign he was stressed. Since he'd been sick, he'd been delegating more and more to me; the fact that he was out on the road with me told me how serious this was. That and the fact he was white-knuckling the steering wheel.

'There are four cursed objects that keep the barrier up around Portlock,' Gunnar told me. 'They are placed in four key places, and each one is guarded by one of four of the supernatural groups in town. The fire gem is guarded by the vampires, the water gem by the magic users, the earth gem by the water shifters, and the wind gem by the land shifters.'

Uh-oh: now I had some context for the panicked call. The fire gem – one quarter of the magical gemstones powering the barrier – had been stolen. 'Is the barrier going to fail?' I could hear the quiver in my voice.

'No, it'll take more than that, but it'll be impossible to strengthen it to its full force until we can return the fire gem to its place.'

That was something: death by barrier monster wasn't imminent, though it felt like only a temporary reprieve. For the last few weeks Liv had been dashing about like a mad woman shoring up places where the barrier had thinned, been ripped or otherwise damaged. It seemed undeniable: someone was deliberately trying to bring it down.

We pulled up to a single-storey log cabin that was almost invisible in the trees. Next to the house, behind a couple of other vehicles, was a familiar white truck with Kamluck Logging on the side: Connor. Of course he'd be there: the fire gem was the vampires' responsibility and it had been taken on his watch. I winced. He was going to be pissed off.

Despite knowing that, I still had butterflies flitting around my stomach at the thought of seeing him. The butterflies didn't get how serious the gem thing was.

Connor and I – we were complicated. We hadn't been able to get around to our planned date out of town yet, but there was something between us that was so strong that it felt almost inevitable. Even so, I still wasn't quite sure how to act around him. I craved him even more than my morning brew, and the one kiss we'd shared had been *fire*. I'd thought about that kiss more than was healthy, replaying the moment with my blessedly sharp memory.

Every time we accidentally touched, it was electric. Literally. There was a little zing between us that Connor had promised to explain on our date. My curiosity was killing me, and since I wasn't quite sure when the date would be, I'd taken to snooping through Gunnar's books to find out more about that little electric flash. So far no dice, but it wasn't for want of trying.

As always, Connor's curly hair was tousled and he was dressed in jeans, boots and flannel. I had recently discovered that I had a thing for flannel. Despite the seriousness of the moment, he gave me a lopsided smile that heated me in all sorts of interesting places.

'Hey,' I greeted him, my voice a little too seductive for a scene of a crime. I cleared my throat. 'Hey,' I tried again.

His smile widened. 'I preferred the first one.'

'Any signs of the intruder?' Gunnar interrupted our flirtation.

I already knew the answer: Connor wouldn't be making eyes at me if the thief was still around. 'None,' he confirmed, turning businesslike.

As we walked up to the front porch, Connor moved next to me, not touching but close enough to feel like I could touch him if I wanted to. I wanted to but it wasn't professional, so I didn't.

Gunnar knocked on the solid front door.

Before it opened an explosion rocked us. We all ducked instinctively. It hadn't come from the property but a few blocks away. A plume of fire and smoke was already rising. Gunnar was visibly torn.

'I'll stay here,' Connor offered. 'You two go to the explosion.' Gunnar clapped him on the shoulder and we ran back to the SUV.

'What blew up?' I wondered aloud, after my ears cleared. I didn't think there was a factory or a business anywhere in this area that would cause such a violent explosion.

'Let's go see,' Gunnar replied, and we took off to where we could see flames broiling and smoke rising. It was only three blocks away so we arrived in record time. We parked at a safe distance from a house that was a total shambles and burning swiftly.

I jumped out of the car to see if there was anyone to save, but as I walked towards the house the heat hit me like a truck. The fire was already burning so hot – too hot? Something in my gut awoke and stirred, and suddenly I yearned to add to the fire.

I watched the flames dance and crackle: they were majestic, hypnotic.

Gunnar snagged my wrist, breaking the moment. I took a deep breath and willed the heat in my stomach to go away. 'There's nothing we can do right now,' he said regretfully. He was right. Thankfully the fire engines' sirens were already audible.

Neighbours were gathering at a safe distance, gawking. 'Does anyone know who lived here?' I yelled.

'It was empty,' a man called back. 'The family moved to Anchorage last month. They had it up for rent.'

Empty. Thank God. Knowing no one was dying in the flames, I relaxed a little. I looked at Gunnar. 'I wonder what caused the fire?'

He shook his head. 'No idea. Gas, maybe?'

That made me smile faintly. When I'd accidentally-on-purpose set my house on fire, I'd blamed it on a gas explosion, too.

I was still keeping my fire magic under wraps – even from Connor. He knew though that I was a different kind of vampire. Yay: I was back to the label I'd borne most of my life. Lucky me.

The fire engines screamed in and the fire officers piled out. In minutes they'd ascertained that no one was in the property, they had a hose aimed at the flames and the true battle began.

Gunnar approached the fire chief. 'Let me know what you find about the cause of the fire.'

The chief nodded amiably. 'I'll copy you in on my report, though I'm going to say that this fire is too hot to be natural. It was started by magical means.'

In my head I pictured the poison witch, Shirley, and her fireballs. And me with mine.

'Appreciate that.' Gunnar turned to me. 'Since they don't need us here, let's head back to the other situation.' He was clearly choosing his words carefully in front of the fire chief; he didn't want to start mass panic about the jewel theft.

When we climbed into the Nomo vehicle, Fluffy whined a little and gave me a glare. 'Sorry we left you, bud,' I told him. 'No one lived there, so it's okay.' He gave a sharp bark and a doggy grin. I was forgiven. Dogs are the best.

We drove back to the break-in and this time we actually made it into the log house. Progress. One step forward: here's hoping it wasn't followed by two steps back.

Chapter 4

Connor opened the door and paused for a second, sweeping me over for signs of injury or distress. Finding none, he turned back to business. 'What was the explosion?'

'A house a couple of blocks over. No one was in it,' Gunnar confirmed.

'Well, that's something at least.' Connor stepped back and let us in.

'You okay?' I asked softly.

His jaw was tight with tension. 'I've been better,' he murmured, letting Gunnar take point ahead of us so we could talk privately. 'The fire gem has been stolen on my watch. It's not a good look.'

I reached out and squeezed his hand. 'We'll get it back.'

He flashed me a grim smile. 'Damn right we will.' He didn't say that heads would roll, but that was definitely the vibe I was getting. The perpetrator better hope we found them before Connor did.

'What happened?' I asked.

'The fire elemental witch lost the damned stone.' Connor couldn't keep the anger and frustration out of his voice. Maybe he wasn't even trying to.

'They *lost* it?'

'It got taken,' Connor conceded. 'Supposedly. I'll let you make up your own mind. Come and meet Kos.' It was clear that he knew the witch well, and I tried to suppress a twinge of jealousy.

'Is the witch unharmed?' I asked as he showed me into a room where a man was sitting. Huh, the witch was a *dude*. For some reason the label 'witch' still made me think female, even though I knew men could be witches. Popular culture has a lot to answer for.

Kos looked downright miserable. He was dressed in a conservative light-blue, button-down shirt with a red bow tie; the shirt was tucked neatly into a pair of navy-blue corduroy trousers with red suspenders. His dark hair was slicked back and he was wearing trendy, red-framed glasses. He looked like he was everyone's favourite schoolteacher.

Next to him was Connor's new second, Lee Margrave, who'd taken the job after Juan Torres had been killed. Margrave looked like a tough guy: the scar down his face gave that impression even without his bulk, and with his huge muscles he looked like someone to avoid. Next to the neatly presented witch, he looked downright evil. If he were in a Disney film, his background colour would have been green.

Kos was staring into space. His eyes refocused, then he looked at Gunnar wide-eyed and panicked. 'It's gone.' He started wringing his hands. He seemed surprised, as though he'd discovered it this instant and couldn't quite believe it. I recognised his voice: this was the man who'd called the theft into the office.

Gunnar looked at me and jerked his head towards Kos; apparently this was my show. Fuck: I didn't want this to be my show – I needed to start with some smaller shows like Punch and Judy. That was more my level.

I'd enjoyed leading the investigation when Gunnar was in hospital and relished the challenge, but this was the gemstone that could lead to the whole barrier falling. This shit wasn't for amateurs, but evidently Gunnar had decided I wasn't one. I appreciated the vote of confidence even though he was totally wrong.

'Right.' I cleared my throat. 'I'm Officer Bunny Barrington.'

'Bunny?' The witch looked down his nose at me. 'How did you get a name like that?'

'At my birth, a seer gave a prophecy about my life,' I lied. 'My mum was so high on gas and air that she couldn't remember anything other than the word "Bunny".' I gave a light shrug. 'And what's your name?'

The witch looked at Gunnar with irritation, but when my boss glared a little he turned back to me. 'Kostas Spencer.'

'Can you tell me what happened, Kostas?'

He looked at me and then at Gunnar again. Gunnar was standing slightly behind me with his arms crossed. He gave a firm head tilt towards me.

'Well, I went to work, and when I came home I checked on the box that held the fire gem as I do twice a day,' the witch said. 'That is – *was* – my job and responsibility for the magic users group. But today it wasn't there.'

'The box, the gem or both?' 'Both.'

I nodded. 'It was there this morning?'

'Yes. I checked on it before work, same as always.'

'What time did you go to work?'

'Seven forty-five, same as always.'

I wondered if he would answer every question with 'same as always'. Should I tell him that it was extremely annoying? 'Where do you work?'

'I do the books at Kamluck Logging.'

Same as always, I added mentally. I estimated he had a fifteen-minute commute. Not far. 'Did you come home for lunch?'

'I do sometimes, but not today.' He looked miserable and his shoulders sagged; I wondered if he was about to break down and cry. I'd cry too if I had to tell Liv I'd lost something so important to the magic users.

I pushed on. 'When did you get home?'

He cleared his throat. 'Five-fifteen, same as always.'

The 'same as always' was back – I'd almost missed it. 'Was anything else missing?'

'I–I haven't really looked. I freaked out a little and called Mr Mackenzie and then the Nomo's office.'

'That's fine. We'll go through the house with you and you can point out anything that is out of place or missing. Can you do that?'

He took a deep breath. 'Yes.'

'Good. First, show us where the stone was kept.'

Kostas appeared a little calmer now that he had a focus. He went to a walk-in closet in the corner and opened it. There was nothing inside it, save for a carved stone pedestal that looked like it weighed more than I did. The plinth was wholly incongruous in those surroundings. 'This is where it was held,' Kostas confirmed.

I made a move to lean in. 'Stay back!' he hissed, holding out a hand to stall me. 'I haven't dropped the wards.'

I frowned but let him push me back. If the wards were still active, how did someone steal the gem? I looked at Gunnar, who shrugged; he was frowning too. I reached up absently to scratch at my scalp, which felt itchy. If I had head lice, I'd die of embarrassment.

Kostas stood back so we could examine the area without touching the wards. I took several pictures then looked at the door lock. It wasn't fancy; in fact, even without any training in lock-picking, I bet I could get in the closet in under five minutes with a credit card or a hairpin – as long as the wards didn't fry me. Though given how jittery Kostas was, they would probably fry me sunny-side up.

Gunnar and I searched the whole place with Fluffy's help as Kostas looked for anything out of place or missing. When we moved further away from the closet, the itching in my scalp stopped abruptly. Was I allergic to something in that area?

We found nothing; nothing was out of place or missing except for the box containing the fire gem. After we'd searched the modest home, we stood by

Kostas as he carefully lowered the wards around the pedestal. He was sweating the whole time, and he swayed as they fell. The faint itching on my scalp stopped. Huh: could I somehow sense wards? *Focus, Bunny!* I told myself. *This gemstone shit is a big deal. Worry about sensing wards later.*

'How close to the fire gem do the wards get?' I asked.

'They are only on the perimeter of the closet,' Kostas said. 'They're gone now. You can enter safely.'

Before I could go in, Fluffy barrelled forwards. I shouted, but luckily he didn't come to any harm. Silly pup, risking himself like that. Thank goodness the wards really *were* down.

He sniffed pointedly around the podium and the floor, gave two decisive barks and looked at me excitedly. He'd found a scent that wasn't Kostas's! 'Where does it go?' I asked urgently.

My boy put his nose to the floor, sniffed a few steps forward then stopped looking confused. He did that three times: got the scent, pointed and then ... nothing. 'Can supernats mask their scent?' I asked.

'He's definitely finding something new and then it disappears.'

'It's possible,' Gunnar confirmed.

'But pricey,' Kostas interjected. 'Very pricey. No one up to anything good needs that potion. It's difficult to make and even harder to buy – just finding the black market is tricky.'

'Do *you* know where it is?'

He shook his head. 'I've never been, though I know it exists.'

I made a note to ask Gunnar about it later. Still, a potion being difficult to acquire didn't rule it out; difficult wasn't impossible. 'Can anyone else drop or replace the wards?' I asked.

'No. I'd know. The wards I lowered were mine, and nothing or no one had touched them.'

Well, wasn't that a head scratcher?

'How often do you reset them?' Gunnar probed.

'Every few weeks.'

'When did you last do it?' I asked.

'This morning,' he admitted.

I gave him a flat look; that was clearly relevant yet he hadn't volunteered the information. Somehow someone had slipped in between the time he'd lowered and reset the wards: a quick theft but not an impossible one. And that still didn't tell us why Fluffy couldn't scent the intruder. Still, it was a starting point.

'Who knows your warding routine?' I demanded.

He gave a one-shouldered shrug. 'No one, but I suppose someone could make an educated guess when I bought the various ingredients for a warding as powerful as this.'

'Does anyone have a key to this place?'

He drew himself up prissily. 'Obviously not. I take my role as the gem guardian very seriously.'

Not seriously enough. The uncharitable thought slipped out and I knew it was unfair. He'd warded the place to high heaven. What else could he have done besides live in a secret underground bunker?

'The wards,' I started. 'Did you have to kill something to power them?' Maybe someone was mad at him for killing their pet chicken called Clive. Maybe this was all some sort of petty retribution rather than a sinister plot to bring down the barrier and doom us all. Yeah, right.

He gave me a look of abject horror mixed with affront. 'I'm a *witch,* not a necromancer!'

Having mortally offended him, I turned my attention back to the plinth but saw nothing that could be considered a clue. Gunnar dusted it and the closet doorknob for prints while I rolled the carpet around the podium with a tape roller to see if there were any stray hairs. I covered the roller with plastic wrap and tucked it in a bag to check when we got back to the office.

'Can you describe the box and the gem?' I asked Kostas.

'It's metal, about this big.' He indicated a foot square with his hands. 'The fire gem is a brilliant-cut ruby about the size of my fist.'

My eyes flew wide open; not only was the stone part of our barrier protection system, it was also extremely valuable. The motivation for the theft might have nothing to do with the barrier.

Gunnar took fingerprints on both front and rear doors, neither of which showed signs of forced entry. Either our suspect was a ghost or they'd unlocked doors with magic – which was entirely possible in this town. My boss was an expert at that particular trick, and I doubted he was the only one.

We left with a few prints, some forensics from the carpet and a lot of questions. How the heck had the thief got in? And what was their motivation for stealing the huge ruby? Was someone focused on a big payday or the wanton destruction of us all?

I prayed that it was the former.

Chapter 5

Whilst we worked the scene, Connor had kept a respectful distance and forced Margrave to do the same. When we were done, he followed us out to the Nomo vehicle. 'Any thoughts?' Gunnar asked him.

Connor ran his fingers through his unruly hair. 'No signs of forced entry. I'm leaning towards the idea it was someone Kos knew. They got a key somehow, knew about the wards being redone. I keep coming back to those protesters. They want the barrier down and stealing one of the gems that powers it is a sure-fire way to do it.'

The protestors were upset because it cost them money to pay the magic users who kept the barrier powered up and working properly. Several members of the community thought it was exploitative; they believed the Portlock monster was a myth or a superstition, that if it had once existed it no longer did. The barrier was just a good earner for the magic users.

They were totally wrong. Gunnar, Thomas and I had gone through the barrier looking for two missing hunters, and though we'd found them they hadn't come back alive. The beast beyond the barrier had seen to that. I still had nightmares about thick, cloying, black smoke pouring through the tear...

A chill ran down my spine at the thought of the barrier failing. We needed to find the gem, and we needed to make sure none of the other gems were stolen. 'Can you make sure the remaining gemstones are heavily guarded?' I asked Connor.

His jaw tightened. 'You think they'll go after another one?'

'Maybe someone wants a huge ruby to sell – but if not, it doesn't bear thinking about. We can't lose *two* gems. The barrier can't fail.' No doubt the fear was showing in my eyes.

He gave my shoulder a reassuring squeeze. 'I'll see to it.'

'Good. In the meantime, we'll look into the protestors,' Gunnar said. 'Time for some basic police work, hitting the pavement to try to round up a suspect.' He climbed into the SUV as I let Fluffy onto the back seat.

I'd already placed my hand on the passenger door when Connor called my name. 'Bunny, be careful. If someone is going this far to bring down the barrier, who knows where they'll stop?'

'I'll be fine. I'm undead already.' I sent him a cheeky wink.

He shook his head slowly. 'You might not be,' he murmured quietly. 'You have a pulse.'

'Yeah. Anything new on that front?' I tried not to sound hopeful. Connor had found nothing in his personal files so he'd started searching through other resources, but I didn't know what those were.

'Nothing yet, sorry.'

'No problem,' I lied.

He leaned into me and the electricity between us was like a lightning storm. His eyes were dark, more night sky than their usual ice blue. 'Be safe, little doe. I couldn't stand it if anything happened to you.' His warm lips brushed my cheek and my brain short-circuited.

'Does are deer,' I blurted. 'There's even a song about it.'

He gave me a lazy smile which warmed my insides. 'Does are also female rabbits. Bucks are male rabbits.'

'You're a fount of useless information.'

His smile widened. 'After a few centuries, you'd be surprised at the nonsense your brain chooses to remember. And what it chooses to forget.' His eyes looked deeply into mine. 'I could live a millennium and I still wouldn't forget you.' With that parting shot, he sauntered back to the house leaving me clinging to the car to stand upright. The man made me weak at the knees in the very best way.

I forced my mind to focus. *Think about the case. You can think about Connor later.* I opened the car door and climbed in. Gunnar was looking amused and my cheeks warmed. 'Sorry,' I muttered.

He turned on the engine. 'No problem.' His smile faded. 'Just … be careful with him, won't you?'

It wasn't the first time Gunnar had hinted a warning about Connor, but unfortunately all it did was push me further into Connor's arms. Give me a bad boy any day of the week; make him a *forbidden* one and I was a goner.

'I will,' I lied airily. I looked around for a way to change the subject and my eyes alighted on Fluffy. I was sure he had scented the thief when he'd whined in the closet with his nose to the rock pillar. He hadn't been able to track them out, but maybe we could use the scent in another way. 'Gunnar, if we call in each protestor for an interview, maybe Fluffy can sniff them and identify the thief.'

'It's worth a shot. We need to interview them all anyway, so we might as well give Fluffy the chance to get up close and personal at the same time.'

'Nothing says hello like a sniff in the crotch.'

Gunnar laughed. 'Don't say that to Liv,' he muttered.

'Agreed. She doesn't need any encouragement to try and get her face in your crotch.' The words slipped out and he grimaced. I instantly wished I could call them back.

Since we were on the topic of Liv... 'Do you think we should call her about the fire gem?' As the head of the magic users' group, she was the most logical next call.

'She already knows all about it – that witch probably called her first. I wouldn't be surprised if she's waiting at the office.' We were silent for the rest of the drive, both wondering if his prediction would turn out to be true.

I was disappointed that there was no sign of Liv when we parked out back; I always prefer to get an unpleasant task over and done with.

When we got into the office, Shadow let out a plaintive yowl from his carrier. I obligingly opened the door and he pointedly turned around, giving me his back and refusing to come out.

'A moment ago you were yowling to be let out,' I sassed, 'and now you're staying in to spite me. I thought *I* was contrary.' I rolled my eyes at him then turned to Gunnar. 'I've got our list of protesters. I'll start calling them in for interview.'

'Great. No doubt Liv will be by soon.'

Almost like magic, the front door opened and we both looked at it expectantly but it wasn't Liv: it was Stan. He gave me a slightly too-warm smile then he and Gunnar did a manly hug thing. Gunnar drifted back to his office, not so subtly giving us some privacy. It was entirely clear whom he would prefer me to date.

Stan and I had gone out on one-and-a-half dates already. They had been okay but had lacked the spark I craved. I'd finally had to tell him that I thought of him more like a brother. Stan was a great guy, but – he wasn't Connor.

'Hi, Stan,' I greeted the shifter leader, keeping my tone professional. 'Thanks for the help with the protestors.'

'Bunny.' He tempered the smile a little then it brightened when he remembered something. His eyes twinkled with mischief. 'Why did the rabbit pursue a career in stand-up comedy?'

When I'd shot Stan down on the dating front, he'd promised that he would stop pursuing me but that he'd also subject me to a raft of bunny-related jokes. I sighed. I knew this one. 'Because she's very *bunny*.'

Stan grinned. 'Next time I'll get you with one you don't already know.'

I doubted it; I'd heard them all. 'I can't wait,' I said drily. 'What brings you in tonight?'

His face grew serious, which was rare. 'Connor rang about the fire gem theft. He was annoyingly close-mouthed about the circumstances, but the land shifters guard the wind gemstone. Is there anything I need to know about the break-in?'

'Well for one thing, it doesn't appear to be a break-in. No signs of forced entry.'

Some tension left his shoulders. 'So it was probably a one-off insider job.'

'Maybe. It feels too coincidental that there was a huge barrier protest around the time the gem was stolen. Anti-barrier sentiment is rising. At this stage we can only surmise the intentions of the thief, but my gut says to put more shifters on patrol and tell the other groups to do the same as well.'

He nodded and leaned on the counter. 'Good advice, Bunny.' Ugh: Portlock politics. Connor had already rung Stan to say exactly the same thing, yet here he was wanting to hear it directly from the horse's mouth.

I sat at my desk and pulled out a notepad. 'Since I've got you here, talk to me about the stone. What is the wind gem, and is it kept in a metal box about a foot square?'

Stan laughed. 'You're always working, aren't you, Bunny? All work and no play make for a dull day.'

'I'm on shift,' I said drily, 'and I play plenty.' *Just not with you.* 'The gem?'

'It's a diamond about the size of your fist.' Measuring things by fist size wasn't totally accurate because Stan's fist and mine were very different. He had huge paws.

'Has the gem been cut?'

'I'm not an expert on precious stones, but yeah, I'd say so. I saw it once. It was very sparkly.'

'Any idea what it's worth?'

He shook his head. 'No idea, but it's priceless to us.'

Good point. Any Portlockian would value the jewel highly, but I suspected an outsider would think it had significant monetary worth. The British crown had some large, spectacular diamonds and they were worth several billion. If this diamond was the size of a fist, had been cut and had few inclusions, it could be worth billions, too.

I wondered how much the ruby was worth. I'd never heard of one as big as the fire gem, but I had no doubt it was millions.

I looked at my file of protestors. 'I have a couple of people that I haven't managed to ID. Gunnar knew most – the repeat offenders – but not all of them. Do you know these guys?' I pointed to the few unknowns.

'That's Flynn, he's in the siren group.' He tapped the next guy. 'That's Howard. He's a vamp. The last guy is Snow. He's one of mine.'

'Your impressions of him?'

'He works for me. He's a hard worker and I trust him, even if he hates paying his taxes.'

'Shifter type?' I pushed.

Stan's lips pressed into a line. It wasn't the done thing to share things like that with non-shifters but it was relevant. If Snow could become a mouse, maybe he could wriggle undetected into the witch's house.

'He's a moose,' Stan looked uncomfortable at divulging the information and he swiftly changed the topic. 'How about a trip to Homer for a movie? Just as friends,' he tacked on when he saw me stiffen. He held up his hands. 'We could ask Sidnee to come, too.'

'I do love the movies,' I admitted, 'but I can't leave Portlock right now. The gem has to be my priority.'

'No problem. We can go another time when there isn't an emergency.' He snickered even as he said it; we both know emergencies happened on a frustratingly regular basis here.

Stan headed out. He was right: if I waited for things to be calm, I'd never go to the cinema. Even so, I didn't think it was a good idea to go with Stan because I was still worried he'd get the wrong idea. His smile had been a little too bright when he saw me and, although he'd been nothing but friendly, I wasn't sure his crush on me had died a death yet. Why were things so complicated?

I leaned down and thunked my head against the desk a couple of times. I was still thunking when Liv breezed in.

Chapter 6

'Trying to knock some sense into yourself?' she asked derisively.

Charming. I straightened up. 'Liv, how lovely—'

She held up a hand to silence me. 'Is he in his office?'

'Yup.' Poor schmuck.

She swept to Gunnar's office like she owned the place – and I wasn't about to stop her. The whole place warmed a degree or two as she left a hot desert wind in her wake; it was creepy as fuck. Even Fluffy laid down as low and flat as he could. I put a hand down to pat him. 'I know,' I murmured. 'She's scary.'

Shadow chose that moment to leap onto my lap, presumably to view the scary woman. I ran my hand over his silky fur. He had grown a little, and his smoky coat was glossy and his golden eyes bright. I rubbed his ears and he burst into a raspy purr; I'd been forgiven for my temporary abandonment. He stayed on my lap as I did the glamorous job of filling out the reports about the theft and contacting the protestors to make appointments for them to come in.

As I worked, I heard Liv's raised voice arguing with Gunnar. Half the time she was trying to tempt him into a tumultuous affair, the other half she was all pointy and sharp. She confused me, but no way was I going to confront her about it. She was a necromancer and I was undead – or at least mostly so.

She stormed out about ten minutes later without so much as a glance at me. I put Shadow down to snuggle down with Fluffy and went to find out what she had wanted. Gunnar was sitting at his desk, his head in his hands, looking tired.

'You survived her then?' I only half-joked.

He looked up at me. 'Only just. She wants my head on a pike.'

'A pike? Is that an Alaskan thing?'

He laughed. 'No – here we shoot you. I thought it was an English thing. You know, the Tower of London and such?'

I grinned. 'Oh, sure. We're hardcore like that in London. You can't look around Tower Bridge without seeing a head on a pike.'

'I know you're joking, but it would add a certain something to the atmosphere.'

'Yeah,' I agreed. 'The smell of rotting flesh.'

He wrinkled his nose. 'Good point. Okay, no heads on pikes.'

'Glad we're in agreement. So what did Liv want?'

'She's worried that someone will go after the other gems. If they do, we're in real danger of the barrier failing and then we'll all be screwed.'

The barrier failing was my worst nightmare and I shivered as I vividly recalled the thing that lived beyond it. 'Stan is worried about the same thing. Connor has already called extra security measures. Maybe that will be enough.'

'Maybe, but I'm calling in the heads of all the supernatural council members for a private meeting. If we force them to put more security in place, we'll set some minds at ease. While I do that, can you deal with the protestors? Interview them and eliminate anyone with solid alibis?'

'Yeah, can do.'

We had names and numbers for close to thirty protesters now that Stan had identified the last few and I'd already set up appointments with a lot of them. I returned to my desk and called the rest, making notes for Sidnee about any I couldn't get hold of so she could chase them during her shift. Some of them might keep to a daytime routine; that was rare in Portlock, but it was possible.

Once I'd finished, I went to the evidence locker. I didn't want to risk contaminating the evidence but I looked carefully at the barrier tape through the clear bag it was sealed in, even putting it under a desk light and looking at it with a magnifying glass. After I'd had a good look, I'd ship it to the lab for them to examine.

Kostas had dark hair, which was most of what I could see on the tape. I spotted a few short grey hairs that could be from a pet. I was intimately familiar with that since I was currently living with a growing kitten and a large, shaggy dog.

And that was when I spotted a long, nearly colourless strand of hair that was definitely too long for a house pet, unless it was something like a yak. Did people keep yaks as pets in Alaska? The hair was at least a foot long, maybe even two. It was impossible to tell without taking it out of the protective bag.

I cast my mind back. I'd seen a few Portlock inhabitants with very long hair, but the only one I had a name for was young Aoife Sullivan who had called in a fisheye deal to the hotline. The likelihood of the Goth teen being involved seemed slim but I made a note to check her out if the lab found out something useful on the hair. Having a root on a hair sample was rare and without it we couldn't get a DNA match, but even without it the lab could at least tell us if the hair came from a male or female. It wasn't much but it was something.

Now I needed to check whether the hair was there by means fair or foul. I dialled the fire witch's number.

'Hello?' Kostas answered, his tone reserved.

'Hi, this is Bunny from the Nomo's office. I need to verify some information.'

'Sure, anything if it'll help.'

'You live alone?'

'Yeah, it's me.'

'Do you have a pet?'

'Yes, my familiar. A grey cat.'

I doodled a cat on my notepad. That was the short grey hair most likely taken care of – but the long one? 'That's very helpful. Can I ask how long you have lived there?'

'My whole life. My parents raised me in this house,' Kostas replied.

Damn: it could be the hair of an elderly family member. 'Are they still alive?'

'No, they were both killed in a plane wreck when I was a teen.'

'I'm sorry to hear that.' I said. As calm as I sounded, excitement was fizzing in my gut. The long hair really might be a clue. 'Do you have any friends who come round to your place with long blond or grey hair?'

'No, I told you. I don't invite people round to my house.' There was a beat then he asked suspiciously, 'Why?'

'I'm trying to identify some hair I found at the scene. I'm sending it to the lab but it would be good to have some information in advance. Thank you for your time.'

'No worries.' We ended the call.

If Kostas didn't have visitors, or elderly long-haired parents, this strand of hair could be the thief's! I finally had a clue. Portlock couldn't have *that* many people with long pale hair…

Surely this was going to be easy!

Chapter 7

Fifteen protestors later, my smugness was gone. I'd had a whole line-up of grumpy people who hated the barrier tax and thought the barrier should be ripped down and a mighty dance held on its grave. And so far no one had long grey or blond hair and everyone had an alibi. Worse, some of the interviewees had given up names of their protestor buddies, so I had even more people to investigate. Damningly, Fluffy had sniffed each one and shown no apparent interest.

I was starting to think we were on the wrong track when the next two drifted in for the interview. They had long, colourless hair – ding ding! We had a winner! Or two winners, perhaps.

Fluffy sat up sharply and whined. He looked at me, then at the women, then back at me. *I get you, bud*, I wanted to say, but I held my tongue because talking to your dog in front of non-dog people makes you look weird. Dog people understand because we all talk constantly to our dogs, but non-dog owners not so much.

I recognised one of the women instantly: Aoife Sullivan. I checked my list for the other lady's name: Nora Sullivan. I didn't need the matching surnames to know that they were related. Looking at all that long hair, I tried to contain my growing excitement under a wobbly poker face.

I gave them my best I'm-not-threatening-at-all smile. 'Hello, I'm Bunny Barrington. Please come on in.'

'I'm Nora Sullivan and this is Aoife – I'm her mother. Here as requested, for an interview.' Nora's voice had an odd quality that provoked something visceral in me but I couldn't place what was strange about it and why it made me uncomfortable.

She thrust out her hand for me to shake; her nails were short and unmanicured but her skin was lovely and soft. Despite that, she squeezed my hand like she bench-pressed 200 kilos. Ouch.

'Great. Follow me.' I took the two women to the interview room. They were both so pale skinned that I could see traces of blue veins under their skin. Their hair was so white-blonde as to be colourless. Norah's age was hard to judge, but she didn't appear to be particularly old.

Aoife was one of the two teenage girls who'd called the fisheye hotline when a drug deal was going down. Her friend Joanne had been bouncing with excitement at meeting me; Aoife had been less bouncy but no less excited. When I'd first encountered her she'd been dressed as a Goth, but now she was wearing conservative clothes. There were no signs of the grinning enthusiasm she'd showed before; in fact, her whole body language told me she was pissed off. Aoife Sullivan did *not* want to be interviewed by the Fanged Flopsy.

She got straight to the point. 'We didn't do anything wrong!'

I smiled. 'We've met before,' I reminded her.

She looked back sulkily. 'Yeah. You were cooler when you weren't arresting me.'

With an effort, I kept smiling. 'You're not under arrest. We aren't accusing you of anything, we're interviewing those involved in the protest because we've had an incident related to the barrier.'

'Well, it isn't us. Good chat.' Aoife stood up to leave but her mother grasped her arm, yanked her back down and shot her a quelling glance.

Norah sighed softly. 'Forgive my daughter. The banshees are a small group and we've experienced our fair share of bigotry. She's a little sensitive.'

Her pale eyes steely, Aoife scowled at her; she looked about as sensitive as a brick in the face. 'This has nothing to do with being a banshee and everything to do with the Fanged Flopsy here being *wrong.*'

I didn't know a whole lot about banshees and I wondered how many were in town. Was white-blonde hair specific to the Sullivan women, or was it a banshee trait? If it was, that opened up the suspect pool still further – though Fluffy had indicated he'd smelt one of the women at the scene. Was it possible that he'd picked up a banshee scent rather than a specific person's smell? At times it was very inconvenient that my dog couldn't speak.

I kept my tone mild. 'As I said, you're not under arrest.' *Yet*. 'I'll record this interview for posterity,' I said lightly. I clicked on the camera, casually read them their rights then dived straight in. 'Where were you yesterday between the hours of eight in the morning until five at night?'

Nora answered first. 'I was at work at the fish plant. I'm sure my supervisor can vouch for me.'

I looked at Aoife. 'And you?'

She slumped lower in her seat and didn't look at me. 'I was at school.'

'Where do you go to school?'

She huffed and folded her arms. 'I'm taking college extension classes at the high school.'

I glanced down at the information I had on her; she was nineteen, only four years younger than me. It felt like centuries. 'Who runs the program?' I asked.

She shrugged. 'It's mostly online but we meet twice a week for a regular school day. It's through the University of Alaska.'

I jotted down a note, more for their benefit than mine. 'Do you know Kostas Spencer?' They both shook their heads. 'Please answer verbally for the recording.'

'No.'

'No.'

'Thank you. Have you ever attended his property?'

'No,' Nora confirmed.

'I don't go to strangers' houses.' Aoife gave me a bratty, insincere smile.

I made a mental note to ask Kostas if he knew either woman. 'How do you feel about the barrier?' I asked, directing the question to Nora.

She gave me a flat stare. 'I was there protesting about it. You know how I feel about it.'

I raised an eyebrow. 'Tell me *why*.'

'Why? It is nothing but a con!' She slammed a fist on a table. 'A con by the witches to make hard-working folks pay through the nose for their supposed "protection". It's an absurdity. We are all supernats here, we don't need their protection!'

'There are some humans in Portlock,' I pointed out.

She waved that away. 'They are few and far between. The barrier is a waste of time, energy and *my* money.'

I looked at Aoife; she was silent, admiring her nails, expression bored. My radar hummed. If Nora was the thief, she'd probably have the sense to keep her vitriol about the barrier quiet, so she wasn't an obvious suspect in its sabotage. But staying quiet, like Aoife was doing right now...?

'What about you?' I asked her pointedly. 'How do you feel about the barrier?'

She slid a glance at her mum. 'Whatever,' she muttered. 'I don't care. I don't think Mum cares all that much either, she just wants to get into Ezra's pants.'

'Aoife! Show some respect,' her mum barked, aghast. She also flushed red. Aoife wasn't wrong about the pants' thing.

'Sorry,' Aoife drawled. She wasn't sorry. 'You want to get into *Mr Taylor*'s pants.'

Nora glared at her and I quickly interceded. I cleared my throat. 'Right. That's all. We'll be in touch. Thanks for your time, ladies.' I was aiming for casual, but something in me was *sure* that one of them was the thief. Unfortunately I had no hard evidence, only a visual match on a hair that may or may not have DNA evidence on it. I'd need more than a hair to get this case moving and until I got it, I wanted them to think this was all routine.

Gunnar had already told me off for leaping to conclusions but I was learning that ignoring my gut was often to my detriment.

I saw the Sullivan women out and quickly searched the area where they'd been sitting before the next interviewee came in. They weren't under arrest and I didn't have a warrant to collect a hair sample, so if I could find a hair or two from them it might be helpful. I looked around: with two heads of long, loose hair, surely I'd find a few? I shed my long hair like crazy – it was everywhere.

Sure enough, I collected five long white hairs that I bagged, tagged and prepared for the lab. The chain of evidence was vulnerable; I'd been interviewing people all day and I hadn't seen the hair fall from either

Nora's or Aoife's head – but now there was something to compare the other hair to. Better than nothing.

I finished the rest of the interviews, but the two women remained my main suspects.

Gunnar strolled in from speaking to the council. 'How did the protestors' interviews go?' he asked me. I filled him in about the hair and my potential suspects. 'All banshees have white-blond hair like that,' he explained.

Damn it. 'I'll ring Kostas and see if he's friendly with any banshees. Even so, Fluffy definitely pointed to the Sullivans.'

'It's still not much to go on.'

I sighed. 'I know. We'll find more evidence.'

'We'll have to,' he said firmly.

'How did it go with the council?'

It was Gunnar's turn to sigh. 'Not great. Everyone is antsy and there were lots of accusations thrown around. A fair amount of blame was laid at Connor's door for not doing more. Apparently the vampire on the watch shift was on his phone and Connor's not pleased about that. Still, everyone's on high alert now so our thief won't find it so easy to steal another gemstone.'

I bit my lip. 'Should we put some surveillance on Aoife and Nora?'

Gunnar shook his head. 'What have I told you about assumptions? You can't fixate on them as suspects until we have more to go on because it'll close your mind to other possibilities. Besides, we don't have the resources.'

'We could draft in some shifters or vampires,' I suggested. We often borrowed shifter or vamp bodies when we were stretched thin. Both groups had helped to watch the Nomo's office around the clock when it had been holding a load of the dangerous fisheye drug.

'No. If they learn we're looking at the banshees there'll be repercussions. The banshees already have a target painted on their back – vampires, especially, don't like them.'

His lingering gaze told me he was wondering if my suspicions were due to my race. But I hadn't known I wasn't supposed to like the banshees, and I certainly didn't plan on inheriting any problems with *any* of the supernatural factions. They'd have to piss me off themselves.

Gunnar continued, 'If some factions learn that the banshees might be behind this...' He trailed off. 'Just keep your suspicions to yourself, okay?'

I bristled a little, but before things could get prickly Sidnee came in for her shift. Thank goodness: I was tired, cranky and ready for a cup of tea and some trashy TV.

The phone rang. Since Sidnee hadn't even shucked off her coat, I answered. 'There's been an explosion!' the caller started right away. 'I've called the fire department already but you'd best come too.'

'And you are?'

'Henry Davenport. I'm a neighbour. I live opposite the house that exploded.'

'Was the house occupied?' I asked tightly. *Please let it be empty...*

'Nah, it's empty.'

Thank God. 'You got the address?' He gave me an address on the other side of town. 'Thanks, we're on our way.'

I guessed that cup of tea would have to wait.

Chapter 8

The heat from the fire was broiling but some part of me almost basked in it like a cat curling up and purring. The sensation was unsettling. The urge to add to the flames rose up and almost took me by surprise. I gulped down a breath and focused on the earth in front of me.

Gunnar looked at me with concern. 'Okay?'

'Sure,' I lied, wrestling with the urge to burn shit down. 'Totally fine.'

He didn't look convinced but he turned back to the house that was on fire. The red light lit up the dawn sky. We'd arrived after the fire officers, but they were still battling the flames.

'Is this a coincidence or a pattern?' I asked as we watched them trying to put out the flames. 'Another unoccupied house – have we got a pyromaniac on the loose?'

'Can't say for sure unless there's a third one,' Gunnar said grimly. 'But it sure seems likely.'

I stared into the flames. A shadow passed behind the house and ran towards the woods. 'There's someone out there!' I said urgently. 'Watching!'

'Probably a rubbernecker.'

'Or it's the pyro watching their work!' I dashed after the shadow, using my vampire speed for all it was worth. Gunnar called after me but I ignored him. Fluffy was with me, running full tilt a few steps behind.

I chased the figure that was trying to escape. The flames illuminated them: the person was slender and wearing a dark hoodie. He or she was at the edge of the woods, so I turned it up a notch and sprinted. Fluffy did his best to keep up with me.

We got to the trees seconds after the figure disappeared into their dark depths. I looked around but I couldn't see or hear them. A tingle ran down my spine; it was like they had completely disappeared. I looked up into the canopy of the trees in case they'd climbed up but I saw nothing. Even with the dawn coming, the foliage still cast a dark shadow on the land beneath.

Fluffy suddenly rushed ahead, his nose down. He had a scent. Yes! They might have evaded me but they were no match for my faithful hound! I followed him, keeping my eyes sharp. Suddenly my boy stopped and whined. There was a clear footprint right in front of his nose, then after that ... nothing. Bugger.

'Where did they go?' I asked out loud.

Fluffy barked once and then sat; he had no more trail to follow. It was like the person had disappeared into thin air. Was teleportation a real thing? I'd have to ask Gunnar.

I patted Fluffy's head. 'Never mind, boy, we did our best. Let's head back.'

We wound our way through the trees until the flames lit our way again. Gunnar was waiting for us. 'Well?' he asked.

'I saw someone in a dark hoodie but I couldn't see if they were male or female – although they were slender.'

'Hmm.'

'I gave chase and Fluffy had the scent, but then it was like they vanished. Is there a supernatural type with the ability to teleport?'

'There's been rumours about it but I can't say for sure either way. You know how secretive the different species are about their skills.' Yeah, they were about as forthcoming as a politician on election week. Gunnar sighed. 'Unfortunately, the person we need to ask about it is Liv.'

'I can take that one for the team if you want me to,' I offered.

I could see that he was tempted but he shook his head. 'Nah. It makes me a coward if I can't handle it.' He brightened. 'I'll text her.'

I gave him a clap on the shoulder for his solution, but I was still annoyed. Liv was sexually harassing Gunnar and her behaviour was *not* okay. I doubted he'd appreciate me wading in to protect him, but I found that I wanted to.

Liv scared me more than a little. She'd used her necromantic powers around me a time or two, and on each occasion I'd got the feeling that she could play me like a marionette if she wanted to. It wasn't a comfortable feeling but I'd face her for Gunnar if he'd let me; he wasn't alone, even if he didn't know it yet.

'Come on, I'll drop you two home,' he offered.

'I need to pick up Shadow.' The office was in the wrong direction for home.

Gunnar hesitated for a moment. 'You can leave him at the office for the day if you want. Sidnee would probably be grateful for the company.'

She totally would; she loved my lynx kitten. 'If you're sure?'

'It's fine. Then you won't need to haul him to work in the pram tomorrow.'

His comment made me grin. He clearly expected me to bring Shadow to work from now on. 'You're the best boss ever, you know that?'

'Yeah, well, don't spread it around. I have a tough-guy reputation to protect.'

I smiled. Gunnar had a reputation for being formidable but fair, though anyone who was close to him knew he was giant marshmallow on the inside.

He dropped Fluffy and me home and made sure we were safely inside before he drove off to his own bed. I fed my boy, grabbed some blood and a microwave meal and then made my much-needed cup of tea.

Fluffy lay next to me as I sipped it, but I missed Shadow's quiet purr. How quickly the little thing had inserted himself into my heart. He would be cranky at me tomorrow for leaving him at the office. I made a note to take in a tin of tuna to bribe him back into loving me. I was absolutely okay with buying his love; that's the way I'd been raised, after all.

I pulled out my phone and rang Connor on the off chance he was still awake. 'Hey, Bunny.' His voice was warm.

'Hey. Are you okay after the council meeting? Gunnar said it was rough.'

'It wasn't great,' he admitted. 'But Vlad really dropped the ball.'

I paused. 'Vlad? Really?'

'I know,' he sighed. 'He's young and he chose a ridiculous name for himself when he got turned. Give him a century and he'll regret it.'

'I'd regret it after five minutes. Is Connor your vampire name or the one you were born with?'

He hesitated a second and I wondered if I'd inadvertently been rude. 'Both. I've always been Connor Mackenzie.' He sounded a little bitter, which reminded me that I knew very little about his background.

'You want to talk about it?' I offered.

'It's complicated. Not now, okay? I'd rather do this in person.'

'Okay.'

There was awkward silence. 'What'll happen to Vlad?' I asked to break the tension.

'He'll be on logging for the next few months until he proves himself. If he does well, I'll let him have another try at security.'

'You don't hold grudges, huh?' I tried to say it lightly, trying to inject some levity into the conversation.

'No. I've seen enough grudge holding to last a lifetime. I try and let stuff go. What about you?'

'I'm slow to anger, but once I'm there I cling to it with all my might,' I said cheerfully.

He laughed. 'Good to know. I'll have to do my darndest not to make you mad.'

'Sounds like a plan.' I sipped my tea. 'What are you doing now?'

'I'm outside Kostas's house.'

I blinked. 'Isn't that shutting the barn door after the horse has bolted?'

'Maybe, but criminals sometimes return to the scene of the crime. If they do, I'll get them.'

I wanted to tell him about my banshee suspicions but Gunnar's warning had me holding my tongue. 'I'd better go. It's been a long day.'

'It has,' he agreed. 'I'm going to bed soon too.'

The picture of Connor Mackenzie shirtless in bed flashed into my mind with a vividness that made my mouth go dry. 'Sleep well,' I managed, but my voice had turned breathy.

He gave a low chuckle. 'Dream of me.' He hung up.

As if I had any choice in the matter. Lately all my dreams had been about a certain tousled-haired vampire with eyes like ice, eyes that always seemed to see to the heart of me. And surprisingly, he seemed to like what he saw.

Chapter 9

I had to wait until my next shift to see if Liv had replied to Gunnar's question about teleportation. I hustled into the office half an hour early because my curiosity was getting the better of me.

Sidnee was at her desk and Shadow was on her lap. He gave a squeak and hopped down to say hello to me. When I stroked him and gave him a scruffle under his chin, he let out a loud purr and wound himself around my legs. 'I bought you tuna,' I whispered, 'so you definitely can't be mad at me.'

Affection duly dispensed, Shadow went to Fluffy's bed. Fluffy went over so the two of them could lie together. They were super sweet.

'Are you okay?' I asked Sidnee casually. 'How are things?'

'Busy. I spoke to a couple of the protesters – my notes are on the system. Nothing interesting to report back, I'm afraid.' She looked glum, so unlike her usual sunny self.

'You sure you're okay?' I asked.

'I'm fine.'

'You're not. Since Chris—'

'Bunny, I do *not* want to talk about Chris,' she snapped. 'Just leave it. I'm processing, okay?'

I'd never heard her snap before. I felt awful – I hadn't meant to upset her, I just wanted to be there for her. Man I *sucked* at this friendship shit.

Sidnee blew out a long breath. 'I'm sorry. You and Gunnar are both kind of hovering around me. I get that it's from a place of love, but I'm dealing in my own way.' She managed a tight smile. 'It's been a long day. The phone's been ringing off the hook – you know how it is. I'm ready to clock off now you're here. You mind if I go early?'

'No, you're good. Go ahead.'

She packed up and left without saying goodbye to Gunnar. I knocked on his door and went in, Liv suddenly taking a backseat in my mind. 'I'm worried about Sidnee,' I announced.

Gunnar sat back in his chair and stroked his beard. 'Me too,' he admitted. 'I hate seeing her this way.'

'She seems down.'

'She has reason to be,' he pointed out gently.

'Of course she does.' I wasn't dismissing what she'd been through with Chris, but I *was* worried. 'Has she talked to you about it?'

'No, nor to Sigrid. And Sig's been trying.'

'Me too,' I admitted. 'She keeps blowing me off for lunch, and just now she basically lost it with me and told me to mind my own business.' I was paraphrasing, but that's how it had felt.

'She'll come round,' he said.

'I've never really had friends,' I admitted uncomfortably. 'Am I doing enough? Should I do more?'

His eyes softened. 'You're doing great. Sometimes people need space. She knows she's loved and supported, and she'll talk to us when she's ready. We need to keep on being there for her.'

'Okay. Thanks.' I cleared my throat and changed the topic to a more comfortable one like terrifying necromancers. 'Did Liv get back to you?'

'She sure did. She says the only ones she knows that can teleport are banshees.'

Bingo! I was buzzing with excitement as things fell into place. 'Gunnar, the fires and the theft – they're linked. They have to be! A banshee teleported in, snatched the fire jewel and now random fires keep starting? It has to be because of the jewel!'

'I reached the same conclusion. I've asked the council for a search warrant.'

I grinned triumphantly; we might even get this case wrapped up by the end of my shift. 'So besides teleporting, what else do you know about banshees?' I asked. 'Are there any male ones?' What little lore I knew was from the pedestrian world, but in fiction banshees were always female.

'I honestly don't know much about them, but I've never heard of a male one. That doesn't mean they don't exist – you know how closely each species guards their secrets. It's possible that male banshees exist but don't have the same colouring as the women, or it could be a wholly female race.'

I'd thought banshees were spirit creatures, not physical beings like the two I'd met. I figured the folklore and the reality were rather far apart, and I was doing my best to cut down on making assumptions. 'Our whole case is pretty flimsy. Circumstantial.'

'It is,' Gunnar agreed. 'But I've sent the evidence from the scene to the lab, plus the extra hairs you got after the interview. Fingers crossed both have DNA attached.' He grimaced; he obviously didn't think it was likely.

'What are the chances of an intact hair root?' I pressed.

'Honestly? Slim to none, but we have to try. Hopefully we'll get the search warrant and find our missing gem. That's more important than building a solid case right now. We need to get the barrier back to full strength before the beast realises it's weak.'

I swallowed hard; that would be my nightmares come to life. 'Yeah. I hear you,' I said faintly.

The phone rang so I went back to my desk. When I answered it, someone hung up. I tried to redial but the number was withheld. Weird.

For the next hour I read through Sidnee's notes of her interviews with the other protestors, but nothing jumped out at me. I checked the phone log but it was blank. I frowned; Sidnee had said she'd had loads of calls, but if that were true she hadn't noted a single one. That wasn't like her: she was meticulous. My worry about her deepened.

Gunnar burst out of his office looking triumphant. 'We've got it! Let's roll!'

'The warrant came through?'

'Bingo!' Gunnar looked like the weight of the world had been taken off his shoulders; like me, he was expecting to have the fire gem in its box and safely returned to its pillar by the end of our working day. Things were cooking!

I had two known barrier protestors, hairs at the scene and a supernatural race with the ability to teleport. It was the perfect trifecta: means, motive and opportunity. I'd have the thief in jail and the barrier back up and running in no time!

I was almost giddy. *Easiest case yet*, I thought smugly.

Chapter 10

Gunnar suggested I take Sidnee with me to search the Sullivan residence. She'd already finished her shift, but we all knew there were no such things as set hours in this job; besides, she might need the distraction. I called her on the off chance that she wanted to keep busy and she readily agreed to ride shotgun.

With our schedules overlapping more and more lately, we'd advertised for someone to take over the paperwork and filing. So far there'd been no qualified takers; it was a poorly paid job, so it either attracted very young job seekers or desperate ones with no skills. Gunnar wanted to take on the latter and give someone a much-needed chance, but no one had struck the right chord with him.

When Fluffy and I picked up Sidnee, my brand-new Alaskan driver's licence was burning a hole in my pocket. It had been surprisingly easy to get one: I'd had to show my passport and visa, my British licence – and pass the test, of course. After one read through of the driver's manual, I had passed with flying colours.

I carefully pulled onto the road. I still had to think about staying on the wrong side, but I was getting the hang of it.

'Do you think we'll find the gem at the house?' Sidnee asked. She seemed brighter, almost bouncing on her seat with excitement. Maybe she'd just needed some downtime to recharge.

'Yeah.' I flashed her a grin. 'I really think we will.'

'This is going to be epic!'

I laughed and Fluffy barked loudly. We were all thinking the same thing: this would be a slam dunk! I was trying to play it cool but I was really excited to find the gem, especially before it set any more empty houses on fire.

We pulled into the driveway where a battered old dark-grey Subaru was parked by the house. I stopped behind it so nobody could make a quick getaway.

Sidnee frowned. 'Would you have a car if you could teleport?'

'No way! I'd be so annoying, zipping everywhere.' I frowned at the car, too. 'Maybe the teleportation range is short.'

'Or they can't teleport at all,' she muttered darkly.

'It's a reported ability, not a guaranteed one, although the signs point to at least one of them being able to do it. I'm sure we'll soon find out. Arresting someone that can zip away might be tricky.' Maybe Gunnar had sent us because he didn't feel like doing a chase that should be linked to the Benny Hill theme tune.

'So how *do* we arrest someone who can teleport?' Sidnee asked.

I did have an answer for that one. 'The magic-cancelling cuffs. Slap 'em on quick.'

'Let's hope we can hold them still long enough to get them on.'

We pulled on plastic gloves, grabbed the scene-of-the-crime bag and opened the car doors. The outside of the house was neat and well kept, so it was noticeable that a bin had been pulled over and rubbish had spilled out of it. I set it upright then knocked on the carefully painted front door.

Nora answered it and gave me a polite but quizzical smile, which made me feel like a twat for what was coming next. 'Nora Sullivan, we have a search warrant for your house and grounds,' I stated.

Her brows drew together. 'Why?' She looked completely perplexed.

'We suspect that an item has been stolen and is being hidden here.' The council was trying to keep a lid on the fact that the barrier fire gem had been taken, so I didn't want to clarify *what* had been stolen.

She looked at my documentation then grudgingly let us in. She was shaking but I wasn't sure if it was from fear, guilt or rage.

'We'll try to be careful so we don't disturb you more than we need to,' I promised gently. She shot me an unfriendly look; I guessed a search warrant wiped out welcoming smiles. 'I picked up your rubbish bin,' I said in an effort to curry favour. 'It had been knocked over.'

She paled. 'The keelut.'

I blinked. 'It could have been something else,' I suggested. The keelut was a magical creature, a harbinger of death, though it seemed a bit incongruous for it to be a harbinger of death and a scrounger of bins.

'My neighbour said she saw it.' Nora licked dry lips. 'I thought she was lying but now...' She looked spooked.

'Sorry,' I said. 'Can we come in?'

She stepped back. 'I suppose I have no choice.'

Sidnee, Fluffy, and I started at the back of the house. It was a simple bungalow, not much different from mine: three bedrooms, two that were in use and one that was obviously a spare. There were two bathrooms, a kitchen diner, and a modest living room.

We started in Nora's room. Sidnee took the bathroom and I looked in the closet. Fluffy had a good sniff around whilst I checked inside Nora's shoes and rifled through the pockets of her clothes. Remembering the boys who'd vaped fisheye, I checked the same hiding places: under the mattress, under the bed, the dresser drawers, the nightstands, and even the window seat. Nothing.

'Nothing in here,' Sidnee noted glumly. We moved to the next bedroom – Aoife's – which had a bathroom across the hall. This time Fluffy and Sidnee took the bedroom and I took the bathroom. It was much smaller than Nora's, but I took my time to check the cabinet and between every single towel; I even looked in the toilet cistern. Nothing again.

My certainty that we'd find the gem wavered a little, but just as I was sinking into the doldrums I heard a triumphant bark from Aoife's bedroom. 'Bunny, come in here!' Sidnee shouted in panic as I was searching the bathroom bin.

When I joined her, she was staring at something on the floor on the other side of the bed: it was the metal box that had held the fire gem. 'Great work!' I said, but Sidnee's face was grim. What was I missing? 'What's wrong?' I asked as I took some photographs.

Sidnee sighed and flipped open the lid. 'It's empty.' We stared inside the box. Damn it! 'This isn't good,' she murmured. 'It's *very* not good.'

'We'll find it,' I said with false bravado. 'It's got to be hidden around here, or maybe Aoife has it in her pocket.'

'You don't understand,' she whispered. The look on her face was indecipherable as she licked her dry lips. 'Bunny, the objects, the four gems – they're cursed.'

I blinked. 'Gunnar mentioned that. Why is it a big deal?'

'The boxes don't *hold* the gems – they *protect* everyone from them. While the jewels are in their boxes, their magic powers the barrier. But when they're outside their boxes? This is bad. Very, very bad.'

'Is Aoife in danger?'

'We're *all* in danger. Grave danger.'

A chill ran down my spine and I felt the hairs on my neck stand up. I ran to the living room with Fluffy on my heels. Nora was sitting on the sofa, wringing her hands. 'Where's Aoife?' I demanded.

She folded her arms defiantly. 'I don't know – and I wouldn't tell you if I did.'

'She's in danger,' I said urgently. Spreading panic about the stone be damned: Nora needed to understand the severity of the situation. 'We think that Aoife stole the box with the fire gem inside but then she took it out. The gem is cursed and the box protects us from it. Aoife is in grave danger!'

Nora looked worried for a beat but then she seemed to shrug it off. I waited for her to wail and gnash her teeth but she merely said, 'She'll be fine. Not many things can harm a banshee.'

I wanted to shake her; how could she not get it?

Sidnee heard the last bit as she joined us in the living room. She was carrying the metal box in an evidence bag under her arm. Nora's eyes widened and her mouth dropped open at the sight of it. She hadn't believed me until now. If Nora was shocked to see the metal box then she hadn't been an accomplice in her daughter's theft.

'Not much can harm a banshee,' Sidnee agreed, 'but it could hurt someone around her. It's the *fire* gem.

I'm not sure what the curse is or what it does, but it involves fire. Can banshees burn? And even if you can't, your house sure can.'

Things started slotting into place. The fires around town: both properties that had burnt down had been unoccupied, but was that by accident or design? Both had been available for rent, and I suddenly wondered if Aoife was house shopping. Had she gone to the empty properties looking for a place to rent and lost control of the gem? If so, she had to be carrying it around with her. The thought of walking around with a cursed gem in my pocket made me touch my nana's protective charm that hung around my neck.

'Is Aoife looking to move out?' I asked Nora.

Aoife's mum was still staring at the box under Sidnee's arm. 'Yes,' she said almost absently. 'How did you know that?'

I looked her straight in the eye. 'Because Portlock has had two houses burn to the ground since the gem was stolen and each of them was empty and up for rent.'

For the first time Nora looked worried.

'Where is she?' I asked. Nora said nothing. Bad cop it was, then. 'Do you think she can afford to replace the destroyed properties?' I asked harshly.

She pressed her lips together tightly. 'No,' she admitted grudgingly. 'She can't.'

Unless Aoife sold the stolen gem to make an absolute killing – but how would she go about fencing the jewel? She was nineteen and a student, not a hardened criminal. 'So, where is she?' I demanded again.

Her mum answered reluctantly. 'Her boyfriend's house, I think.'

'Who's her boyfriend?' I pressed.

'His name is Luke Savik.'

'Related to Lukas or Akiak Savik?' I frowned. The dead hunters we'd retrieved from the other side of the barrier had been Saviks. How many Saviks could there be in this small town? I remembered from Lukas's file that he had a son called Luke. It couldn't be a common name.

Nora confirmed my suspicions. 'Lukas was his father.'

The Savik brothers had died when they were hunting on the other side of the barrier. If Aoife was dating Luke, she must know that the monster was real. Why on earth would she try to bring the barrier down?

If she was with Luke, the most pressing issue right now was his family and their safety. The gem was deadly and Aoife was strolling around with it in her pocket. The last thing the Saviks' deserved was for their family home to go up in flames.

'We'd better hurry before the gem incinerates a house full of people,' I said urgently to Sidnee. She nodded and we ran out to the car, Sidnee still carrying the box. I opened the car for Fluffy to jump in and we sped off.

I prayed we'd get to the Saviks' house before the gem did its thing and burned everything in its path.

Chapter 11

Sidnee got the address from the Nomo's database and I drove as quickly as I dared to Lukas Savik's house. I'd been to Akiak Savik's house twice before, once to get the information on the missing men and the second time to inform the two widows of their husbands' untimely deaths. The second time haunted me: it had been hard to deliver that news. I'd never been to Lukas's house. I hoped I wasn't going to deliver any more bad news.

We screeched up, dived out of the car and I knocked on the door, Sidnee on one side of me and Fluffy on the other. When Lukas's wife, Olena, opened it she looked panicked to see me. I couldn't blame her: the last time we'd spoken, I'd told her that her husband was dead.

'Ms Savik, is your son at home?' I asked urgently.

Her lips trembled and one hand fluttered to her heart. 'Is he okay? Is he in trouble?'

I shook my head. 'He's fine. I'm looking for his girlfriend, Aoife Sullivan. It's possible she's carrying around a dangerous artefact.'

'Aoife? She's so sweet. She wouldn't...' She trailed off. 'I'll call them down. I'm sure this is all a big mistake.' She left us waiting on the porch as she went to holler for Luke.

I heard a distant, 'What, Mom?'

She sounded exasperated. 'Please come here immediately. The Nomo's office is at the door.'

I heard quiet whispering then a ruckus and knew immediately that Aoife would run. Sidnee had heard it too. I gestured for her to go left around the side of the house as I ran right, Fluffy by my side.

Both kids were heading down the street behind the house towards the trees. The boy might be human but Aoife was definitely supernatural – though that didn't seem to translate to speed. Luke was athletic and he pulled ahead, but I was a vampire and I caught up with them in no time. I snagged them by their jackets and Fluffy growled threateningly to stop them trying to bolt again.

'Why did you run?' I asked grumpily. 'I only wanted to talk.' And arrest Aoife.

Luke shrugged but his eyes shifted to Aoife; she was clearly the ringleader here. 'Why are you following me?' she demanded, contempt pouring from her voice. 'I already had an interview with you. I told you everything I know.'

Sidnee was panting as she caught up. 'That's not true, is it, Aoife?' She kept her voice soft and friendly. 'Hon, we know you took the fire gem. It's dangerous and we need it back immediately. It's cursed.'

Everything about Aoife's body language shouted disdain. 'That's ridiculous. You can't prove that I took anything.'

'We found the empty box in your room.'

'I found it in the trash,' she lied, eyes wide, suddenly looking less certain of herself.

'Don't take us for fools,' I snapped. 'Return the gem and I promise it'll be a slap on the wrist. If you don't, it'll be far more serious.' I wasn't sure I could promise that, but if she handed over the gem I'd do my best to persuade the council to go easy on her.

She looked around nervously. 'I don't have it on me.'

Annoyingly, I believed her. 'Will you let me search you?'

She nodded and lifted her chin. 'I've got nothing to hide.'

I patted her down briskly and checked her pockets. Nothing. 'The houses that burned down – you've been to them, haven't you?'

Her lips thinned. 'You can't prove that.'

'Yes, I can,' I said firmly. 'Estate agents keep notes of appointments.'

Sidnee moved towards Aoife's left to cut her off if she decided to run and the girl watched her with narrowed eyes. 'Oh hell, no,' she spat and took a step back.

'Aoife, please,' I said, channelling good cop for all I was worth. 'We need to locate the gem then we can put this whole thing behind us.' Behind my back I unhooked the magic-cancelling handcuffs, readying them for use.

Aoife took another step back – she was going to bolt! I closed the distance between us. Cuffs outstretched, I reached for her hand and ... she disappeared. Fuck!

Sidnee looked at me, disappointment and excitement warring within her. She was thrilled that Aoife could teleport but frustrated that we'd let her get away. I was plain frustrated.

Looking skittish, Luke licked his lips. Since he didn't have any handy-dandy teleportation magic, I grabbed and cuffed him. We'd interview him at the station; maybe Aoife would follow us there.

'You're under arrest for obstruction and aiding a felon.' I read him his rights. If I recalled correctly from his father's file – which I did – he was eighteen so I didn't need his mother's permission or presence to interview him. The woman had been through hell already, though, so I briefly updated her whilst Sidnee secured Luke in the Nomo's vehicle.

She slammed the door shut and turned to me, a smile playing on her lips. 'That *was* kind of epic.'

'If we had the stone, I'd agree,' I said drily. I felt like an idiot and a failure. I should have cuffed Aoife while I was searching her. Shoulda, woulda, coulda. I put it aside; I needed to channel my energy into finding Aoife and the stone, not beating myself up. There'd be plenty of time for stewing later.

Before I got into the car, I called Thomas and asked for a favour. To my surprise, he agreed easily and I hung up feeling pleased that *something* was going my way.

We headed back to the Nomo's office to interview Luke. I hoped the arrest would rattle him enough to make him talk or that Aoife would be stupid enough to come running to help him. If she did, this time I'd have the damned cuffs ready.

Chapter 12

Luke Savik kept staring at his cuffed wrists, looking lost as he sat in the interview room. His girlfriend had landed him in a heap of shit and he'd lost his father not long ago. My heart went out to him, but I made sure it didn't show on my face.

'How old are you, Luke?' I asked gently, as if I didn't already know. I could remember everything from Lukas Savik's file, including the ages of his children. An eidetic memory often felt like a curse, but it certainly came in handy at times.

'I'm eighteen. I'll turn nineteen at the end of the school year.' School had started; Aoife was robbing the cradle a little here. She'd already graduated and he had one more year to go.

'How long have you been dating Aoife?' I asked, more out of nosiness than to further the case.

He looked at his hands. 'We started dating last year when she was a senior.'

'So you feel that you know her well?'

He nodded, looking miserable. 'We both know that she has the gem, don't we?' I asked quietly.

He continued staring at his hands then glanced up. 'Yeah, but I don't know what she did with it.' He looked at me properly. 'She's a good person.'

'I'm sure she is. So tell me, why was she protesting about the barrier?' I was genuinely curious.

'She wasn't!'

'I have a photo of her at the scene of the protest. She was definitely there.'

'Yes, she was but she was trying to get her mom to go home. She knows the monster is real – it killed my dad. Aoife knows we need the barrier. All of us do or it'll kill us all.' His voice warbled and there were tears in his eyes. He dashed them away angrily.

I squirmed in my seat and wondered if I should pat him on the shoulder. Sidnee would be better at this than me – I was uncomfortable with other people's tears. My parents had never been fond of childhood tears or tantrums; they'd subscribed to the 'children should be seen and not heard' philosophy. As a child, I'd tried to earn their love by shoving my emotions down as deeply as I could. By the time I realised that nothing would ever earn me their love, I was already emotionally stunted. I don't deal with feelings well.

Luke sniffed. 'Aoife knows we have to keep the barrier up. She's trying to save us all.'

'So why did she steal one of the barrier gems?' I asked.

He wiped his face with his sleeve. 'She wants to keep it safe. She's trying to save us!'

That made no sense. I leaned back in my chair. 'How is stealing the thing that keeps us safe going to keep us safe? I don't understand, Luke. Stealing it puts everyone at risk.'

His head was back down. He wasn't going to answer me. Sidnee opened the door and put a bottle of water in front of him then looked at me to see if I wanted one. I shook my head and she left again.

Luke unscrewed the top and gulped down half the bottle. 'Thanks,' he muttered, screwing the lid back on.

'What kind of supernatural are you and your family, Luke?' Their supernat species hadn't been listed in Akiak's or Lukas' files – for all I knew they were human. One sure way to piss off any supernat in this town was to suggest that they were human, whereas the reverse wasn't true. Maybe if I built a rapport with Luke he'd be comfortable enough to answer my questions about Aoife.

He looked up. 'We're Tariaksuq.'

Taria-what-now? 'I'm sorry, I'm not familiar with that.'

He shrugged. 'We're Inuit.'

That was clear as mud. 'Pretend I'm British and I've known about supernats for only a few months,' I said drily.

He smiled for the first time and straightened up a little; he knew more than me and that was a confidence booster. 'We're not that much different from humans, but we can dissolve into smoke for short amounts of time.'

I thought of his dead father and uncle; if they could dissolve into smoke, how had the beast killed them? But then the beast had smoke too, so maybe it hadn't helped them much.

Luke must have read my confusion on my face because he elucidated. 'Most of us can only do it for a few seconds, and not that often.' He looked down at his hands again. 'It's a stupid power,' he muttered.

I didn't know what to say about that, so I let the silence stretch a little. 'Did you know Aoife could teleport?' I asked finally.

He didn't answer. I waited a second and prodded again. 'Why did she think stealing the gem would make us safer?'

He blew out a harsh breath. 'Because if the barrier haters get it, they'll destroy it and we'll all be fucked!' His eyes drifted down to the left. I had no doubt that what he'd told me was true, but he was still hiding something. Was he protecting Aoife in some way?

Aoife had shown some wonderful teen logic. Rather than approach an adult in authority, such as a council member or the Nomo, she'd decided she could do better than anyone else. She'd stolen the gem and in doing so had helped to bring about the one thing she was trying to prevent. Save me from well-intentioned idiots.

I tried not to let my irritation show. 'Does Aoife know who wants to destroy it?'

'She hasn't said,' he admitted, then leaned forward and dropped his voice. 'I wonder about her mom.'

'Why is that?'

'Because her mom hates the barrier. She doesn't believe in the monster and she thinks everyone is trying to screw her over! She thinks banshees are treated as second-class citizens and she wants to put them on the map by bringing the barrier down.' He wrapped his arms around his middle. 'We have to do something. We can't let it fall.'

Now that I understood his reasoning, I could see the weight of the world on his shoulders. Luke was trying to honour his dad by helping Aoife, though all they'd done was put the town in more danger. But they'd conspired to save Portlock; there were worse crimes.

I changed tack. 'When did you last see the gem?'

'I never did, I only saw the box. Aoife said she'd put it somewhere safe and she watches it. That's all I know.' He sounded sincere and I found that I believed him.

I stood up. 'You're free to go,' I said.

Luke looked up in surprise. 'I am? I mean, you're not gonna lock me up?'

'Did you steal the gem?'

'No.'

'Did you conspire to steal it?'

'No, I only found out after Aoife had already taken it.'

'Then you're free to go, though we'd appreciate it if you let us know where Aoife or the gem are if you find them. Let us deal with it. The barrier is in danger until the gem is back in its rightful place.'

'Okay.' He looked uncertain as I uncuffed him and let him go.

Sidnee and I watched him leave the office. 'Was that a good idea?' she asked. 'Just letting him stroll out?'

'Maybe not, but he didn't know anything. I'm hoping he'll convince Aoife to bring us the gem and he can't do that from behind bars. In the meantime, we watch him and find out where she is.'

'How? We're short staffed as it is.'

'I've asked Thomas Patkotak to follow him.'

Sidnee looked at me approvingly. 'Huh. You can be real sneaky, Bunny.' I winked.

My case had become more complicated. Yes, I knew who the thief was and it was only a matter of time before I brought her in, but who was trying to destroy the barrier gems – and why? There was no point in restoring the gem to its rightful place only to have it stolen or destroyed days later.

Sidnee yawned. 'I'm going home for real this time. No more calling me in.'

'Sorry,' I apologised.

Looking more like her old self, she cracked a smile. 'I'm teasing you. Tell Gunnar I'm heading out.'

'Will do. Be safe.'

'You bet.'

I watched her leave, then I sighed and went to chat with Gunnar.

Chapter 13

Before I could say anything, Gunnar said, 'There's been another fire.'

I groaned. This was my fault. 'For fuck's sake! I had Aoife inches from my grasp. Was anyone hurt?'

'Thankfully not. Another empty property.'

'Small blessings.'

Gunnar looked at me expectantly, so I laid out everything that Luke and Aoife had told me. 'Dumb kids,' he muttered under his breath. 'Aoife believes there's a credible threat to the barrier, but Luke doesn't know who from except those who hate the barrier – including Aoife's mother. Is that the gist?'

'More or less.'

'Well, we have about thirty protestors to watch and that's more than the three of us can handle. We'll need to narrow this down. Take that list of protestors and cross-reference it with the database. We're looking for any previous arrests for theft, destruction of property, violence – anything really.'

I nodded. He opened his mouth to say something but his phone rang. He stared at the tiny screen. 'Goddammit, it's Liv.'

'Do you want me to leave?' I offered. Sometimes witnesses were the last things you wanted.

He shook his head, swiped the screen and hit the speaker button. 'Liv, how can I help you?' His voice was polite but distant.

'Have you found the fire gem yet?' she demanded.

Gunnar looked up at me and I wondered for a moment if he was – rightfully – going to throw me under a bus. 'We don't have it yet but we do have a good lead,' he said instead.

'That doesn't help. We need it back in place immediately.'

My blood ran cold. I squeaked out, 'Why?'

'Bunny?' Liv asked.

'Yes, it's me.'

She harrumphed but continued. 'There's been another tear reported. It's small, but we can't seal it permanently without the gems in their places.'

'Noted. We're doing our best,' Gunnar growled.

'Well, your best needs to be better,' she snarled. 'We're all in danger. I'm sending you the coordinates of the tear.' She hung up.

A few seconds later Gunnar's phone vibrated with an incoming text. He looked at it and stood up. 'I'm heading over to patch the tear and put up a camera. You narrow down the list of protestors we need to see.'

Gunnar's magic was unique and mysterious. I knew he could open doors, heal rifts in the barrier and chuck lightening at the monsters. The witches were under huge pressure to fix the growing rifts, so he had been drafted in to help with the repairs. That sometimes left me without a boss, but this really did feel like DEFCON 1.

Part of the problem was that we didn't have enough people to watch the new tears to make sure the creature didn't come through any of the temporary patch-ups. We also wanted to see if someone on our side popped up and try to enlarge them.

Gunnar's face was serious. 'And Bunny? Find that damned banshee girl.' He was starting to walk out as Sidnee walked back in.

'What are you doing here?' I demanded. 'You're supposed to be getting some rest.' Gunnar hovered to hear her answer; he was worried about her, too.

She sighed. 'I forgot to cancel the redirect sending the hotline calls to my mobile. We got a call. Someone thinks they've found a body at the edge of the woods.'

Gunnar hesitated then grimaced at me. 'You'll have to go, Bunny. Start securing the scene. I'll head over as soon as I've put up the camera. I can't leave the tear like it is.'

Liv was being a bitch; she might be short staffed, but *she* could have fixed the tear. Instead she'd put it on Gunnar. I was getting ready to give her a piece of my mind next time I saw her, no matter how scary she was.

The Nomo left and I collected the kit. 'You going back home?' I asked Sidnee.

'And leave you to deal with a dead body by yourself? No way. You can't have all the fun.'

I smiled gratefully. 'Thanks. Are you sure, though? You must be tired.'

'I'm fine. I drank a potion on the way over – it's like an energy drink on steroids. I'll be fine. Heck, I'll be better than fine.' That didn't seem like the best idea, but it was done now so I didn't criticise her.

I debated taking Fluffy with us but, since I knew nothing about the scene, I decided against it. If it was messy, I didn't want to have to tie him up to keep him and his fur away from the evidence. Instead I had him stay on his bed and watch Shadow, who I put in his crate. 'Sorry,' I said to them both. 'We need someone to man the Nomo's office. You two are it.' What a sad state of affairs that we only had a dog to hold the fort.

Shadow sat down with his back pointedly turned towards me. Fluffy looked sad, whined and resignedly put his head on his paws. It killed me, but it was for the best.

We locked up and headed round back where Gunnar had left the Nomo SUV for me. Sidnee gave me the address and we headed out. When we arrived, an anxious-looking woman met us. 'It's back here,' she said. 'I found her while I was walking my dog.'

We followed dutifully. From a distance, the corpse could have been a hillock or an animal lying down, but as we drew closer it was clear that it was a woman. She was lying with her back to us and her long colourless hair had fanned out around her. Oh fuck.

My breath caught. Once we were close enough, I bent down to look at her face even though my gut already knew who it was. My heart gave a sluggish beat. I used a gloved hand to gently brush the damp hair away from her face so I could identify her.

It was Aoife Sullivan.

Double fuck. Well, I'd certainly found the damned banshee girl.

Chapter 14

Next to me, Sidnee made a small noise of distress and I reached out to squeeze her hand. Seeing death was always hard, but seeing it trample one so young was devastating.

My next thought was of Aoife's mum and her boyfriend. Poor Luke, this would crush him. He'd already been through so much; he'd barely had time for the flowers on his dad's grave to die and now this.

I tried to put him from my mind and focus on the body. I had a job to do, no matter how hard it was. If I called it 'the body' then maybe I could distance it from the bright teenage girl I'd met.

Her mother had commented on how hard it was to hurt a banshee so I scanned the body for an obvious wound. There wasn't one but since Aoife was lying on her side, there might be some marks underneath her if she'd been stabbed or shot.

We photographed everything thoroughly and clinically. By the time we were done, Gunnar was back from patching and placing the camera at the new barrier rip. He looked at the body and shook his head sadly. 'Aoife Sullivan. She was what? Eighteen?'

'Nineteen,' I confirmed. It was a damned waste.

'What is this world coming to?' He paused for a moment. 'We'll have to notify the mother.'

'And the boyfriend,' I suggested. Luke deserved that much.

I pushed down my emotions and continued to collect evidence. Once we'd done all we could, we prepared to roll the body to see what, if anything, lay beneath her. Gunnar grasped her shoulders and I grasped her hips.

We were turning her when a ghostly apparition appeared behind the body in front of the trees. We almost dropped the body. The apparition – it was Aoife.

Sidnee squeaked and even Gunnar grunted in surprise. We all looked down at the body then back up at her floating identical twin. What the fuck?

The ethereal girl in front of us lifted a slim arm and pointed into the distance. We looked in that direction but couldn't see anything. When we glanced back, she was staring in shock and horror at the body we were holding. She opened her mouth and screamed.

The sound was so piercing and visceral that the three of us dropped the body and desperately threw our hands over our ears to block it out. It didn't help: you couldn't escape a sound that was penetrating through to the marrow of your bones. It vibrated with such force that I was fully prepared to find that my brain had dribbled out of my ears.

I looked up at Aoife. 'Stop!' I begged her. Then it clicked. She was dead, and whatever happened to banshees on death had taken place. She'd been transformed; she was a *full* banshee now, a wailing spirit intent on proclaiming the dead. Unfortunately, she was the one who was dead. Man, that must suck.

The scream continued; since she no longer needed to take breath, I wondered if it would ever end. I prayed that it would soon because I couldn't take much more. Sidnee and Gunnar were doubled over. Through Sidnee's hands, I saw the bright crimson flare of fresh blood. Fuck.

'Aoife!' I barked. 'Enough!' I didn't know whether she heard me or chose to end it, but she began to fade and her voice fell mute.

It took a long minute after her absence for us to come back to ourselves. I realised I was shaking; her scream had been utterly terrifying and it had fucking *hurt*. 'Sidnee? You okay?' I asked.

She was ashen, staring at her hands. The scent of her blood danced on the air and a sudden hunger took me off guard. My body was aching and it knew blood would fix it. I pushed the urge down ruthlessly.

'I've got some potions. One second, Sidnee.' Gunnar jogged to his truck and rifled in the glovebox. He came back with a small vial and some wet wipes to clean her hands and bleeding ears.

'Thanks.' She gave him a grateful smile then downed the vial in one and closed her eyes as it worked. 'That's so much better. It's a pain sometimes being a mermaid,' she muttered. 'Any other shifter would shift to heal but noooo – I have to find a body of water first. Such a pain.'

'How much water?' I asked curiously. 'Like, would a bath do it? A puddle?'

'A bath, yes. A puddle – depends on the size.'

Gunnar had finished cleaning Sidnee up. 'Can we focus, ladies?' he asked drily. 'We can discuss puddles, lakes and streams another time. Let's turn over the body.' Just like that, it was business as usual.

We carefully turned the body. *Oof.* Well, now we had cause of death. Aoife's side had been crushed to a bloody pulp. Only the remnants of her clothing were holding her insides together. What could do something like that?

'Damn,' Sidnee uttered.

'Yeah,' I agreed.

I scanned the ground under the body and found something small and white. I used my tweezers to pick it up and put it in an evidence bag: it was a fake fingernail done in a French manicure. Something teased the edge of my mind; I'd seen something like that recently but I couldn't remember where. I glanced at Aoife's hands. Her nails were trimmed short, painted bright blue – and they were all there.

The nail was obviously an acrylic. I'd had enough experience with tips and full nail sets to know that they liked to pop off and take most of your own nail with them. I flipped it over, and sure enough it had some real fingernail attached. I'd read that you needed a lot of nail material to get DNA but I hoped for the best. I dropped it in the bag and sealed it.

Then I settled down and went back to work, finished photographing the scene and cataloguing what we'd found. I checked Aoife's pockets and even looked inside the horrible cavity in her body; no fire gem. Her killer had taken it.

'No fire gem,' I called to Gunnar.

His expression was grim. 'It was too much to hope for.' He sighed. 'Call it in.'

I phoned the ambulance and we waited for it to arrive in melancholic silence. We were all shaken by the violence of the death, plus it was somehow harder when it was a young woman like this. All her possible futures had ended abruptly. It was grossly unfair.

The ambulance arrived and loaded up the body to deliver for an autopsy. Now came the worst part: informing her mother. My hands went cold and my throat dry. I couldn't imagine hearing the news that I was about to deliver. I wished I had Fluffy with me for moral support.

As always, I channelled my nervousness into my brain and tried to distract myself. Who could have done something like this? What kind of supernatural would attack in such a way?

They say that most murders are committed by someone the victim knows, most often their nearest and dearest. Distasteful as it was, the only two people who came to mind were Nora and Luke. If Thomas had kept his word it should be easy to rule out Luke – but I still needed to consider him.

'Gunnar, what do you know about tariaqsuks? Luke said they weren't very powerful, but could he have crushed that girl's side in?'

'I'm sure even a human could have done it with a heavy enough stick,' Gunnar said.

I blinked. No way. A stick? No. A baseball bat maybe, but they'd really have to whale on the body for a while to do that amount of damage. How would they get her to stay in place long enough? Whoever had killed Aoife had to have surprised her, otherwise poof – she would have teleported away.

We looked at each other but none of us had any ideas. Another mystery. My simple theft case, which should have been so simple to solve, had rolled into murder – and this murder didn't have an easy solution.

I let out a big breath and walked back to the SUV. Time to inform Nora Sullivan that her only child had been murdered.

Chapter 15

Nora opened the door with a frown. 'What? Do you need to search the house again?' she demanded.

I shook my head. 'Would you mind if I came in?'

'Yes, I would,' she huffed.

Great: the porch it was, then. 'I'm sorry, but we've found your daughter Aoife.' I took a breath. 'She's dead.' Damn, I'd forgotten the whole 'I regret to inform you' bit again. I sucked at this.

'What?' She staggered and I reached out to steady her but she slapped my hand away. 'No, that's impossible. There is already a Sullivan banshee. She must be lost.' Then she let out a wail that didn't have anywhere near her daughter's bite.

'Um, we did actually see Aoife afterwards. Her spirit?'

Nora froze. 'You did?' Hope washed over her as I nodded. 'Oh, thank the Goddess.' She leaned heavily against the doorframe, breathing deeply.

'What does it mean seeing Aoife like that?'

Her gaze sharpened. 'Now isn't the time for questions, is it?' She slammed the door in my face.

I grimaced: she wasn't wrong. I'd made a mess of delivering the news, but something else was clearly going on with Aoife. Had her spirit stayed around because she'd been murdered? Nora had talked about a 'Sullivan banshee'. What did that mean? I hated being ignorant but it was hard to be otherwise when the supernats clung to their secrecy like a stripper to a pole.

Sidnee was watching from the car. Terrific: it was always best to humiliate yourself with witnesses. As I climbed back into the driver's side, she touched my arm. 'Sorry, Bunny. That looked rough.'

'Yeah, she was angry. At least, that's how she came across.'

'I'm sure she's in shock. Grief comes differently to people, but anger is one of the stages we all go through at some point.'

I slid her a sideways glance. She seemed to know all about grief but I didn't know how. I cleared my throat. 'I know we'll have to formally question Nora, but let's give her a minute to get her head around it.' Murders were rarely random; most often it was a family member or a spouse.

Sidnee clearly had the same thought. 'Should we go round up the boyfriend?'

I shook my head. 'Let's do the paperwork and call him in tomorrow. He only recently lost his dad so I can't imagine what kind of trauma he'll go through once he finds out about Aoife. Let's give him one more night's sleep. We've informed next of kin, that's enough for now.'

We were both quiet on the drive back to the office. As we turned the last corner, the fire trucks passed us with their sirens blazing. We looked grimly at each other. Had the fire gem struck again?

Sidnee nodded towards the fire engine and I turned the SUV to follow it. I prayed another empty house awaited us.

Gunnar must have got the call whilst we were notifying Nora Sullivan because he and Fluffy were already at the site. We parked up and piled out. 'What's on fire?' I asked breathlessly.

'It's bad,' he said ominously.

That sent a chill down my spine. Gunnar was Mr Glass Half-Full, casual to the point of flippancy most of the time. For him to say something was bad it had to be virtually apocalyptic. Crap: I'd scared myself.

'What is it?' Sidnee asked.

'The house that's burning holds the wind gem.'

'Fuck,' I cursed. My blood ran cold and Sidnee looked like she'd been punched in the stomach.

'Indeed,' Gunnar agreed. 'I hope you don't mind that I brought Fluffy with me.'

'No, that's fine.' My boy was wearing his K-9 vest and wagging his tail, thrilled to be out and about.

'Shadow?' I asked.

'He's in my truck,' Gunnar admitted. 'I didn't want to leave the little fella on his own.'

'I appreciate that.'

'Let's get to work,' he said purposefully. 'Crowd control.'

People had gathered on the other side of the street from the burning house, milling around, muttering amongst themselves, but they were getting ever closer to the burning building. 'Everyone back!' Gunnar barked.

We spread out and pushed them back, mainly for their own protection but partly to ensure that the firemen weren't falling over people while they did their job. Once we'd taped off the area, I looked around and noticed that most of the supernatural council were among the spectators. For once they weren't fighting amongst themselves, which was probably a sign of how serious this situation was.

Liv was there, as were Calliope, Connor, Mafu and Thomas. Stan appeared to be missing, which didn't look great given that the wind gem was supposed to be his responsibility.

With the scene secured, Gunnar joined the council members and Sidnee and I followed. Connor came to my side and the warmth from his presence helped buoy me. It had been a long, grim day.

'Was anyone in the house?' Gunnar asked.

The mayor, Mafu, came forward. 'We don't think so. We won't know for sure until the fire is out but the wind witch is with Liv, and her family is accounted for.'

Liv was talking to a woman with shoulder-length, wavy dark hair. She had her arm around the woman – she almost looked *nice*. Maybe I'd give her a piece of my mind another time.

Gunnar relaxed slightly when he saw the wind witch was alive and so did I. One death a day was enough to deal with. We might be in a lot of trouble if the barrier came down, but until then the more people we could keep safe the better.

Connor's fingers brushed mine and the zing followed immediately. I gave a small, involuntary gasp that he must have heard because when I looked up at him he gave a quick smile. I wished things were simple enough for me to lean into him; I really needed a hug right at that moment. Instead I stood straighter and put my work head back on. 'Has anyone reported seeing anything out of the ordinary?' I asked.

'No,' Connor replied. 'We're waiting to see if the wind gem and its box are damaged.'

'The fire could have been set to hide a possible theft,' I pointed out.

He sighed. 'Yeah, that's certainly possible, but we can't do anything until the fire is out.' He looked around. 'I think that's why all of the council showed up.'

'Where's Stan?'

'He was out on the boat, fishing. I let him know. He's on his way back in.'

Since Connor and Stan were always an inch from each other's throats, I wondered how that had gone down. At least the rivalry about fishing was older than their recent rivalry over me. Despite that, they'd managed to work together on multiple occasions when the need arose and I guessed this was also one of those times. 'It wasn't his fault,' I said in Stan's defence.

Connor's countenance darkened. 'The hell it wasn't! Wind is his responsibility.'

'So, you still blame yourself for the theft of the fire gem?' I countered, wincing as soon as the words left my mouth.

'Yes,' he growled.

Of course he did. I sighed. 'Well, don't. The fire gem was taken by someone who could teleport. There is no defence against that.'

His gaze softened again. 'Perhaps, but the magic users upped the wards after that. No one should have been able to teleport anywhere near the rest of the gems.'

'What do the wards do if someone attempts to breach them?'

He looked at the flames and I followed his gaze. 'Instant immolation,' he said finally.

I was shocked; that gave the fire a whole different meaning. Could it be a ward-defence flame rather than another fire-gem flame? 'Do you think that crossing the ward could have caused this fire?' I gestured to the burning house.

He shook his head. 'No, because that type of fire would be confined to the person. It would leave a hell of a scorch mark on the floor, but it wouldn't catch on anything that wasn't biological.'

'What if someone's child or pet brushed up against the ward?' I could hear the note of horror in my voice. No wonder Kostas had been so paranoid about making sure the ward was down before we trounced through his closet. Killing the Nomo officers would have been a bad look.

'Don't worry. It would only activate if someone was actively trying to take the gem. Intent is part of the ward.'

I relaxed slightly. Perhaps the gem was still safe in the burnt-out shell of the house. I couldn't imagine how someone could survive that kind of ward long enough to steal the wind gem, but there was a good chance that the person who'd taken the gem from Aoife had been here and tried to steal it. The question remained; had they been successful or not?

Fluffy whined and I patted his head. 'We'll look around in a bit, don't worry.' I wanted to check out the rear of the house, but until the fire was out we couldn't get close enough. I wondered how the stink of the smoke would affect Fluffy's ability to scent anything that was out of place.

Connor shot me a rueful smile. 'We're never going to get out of town for our date.'

'No,' I agreed. 'We can't leave until the barrier is safe again.' I'd never forgive myself if it collapsed and I wasn't there to help Sidnee and Gunnar.

'I hear you. So instead I propose bringing the city to you.'

I turned and stared at him. 'That's a bold claim. How are you planning on accomplishing that feat?'

'Now that,' he purred, 'would be telling.'

I felt a shiver start in my core and it was fanned into delicious flames as his breath tickled the shell of my ear when he leaned in to whisper, 'Be ready tomorrow. I'm done waiting.'

My throat closed off. I squeaked, 'Okay.'

He took my hand, gently raised it to his lips, and the usual zing became a roar. When I met his gaze, his eyes were as hot as the flames around us. He released my fingers with obvious reluctance before turning and walking away to speak to Gunnar.

I was left staring at the burning house whilst my insides burned with an entirely different heat.

Chapter 16

It took two hours to contain the fire and for the firefighters to let us look around the outside of the house. They still needed to check the stability of the inside before they would let us paw through the ruins.

We were about to start the search when Stan arrived in his truck, Bessie. He parked up and Liv made a beeline for him, leaving the shaken wind witch cowering in the shadows. 'This is your fault!' she exclaimed stridently as she marched up to him and invaded his personal space. 'I *lent* the council the stones and look what you have done with them!'

'Calm down,' Mafu urged. 'We don't know yet whether or not the stone has been taken.'

Liv ignored Mafu and narrowed her eyes at Stan. 'If it is gone, I will be back for my pound of flesh. You weren't even *here*. None of your shifters were here! So much for your vaunted protection!'

Stan's eyes flashed and he glared right back. 'Oh hell, no. You don't get to lay this at my door. If someone got in then there was a problem with *your* wards!'

I had a death wish, so I stepped between them. 'Enough! Let's start the search and find the damned gem, shall we?'

Liv stalked off, still visibly simmering. 'Fluffy!' I called. 'Let's go.' He obediently trotted forward, nose to the ground. He started to sniff around but I could tell from his frustrated huffs and sneezes that all he was getting was smoke.

Stan joined me. 'Did you have a man on the house?' I asked quietly.

He sighed. 'Yeah,' he admitted unhappily. 'I had someone who was supposed to be here.'

'Who?'

'Martin Snow.'

'Your moose-shifter who was at the barrier protest?' I asked.

'That's the one,' he agreed grimly.

'Stan, it doesn't look good.' With hindsight, it was obvious that he should have removed the barrier protestor from the gem-protection detail.

'I know. I'll speak to him, then you can have him when I'm done.'

I didn't like his proposed order of events, but supernat politics were murky and Stan *was* Snow's leader. 'Make sure he can still talk when you're done with him.'

'No guarantees,' Stan growled, looking far from the jovial man I knew. He was pissed off and I didn't blame him: Snow had dropped the ball and it looked like he'd done it deliberately. But I knew he wasn't working with the fire-gem thief because Aoife was dead. Was Snow's involvement negligence – or was he part of another gem-thieving plot?

We spread out looking for tracks or anything out of place, but after the devastation of the fire and water any evidence had long since been destroyed. We were still waiting for the fire inspector to give the nod so we could look inside. The crowd had dissipated, leaving the council members waiting anxiously.

Sidnee was bouncing on the balls of her feet and I worried about the effects of the energy potion she'd taken combined with Gunnar's healing potion. If anything, she now had too much energy.

To add insult to injury, the fire – and the smells – were giving me flashbacks to my own house burning down. Every sound made me jump; I probably looked like my namesake hopping about the place. I tried to keep a lid on it, but the vision of Virginia and Jim burning to death was hard to shake.

Several hours later we got the okay to go in. The weepy wind witch, Elsa Wintersteen, showed us where the wind gem had been kept and we searched the area thoroughly; even if the box had burned to ash – which wasn't likely considering it was made of metal and covered in enchantments – the magical gem would definitely be there.

We sifted through ash and rubble but there was nothing to be found other than a scorched, stone pillar. The wind gem was gone. This time, though, our thief wasn't a teenage banshee because she'd been murdered by someone who presumably had stolen the fire gem from her. I was fairly certain that someone was now running around with two cursed stones in their fist.

Life had been simpler when I was serving drinks in a bar, but I still wouldn't have traded my current life for anything.

I needed to keep busy so I took Elsa Wintersteen's statement. Like Kostas, she'd been out of the house; she'd been picking up her kids at school and had come home to find the fire. Her husband was at work. She was shaken and upset and kept throwing nervous glances at Liv. If I'd been in charge of something that I'd lost that was under Liv's command, I'd have been nervous, too.

I wanted to keep chasing leads but we were all exhausted, and by tacit agreement we headed back to the office. Dawn was coming, all three of us had been on shift for way too many hours and we were dead on our feet. Even Sidnee was flagging, despite her potion.

We really needed an extra person to cover the office for times like this. Gunnar said he'd call in someone from the mayor's office to answer the phones for the day.

Tomorrow was supposed to be my day off. I hadn't had one in a long time, and now that I knew Connor had our date planned, I was looking forward to it. But there was the small matter of Aoife's murder and the theft of the wind gem, and I didn't know what to do: my head said to cancel the date but my heart said to keep it. There hadn't been a quiet week since I'd arrived here; if I kept waiting for a break in the mayhem before I took time for myself, I'd never have a personal life.

'Hey,' I said quietly to Sidnee. 'I'm supposed to be off tomorrow, but with everything going on...' I trailed off.

She rolled her eyes. 'Don't be stupid. You need time off or you'll burn out or make stupid mistakes because you're over-tired. Sig is already lined up to cover your shift, so take the day off.' She fluttered her eyelashes. 'Spend it getting sweaty with Connor.'

I blushed and ducked into Gunnar's office where he was packing up for the day. 'I'm supposed to be off tomorrow,' I started awkwardly.

'Then you're off.'

'But Aoife—'

Gunnar held up a hand. 'Bunny, has it been quiet since you joined us here in Portlock?'

'Well no, not often.'

'Exactly. Shit happens here because there are a lot of factions with a lot of history. There's only so many hours in the day, and we all need downtime. We'll run down leads in your absence tomorrow and I'll update you when you're back in.'

'If there's anything urgent—'

'I'll call you, like we did with Sidnee even though she was off. Go. Enjoy your day. Come back ready to fight crime.'

I gave him a cheeky salute, which made him smile, then headed home with Shadow and Fluffy. I made us all dinner and added a cup of tea for me. I warmed some blood and gulped it down before the meal.

Bed was calling my name. I locked up and pulled the metal shutters down over the windows – a girl could never be too careful – then all three of us tumbled into bed.

Shadow was going mad, yowling at the door and scratching at it. 'Quit it!' I murmured and pulled a pillow over my ears. The yowling continued: he was probably hungry.

With a reluctant sigh, I sat up and immediately froze. Light was pouring into my room through the bedroom curtains. The metal shutters weren't engaged, but I had definitely put them down!

'Fluffy! Wake up! Something's not right!' I shook him and he sat up, instantly alert. I threw on some clothes and patted Shadow approvingly. 'Sorry, bud. I shouldn't have ignored you. Let's see what we've got,' I whispered, trying to sound brave.

I opened the door and a rush of cold air greeted me. A breeze whistled over my skin, joining my fear and making it prickle.

With Fluffy by my side, I sneaked out of my bedroom as quietly as I could in case I still had an intruder. My gun was at work so I grabbed the knife that I kept in my boot and held it tightly. For once my fangs co-operated; sensing my fear, they snicked down ready to rip and rend flesh.

Then Shadow darted ahead of me. *Dammit, cat*! I picked up the pace and burst out of the hallway into the main living area. All the doors and windows were wide open, and my eyes were instantly drawn to the splash of crimson on the walls. Fear made me think it was blood but a split second later my nose told me it was paint.

Scrawled across the walls were the words *Drop the barrier or you'll burn next!* God damn it! Why was it always me?

Even though my heart was beating far faster than normal, I took the time to check every room and closet in the house. All clear. I was freaked out but safe.

For now.

Chapter 17

I checked the main door was still locked – it was – then I closed and locked the windows. To make me feel better I tried to roll down the metal shutters again, but they didn't work: the mechanism had been broken. I kept hold of the knife and called Gunnar.

'Bunny?' He sounded exasperated. 'What did I say about you having time off?'

'Someone broke into my house while I was sleeping. They got the metal shutters up and they painted a threat on my walls.'

Gunnar let loose a barrage of swear words that had me raising my eyebrows; it was rare to hear him curse. 'I'm on my way,' he promised and hung up. While I waited for him to join me I took photographs, careful not to touch anything so we could preserve any evidence.

I was determined not to be a damsel in distress, even if my hands hadn't quite stopped shaking. This was the worst possible violation. Someone had broken into my *home* while I was sleeping. Fluffy and I had been so bone tired we hadn't heard a thing. What good was supernatural hearing if it didn't work when I was out cold?

Gunnar arrived and brushed for prints but, predictably, we found nothing on any doorknobs or handles. The intruders had worn gloves. He confirmed that the metal shutter mechanism looked like it had been deliberately broken and took photographs of it. 'I'll call Ernie and see if I can get him over to change your locks and sort the shutters,' he said.

I shivered. 'You think someone has a key to my house?'

He shrugged. 'It's possible. This is borough housing and they might not have changed the locks after the last resident left.' He watched the questions churn in my eyes. 'Yes, that's the first thing I'll check when I get back. I'll see if the previous resident still lives in town or if they've moved on.'

I bit my lip. 'It could be Nora Sullivan,' I ventured. 'She hates the barrier and she could have teleported in. I told her that her only daughter was dead. She may have some misplaced anger focused on me.'

'I'll check her out,' Gunnar promised. 'Now put this behind you and enjoy your day off. I'll contact the borough insurance and arrange a budget for some paint.'

'Thanks.' It would suck to see the reminder of how my inner peace had been violated while I waited for the borough grant, but I needed to look at it as an opportunity to paint my walls a new colour.

Gunnar left; sure enough, less than an hour later Ernie showed up. 'Hey, Ernie,' I greeted him with a smile.

'Hey, little lady. Heard you had some trouble.' He thrust a takeaway cup of chai latte at me. My favourite.

'Thanks,' I said, suddenly feeling teary at the small act of kindness. There *was* good in the world.

Ernie looked panicked. 'If you cry, I'll leave.'

That was enough to make me grin. 'I'll keep it locked down.'

'Good,' he said gruffly. 'We can't have a vampire crying about town. Mackenzie wouldn't hear the end of it from Ahmaogak.'

'We wouldn't want that,' I agreed.

Ernie was hard to age; I'd put him in his early sixties but he could have been a decade either side of that. He was chewing tobacco but he hacked and spat it out before he came inside.

He hummed and hawed as he examined the locks, then shook his head over the state of the mechanism for the shutters. 'Some people got no respect,' he muttered. 'It ain't right.' He patted me on the shoulder. 'We'll get you fixed up, but you need to get yourself some wards. They're pricey but they're worth paying for.' It had been on my to-do list for a while, but it looked like it was now rocketing up to the top.

A truck rumbled into sight: Connor. He parked up and hopped out carrying a bouquet of flowers. He frowned a little as he spotted Ernie tinkering with my locks. 'Everything okay?' he asked.

'I had a little break in,' I said as cheerfully as I could manage. 'We're all fine. They did some redecorating.'

His jaw clenched. 'May I come in?'

'Sure.'

He passed me the flowers but the gesture was abrupt rather than romantic. Then he pushed past me into the living room and stared at the words on the wall with his fists clenched. 'I will find out who did this,' he promised darkly.

I raised my chin. '*I* will find out who did this.'

Connor's dark rage faded from his eyes to be replaced by amusement. 'You probably will, at that. But can I get a witch here to get this place warded for you?'

'I'd been planning to do the same thing,' I admitted.

'There's a wait list. I'll need to pull some strings to get you to the top of it.'

I bit my thumb. I did want the wards but not at the expense of someone else's place in the queue. 'No, I can't do that.'

He sighed. 'I'll get a witch to do it on top of whoever else they planned to help today. No one will be bumped. Okay?'

I considered that as I looked at the red paint drying on my walls. 'Okay,' I agreed. Only an idiot would say no; I was lots of things but I tried hard not to embrace idiocy. 'Thanks.'

Connor stepped closer and wrapped his arms around me. The delicious zing shuddered through me. 'I'm sorry someone came into your home.'

I leaned into his warmth and let his solid presence settle me. He got it, of course he did. 'Thanks. I'll be okay.'

He pulled back, studying me in that way that he had. A small smile teased the edge of his mouth. 'Of course you will. Do you want to postpone our date?'

I pushed back from him and put my hands on my hips. 'Absolutely not! I'm not missing that for anything. I've been looking forward to it.'

Connor's voice lowered an octave. 'Me too,' he admitted huskily. He pulled me flush against his hard, muscular body; clearly he wasn't done cuddling. I could get behind that plan – I would take all the hugs I could get.

'That's the doors all done,' Ernie said as he strode in. 'Oh sorry. Didn't know y'all were... Well, now.' His ruddy cheeks reddened and I could see him rethinking his earlier remark about Connor.

I flushed. 'Thanks Ernie.' I stepped back. 'Can you sort the metal shutters for me?'

'You bet. I'll get on that now. Right now.' He walked out quickly.

'We embarrassed Ernie.' I rubbed my forehead.

Connor looked amused. 'Ernie's been around a long time. He'll get over it.'

'Thanks for my flowers. I'll put them in water. You'd better go. I need time to beautify myself for later.'

'You're beautiful the way you are.'

'Smooth,' I teased.

'Maybe, but it's completely true. You're beautiful, Bunny Barrington, inside and out.'

That made me blush again. Plenty of people had complimented me on my looks, but this was the first time I could recall someone complimenting me on *who I was.* That felt far more real. Beauty was only skin deep but who I was ... that was everything. And I'd been trying so hard to be a new Bunny, a *better* Bunny. I was on the road to self-improvement and it was rocky, but I was still moving forward and that was a win.

'Thanks,' I said again, but it came out as a whisper.

Connor's eyes softened. He held me again, gently this time, and brushed his lips against my forehead before releasing me and walking away. 'Until later,' he called. He climbed into his truck and roared off, leaving me with Ernie, the flowers and a singing heart.

Chapter 18

Ernie repaired the shutters' mechanism in no time at all. The guy was a fixture in the town: he owned and ran the hardware store/ radio station/ coffee shop and apparently was good at everything, including changing locks and fixing broken shutters. He also refused to accept payment.

'I owe you one,' I said finally.

He gave me a horrified look. 'Don't you be throwing loose favours like that around! There be folks here that'd take advantage of such a thing.'

'Not you,' I said confidently.

Ernie wiped his dirty hands on his overalls. 'Well no. Not me,' he agreed gruffly. 'I'll be seeing you, Officer Barrington. You keep safe now.'

'Thanks, Ernie. I will,' I promised. I hoped I wasn't lying.

With my doors secured and my shutters firmly back down, I went to get ready for my date with Connor. When I checked the time, I shrieked – Connor was due to pick me up in an hour! I wanted everything showered, shaved and smelling sweetly by then; I also wanted my hair, nails and make-up to be perfect but I'd left that a little late. Chatting to Ernie while he worked had distracted me. Never mind: Connor had seen me looking worse. Way worse. I rushed into the shower and scrubbed quickly.

Forty-five minutes later, I'd done my hair and makeup. I looked at my nails and sighed; I didn't have time left for them. My wardrobe was woefully slim since my house fire, but I had a little black dress that I'd found online. I shimmied into it. It clung to my curves – the few that I had – and flared at mid-thigh. It had three-quarter sleeves that started tight and ended in a fluttery ruffle.

I pulled on some black knee-high boots with a chunky, retro heel and admired the effect. I leaned into the black vibes with some eyeliner but then softened it with a smoky eyeshadow. It wasn't my usual style but I liked it.

I wore my blonde hair loose and teased some waves into it with my curling tongs. As always, I wore my necklace with my two charms: one that stopped me combusting in the sun, and one which my nana had given me. I held both of them in my hand for a moment and wondered what Nana would think of my new life. Had she even known that vampires were real?

In Portlock and the other magical towns around the world, supernaturals walked around openly but elsewhere the magical world remained hidden. For me, it would seem utterly bizarre to stroll around a non-magical town.

There was a knock at the door and, after one last check in the mirror, I went to open it. My stomach filled with butterflies and my lazy heart gave a solid beat.

Fluffy and Shadow had been let out and fed, so they were good to cosy up together. I'd warned them I might be home late. I turned on the TV for them.

Shadow was busy playing with a stuffed mouse and flipping it around. Fluffy watched him indulgently from the sofa.

When I opened the door, Connor nearly took my breath away. His dark curls were unruly, which seemed to be their normal state, but he'd clearly tried to do something with them. His eyes were ice blue but they darkened as they raked my body. I could almost feel the caress of his gaze.

He was wearing new jeans and no flannel, for once. Instead he wore a blue shirt that showed off his broad shoulders and slim waist. 'Hi,' he murmured.

'Hi,' I breathed back. He held out a hand and, as I took it, there was that damned zing. We'd have to talk about it – but not now, not yet.

Connor helped me down the two steps and into his truck. That was a hard climb in a short dress and I was glad I'd matched my underwear in case I'd accidentally given him an early peep show.

I shivered with nervous anticipation. He'd said he would 'bring the city to me' but I had no idea what that entailed. Whatever he meant, I was game for it.

This date had been a long time coming and I was more than ready for it.

Chapter 19

Connor drove down the road past town and at first I thought he was taking me to Kamluck Logging. Instead, he turned about halfway there and took us up the hill through the residential part of town. The houses petered out and we pulled onto a long drive that ended at a gated estate. His home, I'd bet money on it.

He clicked a remote and the gate slid quietly open. I was expecting to see a brooding gothic mansion—something dark and mysterious that belonged on a gated estate deep in the woods owned by a sexy vampire leader.

Instead it was an elegant log home that looked almost new. It had a steeply pitched roof and two large balconies that wrapped around most of the walls. There were stone chimneys at both ends of the house, and the glass front looked over Portlock and out to the bay. That was a brag; he was a vampire that wasn't afraid of the sun. Like me, Connor had a charm at his throat that protected him from its rays.

He pulled the truck into a big garage and parked it next to a flashy red Mustang. He helped me out. 'This way,' he said, as he ushered me into his home.

When he led me into the front room, I gasped at the view. 'It's beautiful!'

I looked around. He'd set up the area like a fancy restaurant. There was only one table covered with a black cloth and lit by candles, set with expensive looking silverware and crystal.

He pulled out a chair for me then sat opposite me. 'What do you think?' he asked – did I detect a hint of nerves?

'It's amazing. Your home is lovely.'

'Thank you. I do love it,' he admitted.

A man dressed as a waiter cleared his throat before entering. He carried two bottles of wine. 'Red or white, madam?'

'Red, please.'

'The perfect choice,' he replied smoothly. He opened the bottle and poured the tiniest amount for me to sample. I sipped and then confirmed that I was happy with it – more than happy. It was so long since I'd had a good, full-bodied red. The waiter poured me a full glass. 'And for you, sir?' he asked Connor.

'The same, thank you.'

I liked that. Connor may have hired the guy and set up the whole scene, but he still treated the waiter with respect. In the circles I used to frequent, the patrons considered the staff below their notice. That was probably one of the reasons I'd become a waitress: it was the biggest rebellion I could come up with at the time.

Connor chuckled as he watched me take another sip. 'Better than blood?' he asked.

'Much,' I said emphatically, pulling a face.

He shook his head with amusement. 'Do you have a favourite blood vintage?'

I was confused. 'What do you mean? Can you get it in different years?'

He laughed. 'No, I meant types. I prefer AB. Do *you* have a favourite blood type?'

'No, it's all the same to me. Except deer blood, which is absolutely vile.'

'I was hoping to offer you your favourite blood but my research failed.'

'I'm easy to please. Whatever you have will be fine.'

'No problem. The first course is blood. Since you don't have a favourite, I'll share mine.'

I didn't see him give a signal, but the waiter came back almost immediately with two crystal wine glasses of warmed blood. He placed one in front of me and the other in front of Connor.

His eyes lit up and he flashed me a smile with a tiny bit of fang before sipping then setting down the glass. I knew that was a supreme show of control for a vampire. I looked at my glass. I didn't want to sip it; sipping wasn't a show of control for me, it was prolonging the necessary input of nutrition, nothing more.

Connor watched me, a half grin tilting his lips. He was waiting for me to plug my nose and gulp it down but, since I was born contrary, I took a sip and set down my glass too. The blood didn't taste that bad, but I still didn't like it. The idea was too creepy.

He raised an eyebrow, picked up his glass and downed the blood in one. I laughed and followed suit, plugging my nose and chugging it. Mum would have been horrified. Then I ran my tongue over my teeth: bloody smiles weren't sexy.

No sooner had we finished than the waiter brought out the second course. My foodie eyes lit up. 'Marseille-style shrimp stew,' he announced as he placed the shallow, delicate bowls in front of us.

I took a single bite and my eyes rolled back in my head with pleasure. 'Oh yum. This is fantastic.'

Connor smiled. 'Almost everything was locally grown or caught. I figured it was time to give you a proper taste of Portlock.'

I licked my lips and watched his gaze follow my tongue. I was craving another taste of Portlock, but this hankering had nothing to do with shrimp. With a visible effort, Connor tore his hungry eyes from me and concentrated on his food.

We took the last bite as the next course was brought in. The chef had timed things to perfection. 'Crusty halibut with citrus and fennel salad,' the waiter intoned.

I looked at the colourful salad topped with a piece of delicate white fish, lightly breaded and fried on one side. Halibut fish and chips at the diner was nothing like this. When I took a bite, the flavour exploded in my mouth and the tartness of the citrus with the light fullness of the fish made me groan aloud.

Connor's eyes grew even darker and suddenly a predator was watching me. I squirmed a little but it was with anticipation; I was going to rip that blue shirt off him later. I let the promise show in my eyes and it was his turn to shift in his seat. 'Okay?' I purred.

'My trousers are suddenly tight,' he confessed.

'Too much food?' I asked innocently, batting my eyelashes.

'It has nothing to do with the food and everything to do with the temptress moaning at my table.'

'If you didn't want me moaning, you should have hired a bad chef,' I sassed.

'Oh, I wanted you moaning,' he admitted. 'I flew in the chef from Homer. I'm paying him an extortionate amount – and I'm going to give him one hell of a tip.'

I had a feeling that if Connor hadn't planned all of this and the waiter wasn't there, we'd already be naked and sweaty. The heat between us was palpable and building with each glance. Thankfully – and irritatingly – the waiter interrupted with a tiny scoop of a palate cleanser. 'Mojito sorbet.'

Mint and lime with a tiny hint of sweetness: the sharp flavours cleared my mouth of the two previous fish dishes. 'My God, this is divine. Definitely give the chef a raise.' I made short work of the sorbet and wished there were three more scoops. The one thing I missed from my old life was amazing food – not my parents, not the money, but the food.

The waiter returned with yet another course; many more and I'd pop. 'Moose steak au poivre with red-wine sauce.'

The meat was rare and sliced into slivers with the sauce poured over it, and it was served with three tiny, delicately seasoned potatoes. I had entered foodie heaven. 'This. Is. Amazing!'

Connor gave an indulgent smile; he was enjoying pampering me, and I was certainly enjoying being pampered. 'Which dish is your favourite?' he asked.

'This one. No, the shrimp.' I shook my head. 'The halibut, for sure.'

He laughed. 'You liked them all?'

'I *loved* them all! I haven't had food like this for ages.'

His eyes sparkled. 'Are you ready for dessert?'

I wasn't because I was full to bursting, but I wanted to try it if it was of the same quality as the rest of the meal. There was also the possibility that I was dessert, in which case I was totally on board. I nodded.

The waiter breezed in and presented a tiny cup of something chocolate decorated with a purple chrysanthemum blossom and a berry I didn't recognize. 'Chocolate lavender mousse,' he announced before withdrawing discreetly.

I took a small scoop with my spoon, licked it off and let the flavour linger on my tongue before I swallowed.

It was perfection. Despite my best intentions, I polished off the whole lot.

As the dishes were cleared away, the waiter offered me another glass of wine which I happily accepted, though Connor refused. I raised an eyebrow. 'So I can drive you home,' he explained. His smile had a sad edge to it; he didn't want me to go home. I reached for his hand. I didn't want to go either but it seemed a bit forward to tell him that I wanted to stay.

I heard a heavy door close in the distance and realised we were finally alone: the chef and wait staff had gone. Excitement and nerves warred in my gut. 'You did a fabulous job taking me to the city,' I said. 'Thank you.'

'I'm not done.'

My eyebrows shot up. 'There's more?' I said incredulously.

He smiled. 'There's more.'

Chapter 20

He stood and held out a hand and I let myself be pulled up. He led me through the dining room, down a corridor where one of the doors was being guarded by an armed vampire. Okay, so not totally alone with Connor. My curiosity got the better of me. As Connor took me into another room I asked, 'What's the deal with the guard?'

'That's Cody. He's on security rotation.' Connor hesitated. 'I have some valuable jewels here.'

'Not cursed ones, right?' I was only half-joking.

He grinned. 'Just standard gems. I received a tip-off that someone was targeting them so I put extra security in place.'

'Including Cody.'

'Including Cody,' he agreed.

I looked around the huge space. It was decorated like a club complete with booths, a disco ball, dim lighting and, after Connor punched something into a remote, loud club music. I whirled around and threw my arms round him in delight. A club! He'd made me a club! The one thing Portlock was missing was a place to dance!

'This is so cool! Did you really have this room made for me?'

'Yeah. You like it?'

'I love it!' Impulsively I kissed him, just a swipe of the lips, but then I couldn't help but go back for more. The song changed to a sexy one full of bass and a slow, hip-gyrating rhythm. I pressed my lips to his and let my eyes close as he took what I freely offered.

His tongue plundered my mouth, making me moan again. This was even better than the chocolate mousse. Eventually he pulled back and I could feel that he was struggling with tight trousers again. I itched to help him, but we had all night and the music was calling me. This club needed some dancing.

I turned and leaned back against him as I swayed and writhed to the music. He gave a low appreciative groan. We stood like that for a few minutes as I teased him mercilessly. Then the music changed tempo to something we could *really* dance to.

I'd had ballroom-dance lessons as part of my 'society' education and wanting to learn the tango had been one of my earlier rebellions, much to the amusement of my dance teacher. Thankfully he'd agreed to teach me. He loved dance of all descriptions; having taught me everything on Mum's list, he'd thrown in some extras.

I recognised the strains of Spanish guitar music and registered that the beat was one we could tango to. I took Connor's hand and stepped back. He followed me, his eyes watching the line of my leg as I kicked it forward before drawing it slowly back. He drew me closer to him, masterfully leading me as music flowed around us.

His hands traced a path across my abdomen then swept down the sides of my body. He spun me away but kept pace with me, somehow keeping our bodies glued together. His lips were barely an inch from mine and I itched to close the distance, but before I could he'd spun me away again.

He directed me as we moved seamlessly together. Now his hands were holding my ribcage and brushing the underside of my breasts. I regretted teasing him moments before because he was definitely getting his own back. His hands moved up and down my body, never touching anywhere indecent, yet it felt like the most intimate thing I'd ever experienced.

The dance ended with a deep dip and I let my head fall back. My neck extended in open invitation and finally he took it. His lips scorched a path down my skin before ending teasingly at my collarbone.

I was *so* ready for more, but he pulled me back up. He lifted me, walked us a few steps back until we reached the wall, then lowered his lips to mine. I was lost, drowning in him. My hands tangled in his hair and then that damned zing hit harder than ever. I cried out at the force of it.

It was like a splash of iced water to the face.

I pulled back, chest heaving. 'What is it?' I asked insistently. 'That zing. This *thing* between us. There's chemistry – and then there's whatever the fuck that is.' I searched his eyes for an answer. I couldn't describe the power of it; it was more than chemistry, more than electricity. A couple more zings like that and I'd be a puddle on the floor.

Connor pulled back and I was suddenly cold, bereft in more ways than one. His warmth and the dancing had left me hot and the sudden loss of his body chilled me. His eyes were regretful. Something clenched in my gut. I wasn't going to like what was coming next and he knew it.

He pulled the remote from his back pocket and flicked off the music. I blew out a breath and met his eyes. 'It's bad, isn't it?'

He smiled a crooked smile. 'No, it's not bad, but I expect it'll take you a bit of time to wrap your head around it. That's okay.' He hesitated. 'Can I have one more moment?' he asked.

It seemed churlish to say no, so I nodded. He ran a thumb along my cheekbone and down my jaw and kissed me gently. This time it felt like farewell. But I didn't want farewell! I wanted a horizontal mamba!

'It's not bad,' he repeated. 'But it's not easy. I have two things to tell you. Let's start with the easiest one.' He laced his fingers through mine and pulled me to the nearest leather-lined booth. He slid in first and tugged me in after him. It wasn't lost on me that I could get out; he was expecting me to run, but I was determined to surprise him.

He had kept two secrets from me but I couldn't protest – I still hadn't found the right time to tell him that I was a human flamethrower. 'Okay, hit me.'

'My father, Hamish Mackenzie, is the vampire king of the United States of America.'

That was the easiest one? My jaw dropped then I closed it with a clack. My brain short-circuited with panic. 'You're like *Franklin*?'

'I'm nothing like Franklin!' he said firmly.

'Sorry. I didn't mean that. I mean you're the crown prince or whatever?'

'Kind of. I'm having a ... sabbatical. I came to Portlock for a change of scene and politics. I needed some downtime.' He grimaced. 'But when I arrived, the vampire leader here was a narcissistic asshole who used his power abusively so...'

'You put him in his place?'

'I put him in his *grave*,' he corrected. He sighed. 'And no matter how much I tried to say no, the vampires here wanted me as their leader so here I am with my little fiefdom that my father is happy for me to have – for now.'

'For now?'

'He'll want me back at his side sooner or later. I'm his favourite.'

'Well, no wonder,' I said faintly. 'You're my favourite, too.' I blew out a breath. 'You're a vampire prince.'

'Yeah.'

The question was, did I care? I thought about it for a moment. No, not really, because Connor had obviously broken free from his father's yoke. But Alaska was in America, and suddenly I felt a chill. I'd run far away from the last king, but was I now under a different vampire king's power? Was Connor?

'Do you have to report to your father? Are we his subjects?' My voice quivered.

'No. I took this tiny territory to be *free* of him. He has no control over me unless I give it back to him. Portlock is outside his remit.'

'Okay.' I licked my parched lips. Did Connor's high-born status change who he was? No. Was I comfortable with it? No. Could I get over it? Absolutely. 'It's not like I didn't meet lords and ladies before. It's fine. I can cope with you being a prince.'

He lifted our twined fingers and kissed them. 'I'm glad.'

'But?'

'But it's the next bit that I don't think you'll like.'

I grimaced. 'Try me.'

Connor ran his free hand through his hair. It was a tell of his: he did it when he was nervous or unsure. 'Vampires are one of the few supernatural races that mate for life,' he said slowly.

I relaxed a little. Was this a discussion about monogamy? I was a one-man girl. 'Most humans aim for monogamy too,' I said cautiously.

He shook his head. 'It's not a choice to be monogamous – it's more like nature decides for you...'

My jaw dropped as I connected the dots. 'Fated mates? You're telling me that vampires have *fated mates*?' My eyes flicked to the door and back to him. 'I'm here because you think I'm your fated mate?' My voice was shrill. He wasn't interested in *me*; he was listening to that bloody zing. Like he should do, like a good prince.

His expression was inscrutable. 'Not *think*. I *know* you're my mate.'

Nope.

I was twenty-three and I'd only become undead a dozen weeks ago. Life had been hectic and I barely knew which way was up, let alone who I wanted to spend a freakishly long eternity with. *Until death do us part* had a whole different meaning when you were a vampire. I wasn't ready to commit to a long weekend away, let alone the rest of an insanely long life with him. It was too much.

Connor let my hand go, and it crushed my soul to let his fingers slip from mine. I stood up with shaking legs. All I'd wanted my whole life was to have some independence. I'd travelled halfway around the world to escape one hundred years of servitude only to come here and find someone else trying to lock me down.

'I can't,' I managed.

He smiled and said, 'I know. It's okay.' I could see he was hurting.

'It's not okay. Nothing about this is okay!'

'Poor word selection,' he said carefully. 'I'm ... I'm not trying to pressure you, Bunny. You asked what the zing is and I'm telling you. We may be fated but you can still reject the bond – reject me. You still have a choice.' He was trying to make it better but I was reeling. I couldn't deal with this right now; it was all a mistake, a horrible, horrible joke.

'I need to go,' I blurted out. As I reached for my jacket, I turned back to him. 'I do like you – you know that I like you. But I won't be told by anyone who I can and cannot love. I'm sorry. Thanks for the date, it was amazing until...' I gestured vaguely with my hand.

I spun on my heel and ran to the nearest exit, which was the garage door. Shit! He'd driven me here. I could call a taxi, but at that moment I was feeling rather sick. The walk would do me good. It was a long way back to town but I would do it on my own, much like I would probably live the rest of my life. Alone, alone, alone, like Mary, Mary, who was quite contrary.

I felt a little hysterical. Was I rejecting Connor because I hated being told what to do? Possibly. Was it a huge mistake? Probably. But even knowing that, I couldn't make myself turn around. A band of iron wrapped around my chest and I couldn't breathe. Was this what a panic attack felt like, or what it felt like to walk away from your fated fucking mate?

I made it to the gate before he caught up with me. He took my hand and turned me round to face him. Whatever he'd been about to say died when he caught sight of my face. He reached up and brushed a tear from my cheek. I hadn't even realised I was crying.

'It's okay,' he murmured. 'It's okay. Just breathe, honey.'

I bent double and tried but the air wouldn't move into my lungs. I crouched down, then sat on the gravel. 'I can't breathe!' I panted. The world was swirling around me. Fuck.

'You can. It's okay,' Connor soothed. 'Breathe.' He sat beside me and wrapped an arm around my shoulder, pulling me into his warmth.

I took a breath and then another one. The dizziness faded and my chest started to rise and fall freely.

We sat on the cold gravel for a ridiculous length of time. The silence wasn't heavy or harsh; it rolled around us like a comfort blanket and I wanted to stay wrapped up in it. But I had things to do, murders to solve, pets to feed. 'I need to go,' I said, finally breaking the spell.

'I know. I'll drive you.' He held out his callused hand to me and I met his blue eyes as I took it.

Chapter 21

I scrubbed my face clean and threw the dress into the laundry basket; I couldn't bear to see it. Then I looked in the mirror. My green eyes were miserable, tears close to the surface. I looked like shit.

I left the bathroom and threw myself on the bed, buried my face in my pillow and screamed until my lungs burned. Funnily enough, screaming into a pillow solved nothing. For fuck's sake. I sat up and crossed my legs.

Fluffy came in and whined as he cocked his head back and forth trying to figure out what was wrong. 'Connor told me that we're fated mates,' I told him. 'So I ran away. Awesome, right?'

Fluffy looked at me balefully, then he gave a sympathetic whine and climbed up on the bed next to me. He fixed me with golden eyes, ready to listen. I scruffled his ears. It was easier to be honest with him.

'Besides you, only one person in my entire life has ever loved me for *me*, really loved me – my nana. Mum and Dad … their love is supposed to be all-encompassing and unconditional, but it's not. It never was. They loved me only if I behaved exactly as they wanted, and Mum always looked at me like I was a disappointment. It used to kill me until I learned not to care anymore. But Connor… Am I insane for running away from a man who could really love me?'

Fluffy cocked his head then he barked once. It was hard to tell what that meant. He laid his head on my lap, which made me smile. Even if he thought I was an idiot, Fluffy still loved me; no one loves as unconditionally as a dog. I ran my hand over his coat.

Shadow jumped up on the bed with a squeak and I smiled at him. Maybe cats love unconditionally, too. After seeing nothing fun was going on, he jumped back down and wandered out. Okay, maybe cats *don't* love unconditionally.

I took a deep breath and let it out with a whoosh. 'I think the universe really doesn't like me.' I kept stroking Fluffy's fur, letting that small comfort relax me. 'I don't need one more person to love me because it's an obligation.'

Fluffy looked sad. 'It's okay. You're safe. It's Bunny and Fluffy forever.' I gave a wan smile. 'I know you love me for me,' I paused. 'Well, that and the fact that I feed you.'

He growled lightly and nudged my hand with his nose; I guessed he disagreed that his was cupboard love.

'Maybe I should give up on men.' I sighed. 'I need to focus on work and look after you and Shadow. That's enough, isn't it? I don't need anyone to love me, I need to learn to love myself.' I fell back on the pillow and Fluffy stretched out with his head on my arm.

I eventually let his reassuring presence soothe me and I fell asleep.

My phone jolted me awake: Sidnee. I groaned. I was sure she was trying to catch me to ask about my date so I considered ignoring it, but it could be work related. In the end I swiped to answer. 'Hey, Sidnee, you okay?'

'Yeah. How was your date? You have to tell me *every*thing.'

I really didn't want to think about it and I wanted to *talk* about it even less. 'It was a disaster. I don't want to talk about it.'

Silence for a beat. 'I'm coming over.'

I opened my mouth to protest but she'd already hung up. Since I was in fluffy pyjamas, I hurriedly got dressed, brushed my teeth and switched on the kettle. By the time I'd done all that she'd arrived. There are pros and cons to having your bestie living so close.

When I opened the door she studied my face then instantly pulled me into a hug. 'Oh, love,' she said sympathetically. 'I'm so sorry.'

I tried to hold back my tears as I mentally added Sidnee to the list of people who loved me unconditionally. In truth, I could probably add Sigrid and Gunnar as well.

'I like what you've done with the place,' she said once she'd pulled back.

I looked at the threatening red paint on my walls and laughed, then I started to cry. Sidnee put her arms around me again and I sobbed with all the intensity my bruised heart could sustain.

After I'd cried myself out, she made us tea. Tea made *everything* better, if only by a little. 'So, start at the beginning. What did that asshole do? I promise I can come up with some excellent plans for revenge.'

I took a drink. 'He told me we're fated mates.'

Her jaw dropped and she stared at me, then snapped her mouth closed. 'Ok-ay,' she drew the word out slowly. 'But he didn't try anything creepy?'

'No.'

'He didn't become controlling and try to lock you up in his basement?'

I snorted. 'No, of course not.'

She handed me a cup of tea and turned back to the counter to add milk to her own. 'Did he say he was fighting the bond and that he thought you should stay away from each other and that he secretly hated you?'

'Um... No, he didn't.'

She sat down and sipped her tea. An irritated puff of air escaped her lips. 'So, what's the problem?'

'I...'

She raised her eyebrows.

'Me, I suppose.'

She waited.

'I grew up privileged.'

'I noticed, love, but what's that got to do with anything?' Her brows scrunched together in confusion.

I stood up and walked around the couch because I couldn't look at her. I was well aware that plenty of people had it far worse than me. I hadn't been beaten or abused, I just hadn't been loved, and it was hard to put that feeling into words without sounding pathetic.

'My dad is always working – he runs a multi-million-pound company – and my mum spends her time on charities and social climbing.' I sat back down. 'I was raised by a series of nannies. The only person that regularly checked on me or wanted to spend time with me without being paid was my nana.' I stared down at my hands, afraid to look at her for fear of the rejection and judgement I was sure I would see.

Sidnee cleared her throat. 'So, you feel like being a fated mate is another way someone is being forced to love you?'

I looked up at her, startled. That was exactly it. 'Yes. Precisely.'

She looked at me with compassion. 'I get it, I really do. But it's not Connor's fault that you're fated mates any more than it's yours.'

I closed my eyes. 'I know.'

'Speaking as someone who fell in love with an asshole, got used, abused, and then abandoned, I'd say there are worse things than being destined for each other.' Her eyes filled with tears. 'You have a chance at happiness, Bunny. Don't lose it because of your fucked-up parents. If you do, you're letting them ruin even more of your life.'

She dashed away her own tears and gave me a watery smile and another quick hug. 'I have to go to work.' Then she ran out of my house.

I felt terrible. My problem was that someone wanted me; hers was that someone *hadn't* wanted her. Talking about my shit had reminded her of her own.

If ever I found Chris, I was going to kill him.

Chapter 22

I walked into work early and saw with relief that Sidnee hadn't left yet. I wanted to make sure she was okay after our chat that morning.

Emotional and tired, I'd gone back to sleep after her visit. I'd slept fitfully, burning with guilt about how I'd treated both her and Connor. I knew I could make it up to one of them, at least.

Her eyes met mine as I walked in the main door, then she came flying around the high counter. We both said, 'Sorry!' at the same time and the awkwardness made me laugh. She started snickering, too.

'Let me go first,' I said. 'I'm sorry about earlier. I know you've had it rough. My moaning was a wallow in self-pity and I shouldn't have dumped it on you.'

She shook her head. 'No, I came round and demanded that you talk about it. Friends are supposed to support friends. What I've been through doesn't lessen what you're going through. You have every right to your feelings and I acted like a schmuck. I shouldn't have made it about me.'

We shared another awkward laugh as I touched her arm. 'Look, Sidnee, you shouldn't hold this stuff in. I know you must be hurting. You know I'm here, right? I'm a really good listener.'

She looked sombre. 'Yeah, I know. Thanks, Bunny. I promise I'll be ready to talk soon. Just give me a little more time.'

I nodded. 'Whatever you need.' I understood about needing time to work things through. That was basically what I'd thrown at Connor, and I was still confused about the knot of emotions I was feeling about the whole mess.

'Bunny, are you there?' Gunnar bellowed from the back office.

'Yeah, boss.'

'Come back here,' he demanded.

I smiled apologetically at Sidnee. 'Lunch later?'

'Sounds good, see you then.' She gave me a proper smile, and I really hoped that this time she wouldn't cancel on me.

I dropped my bag on my desk and unclipped Fluffy's lead. When I put Shadow down, he immediately went to Sidnee for a cuddle.

I went into Gunnar's office. 'Hey.'

'Good evening, Bunny. Lab results came back on the hair strand found at Kostas's house. It had a hair follicle and it was positive for Aoife Sullivan. We can prove that she stole the fire gem. Good work.'

Knowing that Aoife Sullivan's body was being sliced up for an autopsy as we spoke eradicated any pride I might have felt. 'Seems like too little too late,' I groused. 'I feel like I'm chasing my tail.'

'You did great police work. It's sad about Aoife, but don't forget our focus. Let's find the bastard that did this to her, and who in all likelihood stole the fire gem and probably the wind gem too.'

I nodded. It didn't make me feel better that we were so far behind the game. We didn't even have a suspect except for her nearest and dearest. 'I've got appointments with her mum and boyfriend in...' I looked at my phone '...an hour and twenty minutes.'

He nodded. 'I've got a meeting with the council. Let's divide and conquer.' As I turned to go back to my desk he added, 'We're also supposed to meet Liv later to inspect the residences where the earth and water gems are being stored. They *cannot* be lost as well. So keep that on your radar – you should have plenty of time for your interviews and even lunch.'

'Got it, boss.'

He gave a dismissive grunt and I left his office. Sidnee had gone for the day so I settled Fluffy and Shadow and went to see what she'd left for me. She and Gunnar had interviewed all the barrier protestors and I scanned their notes. I frowned at Sidnee's call log. Hardly any calls were recorded, so it must have been a slow day.

I called Thomas and asked for a report on Luke's movements, then answered a few emails, did some filing and watched some of the barrier protestors' interviews. I finished with fifteen minutes to spare before Nora Sullivan was due to arrive. She'd been less than friendly when I'd made the appointment and I was dreading her dark looks and snarky remarks, but she'd lost her daughter and it wasn't hard to understand that grief was making her lash out. She still struck me as a little uncaring but maybe I was bringing my own mummy issues to the table.

After prickly Nora I would have to face woefully sad Luke, and I didn't know which one would be worse. I switched on the kettle for tea; that always helped to calm me. It was nearly ready when Nora came in. I added a cow's worth of milk to my brew and walked out to greet her.

'Good evening, Ms Sullivan. If you'd follow me?' I took her around the counter to the interview room. 'Would you like something to drink?' I offered solicitously.

Glaring at me, she shook her head. Her yellow eyes looked pale and creepy under the fluorescent lights. I put down my cup and pulled out my tablet with the questions on it. 'How are you doing?' I asked sympathetically. Something about her rubbed me up the wrong way but I was working hard to be empathetic.

She shrugged. 'I'm fine,' she said abruptly. 'Let's get this over with.'

Fine with me. 'Where were you on Tuesday night between the hours of 10pm and 3am?'

She stared daggers at me. 'You think I murdered my daughter?'

I looked at her squarely. 'Honestly, I don't, but I must say you don't seem as bereft as one might expect.'

She gave a sharp, rueful laugh. 'Of course not! My daughter has *ascended*,' she said triumphantly.

I blinked at her. I had no idea what she was talking about. My ignorance must have shown on my face because she explained. 'Banshees have two life cycles. In our mortal shell we can procreate and live like other supernats, but our next life cycle is not guaranteed. Only one banshee in each family in each generation can ascend. And my Aoife was chosen.' She sounded proud, not sad in the slightest.

Okay, so maybe that explained why she wasn't devastated – though presumably it meant no earthly future for her daughter, no wedding, no grandchildren. Wasn't that worth a little sadness?

'What happens to those that don't ascend?'

She shrugged. 'They move on, leave this world like anyone else.'

'What does it mean to be one of the ascended?' I was curious what effect Aoife in her spirit banshee form could have on the physical plane.

'Haven't you ever heard of our kind, vampire?' Nora sneered at me.

'Of course I have, but I didn't know about your double life cycle, or the one banshee per family per generation thing. Supernats are close-mouthed about their own species.' I kept my voice matter of fact.

She huffed. 'As a regular banshee, she'll wail the deaths of an entire generation of the Sullivan clan. If she's a strong banshee, she'll be able to communicate with her loved ones, both friends and family. And if she's exceptional, as I think she will be, she'll be able to affect the physical world to some extent. She may even be able to communicate with people that she doesn't have a strong emotional connection to.'

Aoife had appeared to us: did that mean she was super strong? I perked up a little. If she could communicate, perhaps she could tell us who killed her. 'You say she could move things around. Is that like a poltergeist?'

'It depends on how strong she is. We have a family story about my great-great-great grandmother. She was almost as physically present as I am.'

'When I told you the news of Aoife's death, you said there was already a Sullivan banshee.'

'There is,' she sniffed. 'But from a different generation. I wasn't sure if there'd been enough time between the last banshee's and Aoife's deaths, but evidently there was.'

I'd had no idea that banshees were so complex. Multiple lifecycles and some of the ascended-spirit banshees could impact directly on the world. I'd certainly seen and heard Aoife, but what I'd seen was a scared girl wailing about her premature death. She had seemed pretty fucking traumatised to me – but what did I know?

Chapter 23

I continued the interview. 'Did you know that Aoife had stolen the fire gem?' I asked abruptly, hoping to shock something out of her.

Nora pursed her lips. 'Not until you told me,' she said flatly.

'Do you know why she did that?'

She smirked proudly. 'To bring that damned barrier down, of course. For years she's heard me talk about that ridiculous tax bleeding our finances dry – and for what? To protect us from the bogeyman? It's absurd. We're supernats, for god's sake. We fear nothing and no one.'

She could speak for herself; I feared plenty of things including spiders, commitment, and the monster beyond the barrier. 'Have you actively done anything to bring the barrier down?' I asked.

She looked down and away from me. My gut told me the real answer was yes even as she was saying no.

'You've protested,' I pointed out.

'And that's all,' she lied.

'How far can you teleport?' I demanded.

'That's none of your business,' she retorted.

'It *is* my business. I'll remind you that this interview is voluntary at the moment, but if you leave some questions unanswered I might have to take it to the next level.' I looked her in the eye. She might think I was bluffing but I really did suspect she had something to do with the theft of the wind gem. She wanted the barrier down.

Now that I knew how banshees worked, I was also suspicious that she might have had something to do with her daughter's death. She could have killed Aoife so that the girl could ascend to the position of family banshee. She hadn't lost her daughter with her death, not truly.

'I can teleport a hundred feet,' she snapped.

'Could Aoife do the same?'

'She's stronger.' Nora's voice was full of pride. 'She can teleport almost a mile.'

I realised she was responding in present tense, as though her daughter were still alive. Maybe I was wrong about her and she *was* grieving, or at least deep in denial. She started to chew on a fingernail and I noticed they were all ragged and short; she was an anxiety chewer like me.

'Have you ever considered having your nails done?' I asked lightly, wondering if it could have been her fake nail I'd found beneath her daughter. 'I used to chew mine until I started getting the fake ones. It stopped when I couldn't chew through them.'

She dropped her hands. 'It doesn't stop me.' My ears pricked up and excitement coursed through me. 'So I quit getting them done.'

Dammit. 'Is there anyone you can think of that would want Aoife dead?'

Nora's face tightened into a scowl. 'No. Everyone loved her.'

The only time I'd met Aoife before all this started, she'd been friendly enough. She'd reported a drug bust and been excited and giggly, although now that I thought back she could have been drunk or high. 'Did Aoife take drugs?' I asked.

'*What*? No, she did not!' Nora stood up, outraged. 'What are you insinuating? Are you trying to blame her for her own death?'

'Of course not. Sit down, please. No, I'm not trying to blame her for her own murder; I'm trying to narrow down a suspect. Drug dealers aren't known for their kind natures.'

She glared at me icily but reluctantly sat back down. 'Drugs?' I prompted.

'I don't know,' she admitted grudgingly. 'She's underage for alcohol and marijuana, so if she did either she kept it from me. She knows I wouldn't tolerate that kind of thing.'

I had no idea if fisheye could harm a banshee, though it had killed a vampire, almost killed a demigod and generally wrought havoc around town. I guessed it was too late to worry about Aoife taking it.

'What about Luke?' I probed.

'What about him?'

'Do you think he could have killed Aoife?'

'No. He's a good kid. He's been through a lot, and he adores Aoife.'

'Do you know where we found Aoife's body?'

Nora paled but nodded.

'Do you know why she was there?' She'd been behind some houses at the edge of the woods and that had been bothering me. The family who owned the property didn't know her and were deeply disturbed about what had happened. There was no logical reason for her to have been there.

Nora shook her head. 'I don't know for sure but I have my suspicions. I wondered if it was a stopping point for her when she teleported from home to wherever. It's at the edge of her teleport range from our house.'

That made sense: Aoife probably stopped in the same places when she teleported. With a range of about a mile, she could get to town from her house with two stops. Since no one had reported her zipping around, she must have kept her abilities on the down-low and paused in discreet places like the woods.

'Is there a limit to how many times you can teleport in a fixed period of time?' I asked.

'It depends on your energy reserves. Aoife was stronger than me in that regard too,' she said proudly.

Since she seemed off-guard, I asked, 'Did you harm your daughter?'

'No! Never!' she snarled at me.

'Did you steal the wind gem or take the fire gem from your daughter?'

'Absolutely not.' She stood up and put her hands on her hips. Her shirt sleeve rode up, exposing her wrist where a fleck of red paint was visible – red paint the exact shade of the threats on my wall. I let my eyes linger there deliberately and she hastily pulled down her sleeve.

'Done any spray painting recently?' I asked mildly.

'You can't prove anything,' she hissed. And then she teleported away.

Chapter 24

Nora's anti-barrier sentiments had been clear in all of our chats and I wouldn't have put it past her to steal either of the gems, but despite her prickly demeanour I really didn't think she'd harm her own kid. Me, however... I was ninety-nine percent sure she was the one who'd spray- painted a threat to burn me if I didn't drop the barrier.

No doubt she'd busted the shutter mechanism to make it appear that someone had sneaked in, then she'd teleported into my home, sprayed the message, opened the windows to look like the intruder had escaped through them – and teleported out.

Luckily for everyone involved, I didn't have the skills or inclination to drop the barrier. She could try and set me on fire if she liked but I had my own flames to bring to the table; I could fight fire with fire.

I had a few minutes before Luke was due to arrive, so I checked my phone. I had a text message from Thomas Patkotak, our resident supernat hunter: *I stuck to him like glue, but he went straight home and stayed in bed for the next fifteen hours, exonerating him of any direct involvement in Sullivan's death.*

I'd half-expected that but I was still disappointed. If it wasn't Nora and it couldn't be Luke, who the fuck had killed Aoife Sullivan?

I dropped Thomas a message thanking him and confirming that he could stop monitoring Luke. He replied and said he'd bill the council for his time.

Luke appeared just as I was making another cup of tea, his eyes red-rimmed and his shoulders slumped. His whole body looked like it was curving in on itself.

I felt really bad for calling him in. According to Thomas, Luke wasn't implicated in Aoife's death and he'd also lost his father less than a month ago. Grief was his new best friend and my heart ached for him.

I took him into the interview room and started the recording. 'I'm sorry for your loss – and I'm really sorry I have to ask you these questions at such a difficult time.'

He nodded. 'I know. I want to help you catch whoever hurt Aoife. She was so amazing – she didn't deserve this – no one deserves this. I can't stop wondering if she died alone and in pain. If she saw it coming, if she was scared.' His voice hitched. 'I can't stop thinking about her. I've barely slept.'

I understood; it wasn't that long since I'd lost my nana and at least she'd lived a full life. I missed her but it was a different kind of grief. Luke was mourning Aoife's potential, the future they might have had together. 'It's a hard time and I'm sorry to make it worse, so let's get the questions over and done with as quickly as we can, hey?'

Luke gave a wan smile so I powered on. 'Where were you Tuesday night between the hours of 10pm and 3am?'

'I was home, asleep in bed.' He sniffed and his eyes filled with tears. I pushed a box of tissue towards him.

'Did you ever harm Aoife Sullivan?' I asked.

'No, never! I loved her.'

The tears really fell then and I felt like a total twat. 'I'm sorry to ask this, Luke, but do you know anyone who would want her dead?'

He shook his head fiercely then stopped suddenly. 'Maybe her dad?'

'Her dad?' Now I was confused because Nora had marked him as deceased on her paperwork. 'Ms Sullivan indicated that he was dead.'

'She might have wished he was dead but he's not. He got out of prison.'

So Nora was a liar, liar, pants on fire. 'Is he a banshee?' Gunnar had said that he'd never seen a male banshee, but it was sensible to check.

'No,' Luke replied. 'Banshees are always female. From what Aoife told me, when female banshees want to breed they find a powerful supernat male to procreate with. Sometimes it works out as a long-time deal, but most banshees don't bother with marriage or family life. They just want a kid – a daughter, to be precise.'

It probably didn't matter now, but Luke had confessed to me that his family weren't powerful.

Young love aside, he and Aoife probably wouldn't have worked out in the long run.

'Did Aoife have any non-banshee half-siblings?' I asked.

'She wondered about that. If she did, she didn't know about them.'

'Tell me more about her father. Is he in town? What's his name?'

'Aoife told me that he got back last week. He's a powerful witch, and I think she said his first name is Curt or Cayden – something like that. I'm almost positive it begins with C.'

'Did he have the same last name? Sullivan?'

'No, I don't think so. Banshees take the name of their family caste.'

'Why do you think he could have killed her?'

'Aoife was worried because she took something from him once and she wouldn't give it back. She said he wasn't a good guy and she always sounded scared of him. She said he was super powerful. I'm a total idiot – I can't believe I didn't think of him right away. You could have arrested him already!' Luke was agitated, pulling at the sleeves of his shirt.

'It's okay,' I soothed. 'We'll find him and speak to him.'

The last remnants of energy left him and he looked ready to drop. His hands were shaking and he was crying again. Time to cut him loose. 'Thanks, Luke. If you think of anything else, please call me. You're free to go.'

He left slowly, moving like a wounded animal. I went to see Gunnar and share the news about Aoife's very much alive and supposedly nefarious dad.

My boss was looking harassed when I knocked on the door jamb. 'Hey. I've got some news.' I ran through both interviews with him. 'Did you know that Aoife Sullivan's dad is alive, and that she stole something from him?'

'Well, now. I thought Nora said he was dead.' He sounded interested.

'She did, but Aoife confided in Luke that he wasn't.'

'You get a name?'

'No. He's a newcomer to town and his name could be Curt, Cayden or something beginning with C,' I recited.

Gunnar grinned. 'Good. We have records of any newcomers.'

'That's supposing he hasn't been here before and registered, and that he's come through the proper channels.'

'True,' Gunnar conceded.

'Either way, we need to search the records. I'll get Sidnee on it – she's a wiz at that. And if Nora is covering for her ex, she's moved up the suspect list with him.'

'She's a distinct possibility.'

I sighed. 'She is, but something is telling me no. She has the means because she can teleport. She has the motive – she hates the barrier tax and she might have wanted to help her daughter ascend and try to bring it down. And Nora had the opportunity because that ability to teleport will be convenient when she's at work. She's also been caught lying about the dad, so we can't trust her when she says her range is about a hundred feet.'

'So what's stopping your gut?' Gunnar asked curiously.

I shook my head. 'I don't know. Maybe I struggle to accept a mum would kill her child.'

'People do all terrible things for the very flimsiest of reason,' he said darkly.

I thought of Fluffy, abandoned and starving in a bin. He wasn't wrong. 'How did it go with the council?'

'As you can imagine, they're up in arms. Someone has both gems and if we don't get the gems restored soon, the barrier will fall.'

My scalp prickled. 'Getting the gemstones needs to be our priority. There's no evidence at the wind witch's house – any evidence was totally incinerated, so we have to follow the trail for Aoife.'

'Whoever killed her took the fire stone and used it to raze Wintersteen's house and steal the wind gem. Even if your gut doesn't like Nora, it's all we've got to work with. We don't have any hard evidence against her, but we do have plenty of suspicion. We need to find something – anything – and arrest her. If there are no more fires while she's in the lockup, it's likely we've got the right suspect. I think it's time for an old-fashioned stake-out but with a dash of modern ingenuity.' He looked at me. 'Stop with the wrinkled brow and say it.'

'How do we watch someone who can teleport? We'd never know how to find her.'

'We'll see if her alleged crimes are strong enough to get us a warrant to plant a camera in her house.'

'That's legal?'

'It's tricky. It's usually only used with suspected terrorists, but if she has those gems and is trying to bring down the barrier that could be interpreted as terrorism. It depends on whether the council agrees. My gut says they will.' He sounded grim.

The idea of planting cameras in someone's home made me uncomfortable, but I had no other smart ideas about how to watch a teleporting supernat. We were too short-staffed for an old-fashioned stakeout.

Gunnar smiled. 'Don't worry, we won't place them in her bedroom or bathroom, but we can put them in the living room and kitchen. We'll also see if there's a good spot for outside surveillance. I wish we had the budget for drones and extra staff with cases like this.' He was right: if we were to keep the other two gemstones safe, we needed a bigger budget.

'When are we meeting Liv about the remaining stones?' I asked.

He rolled his head from side to side and puffed out a breath that moved his beard and moustache. Subconsciously he was limbering up to face her. 'Two hours.'

'Okay. I'm heading to lunch after I do the paperwork from the interviews. Any new applicants for the filing job?'

'Haven't checked. Why don't you look at the computer for me? I'll check the mail.' Gunnar heaved himself out of his chair to head for the post office and I went to see if we had any email applicants.

Only three. I scanned through them. The first was a no: everything on the application was misspelt apart from their name – at least I hoped they hadn't misspelt their name. The second one was spelled correctly, but there wasn't much experience. However it was worth an interview because we were growing desperate. The last one gave me pause: April Arctos.

April was the bear-shifter mother of one of our juvenile delinquents whom we'd caught breaking into the Grimes brothers' trading post and who'd taken fisheye. I'd met her a few times and she'd come across as bossy, controlling and competent. I moved her to the top of the list. She'd get us organised in no time, and right now it felt like we needed it.

Chapter 25

'April Arctos?' Sidnee repeated as she noisily slurped a milkshake. 'She'll either be horrendous or she'll be running the show in a day.'

I laughed. 'My thoughts exactly, but who better to be in the office alone? No one would get away with anything.' I took another bite of my burger.

'She has my vote,' Sidnee agreed.

'If it was a democratic process I'd hire her now, but it's got to go through Gunnar and the council first.' I swallowed down some more tasty beef. 'Hey, I noticed that we aren't getting any hotline calls. Have you had any?'

'Oh, yeah, I was getting most of them during my shift, so I had them sent to my phone. I leave you messages if it's something you need to deal with.'

I'd had a few, but not many. 'So the calls have died down a lot?'

Sidnee didn't look at me; she was playing with the salad on her plate. 'Yeah.'

I nodded, but something was niggling at me and I couldn't put my finger on it. Suddenly Sidnee looked beyond me and glared. I turned to see who had earned her wrath and saw a young man and a woman smirking at her. 'Who are they?' I asked.

'No one. Just assholes.' She speared a tomato with her fork.

'Mermaid assholes?'

She tried to give a nonchalant shrug. 'Yeah.'

'You want me to say something to them?'

She gave me a bitter smile. 'Say what, Bunny? "Please leave Sidnee alone, or else?"' That had pretty much been my plan. Then she grinned suddenly. 'That *was* your plan, wasn't it?'

'I was maybe going to flash my gun, too,' I confessed.

She laughed aloud. 'You're the best! You know that, right?'

'I'm trying. I'm not good at this friendship thing, but I want to be there for you.'

'You are – you have been and I really appreciate it. Come on, let's go. I'm full anyway.'

We paid the bill and I made sure to level a glare at the two mers as I walked past. They didn't look cowed in the slightest so I was tempted to flash my fangs, but luckily the little buggers didn't listen to me and refused to drop down. As the local law enforcement officer, starting a fight would have been a bad idea.

I hurried back to work. Gunnar and I had an appointment offsite with Liv and she didn't suffer fools, let alone unpunctual ones. We headed out about twenty minutes before we were due to meet her leaving Fluffy and Shadow to hold the fort. Shadow was doing the very serious job of snoozing and Fluffy was in guard-dog mode.

Gunnar took me to a side of town I'd not visited before. Portlock was on the tip of the Kenai Peninsula, on the south-east side of Port Chatham Bay, but there was an additional spit of land that jutted into the bay with a few expensive houses on it.

We drove to the last one. With water on three sides it had an amazing view, though I wasn't sure I could have lived there. I'd be spooked in a storm, and the water around the house would be tempestuous.

The house was made of wood and stone and looked very solid, except for its huge windows. We knocked. Liv answered the door and we entered the stylish, nautically themed interior. The homeowner had a love of quotes: things like *Shore is nice!* and *My sense of direction leads me one way: to the beach!* were splashed on the walls. That was how I knew the house definitely wasn't Liv's: no way she'd have anything cute on her walls. She'd have something dead, for sure.

A sturdily built woman stood up. She had dusky colouring, suggesting she was native to the area, and two thick, dark braids that hung to her waist. Her dark eyes were framed with eyelashes that any celebrity would have killed for.

Liv introduced us. 'This is Adelheid Paneok, the water witch. I've been here all day strengthening the wards. See what additional security measures you can put in place,' she ordered briskly. Her eyes lingered on Gunnar but there was no trace of her usual flirtatiousness; she didn't even sashay as she showed us to the room at the end of a hall.

My scalp started to itch as we neared the door. When Liv opened it, we saw that it was a vault. The door was four inches of steel with a complex locking mechanism. I was impressed: this was the most secure location I'd seen so far. Liv showed us that the box containing the water gem was securely on its plinth.

'Are the walls reinforced as well as the door?' I asked Adelheid.

'Yes, reinforced concrete like a bank vault.'

'It's possible that the thief can teleport in. Do the wards go all the way to the box?'

'Yes, we took that suggestion and put it in place. There is only a half-foot buffer between the wards and the box, if anyone teleported in, they'd be fried.'

Some skinny people might have a depth of less than fifteen centimetres, but that was unlikely; one wobble backwards and they'd be incinerated. Maybe we needed to let the would-be thieves know what they were facing to discourage more thefts.

When I said as much, Liv snorted. 'No, Bunny, we're not announcing the measures. It would be like a bank vault putting their blueprints in a newspaper.' Her tone was scathing. 'It would invite a break-in. If anyone tries it and gets incinerated, more fool them.'

'Would you allow us to place a camera inside the vault and outside the door?' Gunnar asked, changing the topic. I shot him a grateful look.

Adelheid hesitated. 'They'd only be in those places?'

'Absolutely,' he promised.

'Then sure, no problem. But I'd have to drop the wards long enough to install them. Would that be safe?'

'Yes. We'll do the installation ourselves. I don't want anyone except those of us in this room to have access.'

'When can you do it, Nomo?' Liv asked.

Gunnar frowned at her. 'Are we expected at the earth gem soon?'

'No, I gave them a three-hour window.'

'Then I can do it now.'

Liv was impressed and her eyebrows rose a little before she schooled her face. Poor Gunnar – his efficiency had probably revived her ardour.

Adelheid started the process of lowering the wards by lighting candles and chanting while Gunnar hustled out to the SUV. He returned with a large tote bag and a toolbox. It took a while for the wards to drop, which made Liv smile in satisfaction. When they were down, Adelheid swayed a little and the irritating itch on my scalp stopped abruptly.

'Okay?' I asked the tired witch.

She flashed me a brilliant smile. 'I will be in a moment. It's nowhere near as bad as putting wards *up*, but it does take it out of you.'

'Can I ask a question?'

The water witch glanced at Liv who gave a nearly imperceptible nod. 'Go ahead,' she said. 'Shoot.'

'What exactly is the water gem?'

'It's a large, brilliant cut sapphire, about the size of...'

'A fist?' I finished for her.

'Well l... Yes.' She gave me an odd look.

'Has anyone new come into your life recently? Has anyone shown an interest in your routine?'

She thought about it then shook her head. 'No, I don't think so, ma'am.'

'Other than yourself, who could lower your wards?'

'Well, obviously Miss Fox here and the other guardians. I suppose another elemental witch who was powerful enough could do it if they had enough time and patience, but there's no one in this town capable of it. Liv has sent for more witch elementals to join us but they won't arrive for a few days yet.' She looked into the vault. 'Watch yourself,' she warned softly. 'The wards aren't there to protect the stone.'

Gunnar started the installation and I stopped chinwagging. I drew my gun and stood beside the pedestal, keeping my eyes on the box the entire time: I didn't want to blink and have a sticky-fingered teleporting-banshee snatch it in a flash. The thief would know we were checking the other stones; if they wanted to try for that trifecta, the time would be now.

Something about the gem was making me uncomfortable and I felt odd – off somehow – being this near to it. It had a malevolent energy that set my nerves on edge, and a hum that rattled my back teeth. My fingers itched to flick open the box and look inside; the need to grab it and run was unmistakable. I planted my feet more firmly and held steady.

Gunnar looked up mid-install and nodded approval. His hands were shaking with the effort of resisting the gem. Jesus, what was up with these damned things?

Once he'd finished installing the cameras, the witch put the wards back up. She was visibly drained.

The itch started again and I pushed down the urge to put a distance between myself and the wards. 'Do you have to do your thing again with the wards?' I asked Liv.

'Of course not,' she said dismissively. 'The new wards were already set. Adelheid is lifting and lowering them, not making them all over again.' It was all foreign to me but I nodded as if she were making total sense.

Gunnar installed another camera outside the door. Both were battery run, motion activated and sent images to our phones; they were also video only, so they didn't suck up a lot of power. Once he'd finished and we'd tested that they worked, we said our goodbyes to Adelheid. She was going for a lie down.

We followed Liv to the home of the earth witch. Apparently Calliope was meeting us there – and I wasn't too thrilled at the prospect. Not long ago we'd suspected Soapy, her second and lover, of being a drug dealer so she probably wasn't thrilled with us, either. Plus, she was a terrifying water dragon and I'd seen her kill someone with one bite.

I'd have to remember not to stand too close.

Chapter 26

The earth witch's home was up the mountain and deep in the woods, close to the Grimes brothers' trading post. Like Kostas's home it was a log cabin, but unlike his it looked brand new. It made me think uncomfortably of Connor but I pushed him forcefully from my mind. Now was not the time to try and sort through my muddled emotions. I needed to be sharp and focused.

Liv walked boldly up to the front door and knocked. The witch opened it – at least, I assumed it was the witch. He was medium height, stocky and had a scowl on his face. Charming. Calliope stood behind him, looking bored.

'Gunnar and Bunny, meet Vitus Vogler, the earth witch,' Liv introduced us.

Gunnar seemed to know him, so it was obvious the introduction was for my benefit. Maybe I was growing on Liv – or maybe she knew how to be diplomatic.

'If you'll follow me, I'll show you the gem's security.' Vitus's tone was impatient; he clearly wasn't messing about.

The house was almost completely open plan. There was a large main room with soaring ceilings; above was a loft, and to our left was a short hallway that led to four doors – bedrooms and maybe a bathroom. The wood-burning stove in the middle of the room, surrounded by chunky leather furniture, wasn't lit. There was a large kitchen with commercial-level appliances.

Vitus led us up some steps to the loft; it was half the size of the house and obviously a family room, with a large TV and comfortable furniture. Off it were two doors: one led to a bathroom and the other was for the gem. Both doors were cheap and flimsy; a strong wind or a firm kick could break them down. The security here seemed low and I was surprised it hadn't been targeted first.

'Is it warded?' I asked curiously. My scalp wasn't itching but that wasn't a reason to plough recklessly into the room; I didn't want to get fried by accident.

'I haven't had it warded,' Vitus said. My jaw dropped and Liv started to vibrate with barely contained anger. 'I live so far out here in the sticks that not many people come by, and the only road is visible from my front windows. I'd know if anyone came around.'

'We called you about the other thefts. One of them was done by someone who could teleport,' Gunnar said.

Liv exploded, 'We told you to place extra wards!'

'The *house* is warded,' Vitus responded.

'*We* walked in here!' I said incredulously.

'What do the wards on the house do?' Gunnar asked.

'They send me an alert if anyone enters the house.'

'An alert!' Liv was virtually apoplectic.

'Relax, Liv. No one would dare attack something under *my* protection,' Calliope said.

My mouth spoke before my brain sparked. 'You got kidnapped a few weeks ago! Someone dared attack not a *thing*, but *you*.'

Calliope gave a chilly smile. 'And I ate him.' She smacked her lips.

'Snacking on a thief after the fact won't get the gem back,' Liv snapped. 'And you had indigestion for a week after eating the general.'

'He was very unhealthy, full of trans fats.' Calliope sighed. 'A moment on the lips, a lifetime on the hips.'

'That is such an outdated saying,' I bristled. 'Eat what you want when you want in moderation and do some exercise.'

Gunnar cleared his throat. 'If we can focus?'

I grimaced and turned to the earth witch. 'First things first. Have you checked that the gem is still there?'

'Of course I have,' Vitus scoffed, glaring at me as if I were an imbecile. I was making friends again. 'I check twice a day – which is the rule.' Clearly he was a letter-of-the-law kind of a guy: he did what was required of him and strictly no more.

'Why don't you take it out and show us?' I said.

He looked at me, horrified. 'I can't take it out! It will cause an earthquake.'

'So how do you check it?'

'I lift the lid briefly.'

I didn't trust his lackadaisical attitude so I opened the door of the closet to check. As with the other three barrier gems, there was a stone plinth with a metal box resting on it. I let out the breath I'd been holding, reached in and lifted the box lid.

The green jewel glittered at me and I wanted to pick it up and run away with it. It mesmerised me, holding me locked in place; I knew immediately that it would definitely help me accomplish my life goals.

Luckily, almost as soon as I opened the box Gunnar reached over and snapped it shut, breaking the spell. 'Fuck,' I said shakily. 'What is it with these damned gems?'

'Cursed,' Liv said drily. 'Remember?'

'It's like they're alive...'

'Something like that,' she agreed. 'Well, thanks to Bunny, we know the gem is there. Now it's a matter of keeping it that way.'

'I'm going to place some surveillance cameras, then you and Liv will place several very scary wards around the gem. Got it?' Gunnar's voice was steely.

A bead of sweat rolled down Vitus's forehead. 'Sure.' He threw a quick glance at Liv; she must run her group with an iron fist. He was scared of her – but I would be too if my security was as bad as his. If his gem had been stolen he'd be to blame, and I was sure Liv's wrath would be terrible. He'd got lucky.

'I've checked the exterior of the house and I didn't see anything out of the ordinary,' Calliope said calmly.

Gunnar gave her a barely perceptible nod and started installing the cameras. His phone pinged, and he unlocked it to see what the message said. 'We've got the warrant to install the cameras at Nora Sullivan's,' he murmured to me. 'I'll drop you back and go straight to do that after here, since I have the surveillance equipment already with me.'

I nodded in acknowledgement, better him than me. I'd be so nervous that Nora would walk in while I was installing them.

While Gunnar worked, I talked to Calliope. She wasn't my biggest fan, but I was worried about Sidnee so I braved the storm. 'Any sightings of Chris Jubatus?' I asked.

She looked at me sharply. 'We will report directly to the Nomo's office if he is seen.'

Her siren group was the one best placed to keep an eye out for the selkie. They were also watching the sea cave where there was a huge stash of fisheye waiting for someone to disarm the explosives around it so we could retrieve it for destruction. The siren group had carried out a huge search mission to try and find Chris and the other members of the stray military branch that had breached Portlock and flooded it with the drug. They'd had no success, and Calliope was still salty about it.

'Any activity around the sea cave?' I pressed.

Her response was more of a snarl this time. 'As I said, if we see anything we will report it.'

'Thanks. And I know I've said it before, but I am sorry about the whole suspecting Soapy thing.'

She nodded tersely and moved away; either she wasn't in a chatty mood or she didn't want to chat to *me*. I suspected the latter but told myself it was the former.

When Gunnar was done with the cameras, Vitus and Liv laid down what I hoped were very thick and very deadly wards. While they were busy, I asked Gunnar, 'What kind of magic do necromancers do? I've seen Liv attempt to raise the dead, but how can she add to or make wards? What does death have to do with that?'

'Death powers her magic. Trust me, something died so she could do this today. It was probably a goat or a few chickens, but something died and she is using its life force.'

Liv must have heard my question because she smirked. 'Do I scare you, little dead thing?'

I shuddered, involuntarily. She absolutely did.

She held up a gruesome doll made of fur, feather and bone, stained with a brownish-red substance that

I could smell was old blood. 'This contains the life force of several sacrifices. It is enough for this work.'

Her magic smelled awful to me: old blood, decay and the stench of rot. I stared at the totem and I could almost see the miasma of death around it like a dark aura. As I stared, a feeling of something slithering around and tugging at my guts began and I swayed on my feet. I forced myself to look at Liv. The smirk was still there and I had the sensation of desert sand scouring my skin.

She put the creepy doll back into her voluminous bag and the slithering sensation stopped. She was determined to let me know that she could control me in my undead – or partially undead – state.

Like I'd ever forget.

Chapter 27

According to the cameras Nora Sullivan hadn't done anything suspicious, and we still hadn't managed to track down Aoife's father, so the case had stalled. To make matters worse, the barrier was weakening. Rifts and thinning spots were being reported all over town and Liv and the other magic users were being run ragged doing patch repairs. We were only treating the symptoms, though; we needed to deal with the cause. We needed to find the missing gems – like yesterday.

At least there hadn't been another fire since Elsa Wintersteen's house had burned down. Maybe whoever had the fire gem had wised up to how dangerous it was and was shielding it.

We had the fire gem's protective box, but presumably the thief still had the wind gem's box. Or maybe they'd put both gems in the same box? But why did they want the gemstones? If it was to bring down the barrier, all they needed to do was sit tight whilst we ran out of time. It wasn't a comforting thought.

Connor had been silent since our disastrous date; either he'd given up on me or he was giving me the space I'd demanded. It had only been a couple of days, so maybe the silence wasn't as much of a big deal as I thought, but I was worried I'd really hurt him by walking away. At the same time, he had to understand that I wasn't freaking out over *him* so much as everything that came with him. An immortal lifespan together would freak out any twenty-whatever year old, even one without my contrary nature and loveless upbringing.

It was best not to think about it because thinking made me tense. I needed to solve Aoife's murder, get the gems back where they belonged and save the town. Easy. I pushed away thoughts of Connor – and that was when he walked into the Nomo's office.

When the door opened, I threw out my usual greeting, 'Welcome to the Nomo's office, how may I...?' Then I looked up. He was standing there in his form-fitting jeans and sexy flannel, his black curls untidy as usual. God, I'd missed the flannel.

My tongue fell silent and my stomach clenched. I looked at him expectantly, frozen in that state of flight, fight or freeze. Apparently, I froze in this type of situation. 'Connor,' I breathed.

Fluffy gave a sharp bark and stood up in front of me, as though protecting me.

'*Et tu*, Brute?' Connor said softly to the dog.

I coughed over my involuntary laugh. His eyes zipped back to mine and we spent a moment drinking in the sight of each other. He looked a little tired but okay, and something in me eased – he wasn't *that* mad at me. 'I brought you something.' He held out a bag. As I took it, he ran his fingers nervously through his hair.

The only gift I'd ever received from a man was sexy lingerie and this bag was way too heavy for that. Plus, I wasn't sure if we were even seeing each other after my freak-out, so sexy lingerie would have been weird. 'What is it?' I asked cautiously.

He gave me a lopsided smile, 'A vest.'

'A vest?' I repeated. That was a first. I reached into the bag and pulled out the object. As promised it was a vest, not of the fabric kind but of the bulletproof kind.

'It's spelled,' he said awkwardly. 'I got it from the MIB. Nothing will get through that one.'

I stared at him, conscious that my mouth was hanging open, but I couldn't get my brain to fire enough to know what to say.

'I don't want to see you hurt again.' He shrugged awkwardly. 'No obligation or anything. It is a gift, freely given.'

My floppy heart beat hard and warmed me from the middle outwards. 'Thank you.' It felt like a big deal. Connor knew I didn't want to be with him because of the fated-mates thing, yet here he was still helping me, still trying to protect me in a way that wasn't overbearing or demanding. He understood how much I'd come to love my job and he wanted me to be safe whilst I did it.

'Here, let me help you try it on.'

I put it over my head and he tightened the straps around the body. It wasn't bulky; I could wear it under my clothes and no one would ever know. His hands lingered for a second on my hip, setting my skin on fire. *ZING*. At the force of it, he snatched back his hands. 'Sorry,' he murmured.

I turned to face him. 'No problem,' I managed, though my knees felt weak. The zing didn't like being ignored and it was trying to push us together with all of its considerable might. I imagined for a second what it would be like to give into it, to feel that delicious shock when Connor and I finally...

He was too close and I could still feel the ghost of his touch on my skin. I took an involuntary step forward. Connor's eyes flicked down to my lips – but then he blew out a harsh breath and stepped back. His chest was rising and falling rapidly; he was as affected by all this as I was. 'Is Gunnar in his office?' he asked huskily.

I blinked a few times and finally registered what he'd asked. 'Uh, yes. Go on back.'

'Thanks.' He strolled away as if we weren't both dying to rip off each other's clothes.

I gave a wistful sigh and looked down at Fluffy. 'Thanks buddy. I wonder what he wants Gunnar for?' I scratched his ears, making him paw at the floor as he tried to scratch an itch that wasn't there. We both looked at Gunnar's door. 'It's probably about the warrant for Nora Sullivan.'

Fluffy barked once. 'That's what you think, too?' I asked. With an effort, I sat down again.

Connor walked out a few minutes later. He didn't ignore me but he walked past as though his business were concluded.

'Connor.' I surprised myself by stopping him. He looked at me expectantly. I wasn't sure what to say but I couldn't bear to see him leave. 'I'm sorry about everything.'

He studied me. 'You have nothing to apologise for. Understandably it was a shock.'

'Yeah, it was.' He turned to leave.

'I'm processing it,' I blurted. 'I feel less shocked already.'

He gave me a slow smile. 'I'm glad to hear it. Take all the time you need. I promise I'll be waiting.' He walked out.

I sagged in my chair. At least he didn't seem angry, even if he was giving me more space than I wanted. Truthfully, I wanted zero space between us but I was trying hard to think with my head and not my hormones.

'Bunny!' Gunnar shouted. We really needed an intercom system.

I went into his office. 'You hollered, boss?'

'The council won't give us that warrant without more evidence. Do you have any of your out-of-the-box ideas?'

I leaned against the door jamb. Nothing was coming to me. Absentmindedly I looked down at my hands; I hadn't had a manicure since my Welcome-to-Portlock party a month or more ago and they needed work. I needed a nail appointment.

Something clicked in my brain. Nails. 'Gunnar, it might be nothing but I'm calling the salon for a nail appointment.'

He gave me a strange look. 'However your process works, I guess.'

I rolled my eyes. 'The fingernail under Aoife's body...! There can't be *that* many places in this town to get your nails done. The nail technician might be able to tell us whose it was!'

'And you're booking an appointment because...?'

'Because technicians chat freely while doing nails,' I explained. 'He or she will be relaxed and I'll get more than I'd get from an interview at the station. Unless you want to go instead?'

Gunnar guffawed. 'Uh, no.'

Good, because – and this was the important part – I also really wanted a manicure.

I got on the phone. Sure enough, there was only one nail salon in town and they had an appointment for the next day. I thought about going over and trying to interview them immediately then and there, but in the end I made the appointment. I didn't want to be rushed and dismissed because I was making their customers wait.

Besides, good things come to those who wait.

Chapter 28

As I hung up from the salon, the office phone rang. 'Nomo, Officer Barrington speaking,' I answered briskly.

'Bunny, grab Gunnar and meet us at the barrier closest to the Grimes'. There's a breach, a big one. We're going to need Gunnar's brand of magic.' Liv's voice was grim. Before I could reply, she hung up; cockily certain that we'd come running because she'd summoned us. Annoyingly, she was right.

A breach? Big enough that they were struggling to close it? My blood ran cold. I bellowed at Gunnar, 'There's a breach by the Grimes', we've got to go!'

I heard him get out of his chair so quickly it hit the back wall and met him at the door, Fluffy at my heels. I looked down. 'No, Fluffy, it's not safe.' He barked;

he didn't think it was safe *for me* either. I looked at Gunnar uncertainly.

'Bring him, he can stay in the car,' Gunnar said.

I didn't want Fluffy that close to the beast; if it had breached the barrier, it could already be through and making its way into town. That thought nearly made me piss myself – but there again, if the monster was careening through town, nowhere was safe.

Fluffy made up his own mind, ran to the door and burst through as soon as Gunnar opened it. Close behind him was Shadow. I didn't have time to take my menagerie back, so I scooped up the lynx kitten and set him on the back seat with Fluffy.

Gunnar drove like a madman and we made it to the barrier in record time, bad roads and all. Shadow crawled under the back seat, hissing after a particularly bad pothole, while Fluffy yipped in surprise as he bounced up and down on the seat. Maybe I should keep their kennels in the SUV for emergencies, but I'd never intended for them to come with us in the first place.

There were three vehicles and several people milling about when we arrived. Gunnar and I shot out of the SUV, trying to shut our doors before the animals could escape. Fluffy didn't like that and barked a protest as we dashed away.

Liv and four others were frantically working at the barrier, facing it with their hands up and chanting. The spot that Gunnar, Thomas and I had dived through when we'd found the dead hunters was gushing smoke and I recognized the inky air that was wafting towards us.

It was the same smoke that the beast had sent through the barrier after us. Fear made my mouth dry; my bulletproof vest wouldn't save me from the monster. The magic users seemed to be stopping the beast from physically intruding, but they hadn't managed to push it's smoke back through the hole.

A tiny, outraged meow made my heart stop and I turned; sure enough, Shadow was at my heels. Fuck! He must have slipped out before I could shut the car door, though I could have sworn he was still in there! I scooped him up. 'What are you doing?' I hissed.

Liv came over to us, for once looking tired and very human; there was no trace of her man-eating flirtatious energy. 'Bring your pet to work day?' she bitched. She didn't wait for me to respond. 'We've been doing regular rounds. It's pure luck that we found the tear before the beast made it all the way through. We made it in time, but only just.'

She pointed to a car parked alongside ours. 'The witch that found it is resting in the car. She's exhausted – she had to hold it off for more than ten minutes on her own. Luckily the rift was small or she wouldn't have made it, but the thing on the other side has widened it.'

'What can we do?' I asked. If the witches were on it and the beast hadn't come through, I didn't know what she expected us to add to the situation. My fire magic had once driven the beast back, but there was no way Liv could know about that.

'I need Gunnar to—' Liv started.

Shadow hissed, then he clawed my arm and leapt away as I dropped him. He ran towards the rift and the dark smoky tendrils whipping through the hole. I ran after him. Stupid cat – he was going to get himself killed! He reached the black smoke seconds before me. I screamed, 'Shadow! Come back!' but he was a cat so he blithely ignored me.

Then something amazing happened. The smoky colouring that covered him somehow lifted from his tiny form, leaving behind the tawny-silvery colouring of a normal lynx. His shadow leapt at the invading smoke and there was hissing and roaring and yowling. It sounded horrendous, but I knew that somehow Shadow was fighting the beast.

We watched dumbfounded as he pushed the invading smoke back through the hole. 'Seal it!' Liv barked to Gunnar. 'Now!'

'Wait!' I yelled. 'Shadow's shadow still needs to come back!'

'Just seal it or we could all die!' Liv roared. 'The barrier is unstable!'

Ignoring Liv – she wasn't his boss – Gunnar waited a beat until the kitten's shadow dropped back to earth. The umbra hovered over Shadow for a moment before they melded into one and once again his fur turned dark like a melanistic lynx. I reached out in wonder, scooping him up securely and kissing his fuzzy – possibly demonic – head.

Gunnar wasted no time. He lifted his hand, mumbled something in Scandinavian and sent a beam of blinding white light straight at the rift. We watched with bated breath as his luminescent magical energy slowly closed the tear. He held his hand out until it was completely sealed then gave a rumbling groan and dropped to his knees.

'Gunnar!' I shouted.

He lifted his shaggy head and smiled weakly. 'I'm all right, Bunny.' The hell he was! His voice wasn't much above a whisper, and he was swaying.

Liv sent her witches to finish the job, and they gathered in front of the patched tear chanting in unison. I put Shadow in the car then turned back to Gunnar. He was on his feet again. He came over to me, taking his time with slow measured steps.

'What's that for?' I gestured at the witches.

'An extra band-aid,' Gunnar replied.

'How long will it hold?' I asked as Liv stalked towards us.

'If the beast keeps pushing here, it won't be for long,' Liv said grimly. 'We can't spare a witch for round-the-clock surveillance – we're already run ragged. What do you want to do?'

Gunnar sighed. 'I'll grab another camera.' He already had some around town monitoring the other rifts and weak spots. Things were getting dire.

'What the hell is your cat?' Liv asked me, her eyes bright with interest as Gunnar walked away.

'I thought he was a lynx kitten.'

'Well, he appears to be far more. I'll buy him from you,' she offered.

I blinked, taken aback. 'No thanks. He's not for sale.'

'Everything is for sale,' she argued.

'I'm glad Shadow's on our side,' Gunnar said as he came back with the camera and Fluffy. Shadow was now curled up on the dashboard, sleeping as though he were exhausted.

Fluffy rushed over and sniffed me to make sure I was alive. Once he'd reassured himself, he sat at my feet and looked alert. I patted his head. 'Sorry, boy. I'm fine.'

Gunnar placed the camera so it faced the rift, though it would only show us a new tear if smoke drifted through again – and by then it might be too late.

I repeated my question to Gunnar. 'How long do you think it will hold?'

'Hard to say – anything from a few days to a week. Hopefully long enough to recover the gems and reset the barrier. Since the Grimes brothers live close I'll ask them to keep an eye on it.'

'I thought they were illusion witches?'

He laughed. 'They are – some of the most powerful I've ever run into. But that doesn't mean they can't muster enough "real" magic to give us time to get someone out here if the patch fails.'

That was a relief: this was a remote spot and it had taken almost thirty minutes to drive here. 'We need more eyes. Should we warn the public?' I asked.

He tensed. 'In some ways that's a good idea, but we also have to protect the citizens from themselves. People will panic if they know the barrier is failing, and we can't have them getting hurt. I've seen many a mob in my time and they're never pretty.'

'But the alternative is that the beast might break free and people get killed!' I pointed out.

'I know. This is one of the aspects of the job that will give you heartburn and, if you're human, a stress-related heart attack. We have to find a balance, and that relies on choosing what looks like the best path. My gut is saying we still have time to find the gems before we have to warn the townsfolk – though we don't have a lot of it.'

I nodded reluctantly. I hated people not knowing, but if we found the gems tonight we'd have started a huge panic over nothing. I guess doing my job – finding Aoife's murderer and the gems – was the best I could do for now.

We turned to leave but before we got in the vehicle Liv stopped us one more time. She was visibly stressed. 'Gunnar, Bunny, you *must* make finding those gems your priority. My people are drained and overworked, and I don't know how much more we've got in the tank. You understand?'

Gunnar nodded abruptly. 'We're trying, Liv.'

'Try harder.' She eyed Shadow. 'And find us more of those damned cats.'

Chapter 29

By the time we'd wrapped up and left the area I was almost due to go off-shift, so Gunnar dropped Fluffy, Shadow and me home. I felt like I'd spent most of my time chasing my tail. We still had very few leads and no hard evidence, but I wouldn't be much help during the morning hours because the daylight exhaustion was unreal. I could battle through it as best I could, but I definitely wouldn't be at my best.

Plus, there was a new mystery: Shadow. I looked at my feline, who was extending his leg into the air and cleaning his asshole with zero embarrassment. What freaky power did he have – and where the hell did it come from?

He put his leg down and curled up into a ball; the poor little thing was still exhausted. So was I.

I made some food and put a video of a roaring fire on the TV. The crackle of the flames relaxed me; fire had always soothed me, though it had taken a momentary hit after my home had burned down. There was something reassuring about it, even when it was only on a video. Like a caveman, part of my brain knew that flames would ward off the monsters and tonight that was exactly what I needed.

As I stared into the dancing flames, my thoughts inevitably turned to the fire within me. Despite snooping through Gunnar and Sigrid's books, I knew very little about my fire magic. If Kostas had been less of a frosty asshole perhaps I would have spoken to him about it, but something about him had set my teeth on edge. I certainly didn't trust him enough to share my secret.

Franklin had turned me – but into what? I wished I could remember what had happened that night but there were only flashes of memory. Was this how ordinary people remembered things, in little fragments? I didn't know, but I knew that I didn't like it.

It was frustrating not to be able to recall that night as perfectly as I could remember almost everything else, but I'd been drunk and then dead. Maybe that was why my memory wasn't as sharp about my turning, or maybe someone had cast some kind of memory spell? Here in Portlock I was learning that anything was possible.

John had said that a witch had hired Franklin to turn me. Had the witch been there that night and spelled me? I'd never know – and I wasn't going to call up Franklin and ask. He hadn't made my Christmas card list.

But elemental fire magic? That was crazy. I took a moment to search within, and as I concentrated I felt a ball of energy at my centre. Anytime I felt angry, it instantly became more evident that I was a ticking bomb that could blow up at any second. I needed to learn how to control it or there was a real risk I'd raze Portlock to the ground. What I'd done to Virginia and Jim would seem like child's play in comparison.

To distract myself from my dark thoughts, I did some cleaning and tidying. I stopped only when I was satisfied I was guest-ready – bar the red threat splashed across my wall by Nora. But that was a job for another day.

The sun was rising and daylight exhaustion was tugging at me. I pulled down the metal shutters, locked the windows and doors and dragged myself off to bed.

Pain flared in my shoulder. I was bleary and disorientated – and I was also on the floor. What the fuck?

I sat up, and that was when I registered that the whole house was shaking. I used the mattress to steady myself and stand up, then teetered around holding onto the furniture until I could open my bedroom door. The house continued to tremble. I heard the kitchen cabinet doors rattling, things falling and smashing. I braced myself in the doorway.

Fluffy's tail was sticking out from under the bed. I had no idea where Shadow was but, knowing the cat, he was probably under there with Fluffy. At least they were safe.

The quake kept on going; this was way stronger than the last one. The glass of water on my bedside table was juddering around like a drunk on a stag-do.

I took a shuddering breath as it finally stopped. I had no idea how long it had lasted but it felt like at least thirty seconds, maybe more since I hadn't woken up immediately. My vampire ass had been dead to the world.

I grabbed my phone and checked for messages. Nothing yet. It was close to the time for me to wake up, so I dialled Sidnee.

'Bunny, that was a big one!' she said before I could even greet her.

'How big?'

'Seven point two.'

'Okay. I don't want to be in another one,' I said tiredly. 'I'm done with earthquakes.' I absently rubbed my shoulder but any bruise I'd got from tumbling out of bed had already vanished.

Sidnee laughed. 'We'll probably get some aftershocks, so be ready.'

I groaned. Just then, a siren started to wail. 'What's that?' I asked anxiously.

'Shit,' Sidnee swore, fear lacing her tone. 'It's a tsunami warning.' My blood ran cold. 'Get to the high school as fast as you can. It's on high ground.'

'See you there.' I hung up then threw on my clothes and yelled for Fluffy to grab Shadow. The high school was a brisk ten-minute walk, but I had no idea how much time we had. I wasn't prepared for a fucking tsunami!

As instructed, Fluffy backed out from under the bed with Shadow in his mouth. My dog was smart: too smart. That was a worry for another day. I grabbed the kitten and shoved him in his carrier then picked up Fluffy's lead.

We bolted out of the house and sprinted down the street. Some people were in their cars, others were on foot, but everyone looked anxious. They were more prepared than me – even the kids had their backpacks. Did they all have tsunami bug-out bags?

We were all moving in a sea of fear up the hill towards the school. Ahead of me, a little girl dropped her teddy. Her scared mum barked at her to leave it, grabbed her arm and tugged her up the hill. I picked up the teddy and ran to the school; I'd kept my eyes on the child so it was easy to find her to pass it back to her.

'Squishy!' she cried, cuddling it to her heart. 'Thank you, Fanged Flopsy!'

My smile was a little strained; I'd really hoped that particular moniker wouldn't stick. 'You're welcome.'

Her mother shot me a grateful smile. 'Thank you, officer.'

The title was a reminder. I *was* an officer. It was time to start acting like one.

'Everyone,' I called. 'Can we please move closer to the school to make room for new arrivals? I know we're all scared but I'm sure it'll be okay. Let's stick together, Portlock.'

I spotted the toweringly tall Ezra standing nearby. He'd been one of the main voices at the protest, so I already knew he could work a crowd. 'Ezra, can you help the people on foot? We need to make sure everyone stays close to the building. Has someone got keys to the school building so we can move inside if necessary?' Hopefully Gunnar and Sigrid would join us soon and my boss could open the doors; if not, I needed a backup plan.

Ezra squared his broad shoulders. 'Harold has the keys. He's the caretaker,' he said briskly.

'Is he here?'

'Just over there.' He gestured to a guy with a trimmed beard and glasses.

'Okay, speak to him and see if he has them with him or has access to a keybox.'

'I'm on it.' Ezra walked off purposefully, calling to people as he went, corralling them into helping with crowd management. The throng moved obligingly closer to the school, making more room for cars and newcomers.

I started to direct cars into the school car park, so at least we were panicking in an orderly fashion. It was the British way.

The sirens stopped abruptly and the silence was deafening. People turned to me for an explanation, their eyes hopeful, but I had nothing to tell them.

I pulled out my phone and called Sidnee again. Her ringtone blared close to me and I realised she was only a few people away. I ran over to her. 'Any ideas why the siren stopped?' I asked.

She looked towards the bay. 'Tsunami warning must have ended.' She hurriedly checked her phone. 'Yup.' She showed me her screen; the warning had been downgraded to a low threat level.

Thank goodness. 'Does this happen a lot?' I asked.

She shook her head. 'No, it's pretty unusual, hence the panic. We only get a tsunami warning once every few years if we get an earthquake that's a seven or more.'

'Has this town ever been hit with one?'

'A tsunami? Yeah, in 1883, an earthquake caused a large landslide that set off a big tsunami. I heard it was pretty bad.'

'Let's get everyone home.' I cleared my throat and raised my voice. 'The tsunami warning has stopped and the threat has been downgraded. You may all return to your homes. Thank you for your co-operation and patience today.'

'Yay for the Fanged Flopsy!' the little girl whose teddy I'd rescued shouted.

Wonderful. The assembled horde burst into rapturous applause and I quickly grabbed Sidnee so she could stand next to me in the limelight. Thankfully the clapping stopped quite quickly; everyone was eager to get back to normal.

I found Ezra as he was leaving. 'Thanks for your help.' I held out my hand. After a beat, he took it and shook it firmly. 'Can you make sure Harold locks up the school?'

'Will do.' He nodded and melted into the crowd. I knew very little about the man but he'd gone up in my estimation. He may not like the barrier but he cared for the people of Portlock and his heart was in the right place. These days, that was the best you could hope for.

I helped direct the cars back into town so that tempers didn't flare if people didn't take turns to drive out. If there's one thing you can say about the Brits, it's that we love a queue; being in a queue was second only to managing one.

I watched the last car go. My work here was done; now it was time for my real work to begin.

Chapter 30

Sidnee was back at the desk when I rolled in with Fluffy and Shadow. 'Sorry I bounced,' she said. 'I didn't want to leave the office unattended for long.'

'No worries. What happened to Gunnar and Sigrid?'

'They were at another gathering point. Gunnar's already in his office.' I hadn't realised there was more than one gathering point but it made sense.

I checked my phone and grimaced when I saw I had three missed calls from Connor. I went into the break room to give him a quick call back. 'Hey,' he answered. 'I was trying to check-in. You okay?'

'I'm fine. I went to the high school.'

'I figured you'd be there. You left your house unlocked so I secured it for you. I'll swing by with the key.'

I flushed with embarrassment at being so careless. 'Thanks, I appreciate that. I ran from the house.' I paused. 'What were you doing there?'

'Checking you'd gotten out okay,' he admitted. 'It can be difficult to wake up when daylight exhaustion has you in its grip, even with the alarm.'

'The quake woke me,' I reassured him. 'Did you go to any other vampire's house to make sure they were gathering?'

'No,' he admitted, 'but the vast majority live in the hills, mostly because of the tsunami risk. Under cover of the forest, they can evacuate their homes even in daylight because the canopy is so dense. In town they can't leave their homes for fear of the sun. A tsunami *might* kill them but the sun definitely would.'

Connor lived in the hills and he'd left the safety of his home to come into the valley to check on me. That felt like a big deal. 'Thank you,' I said softly.

'For what?'

'Checking on me. I appreciate it.' Ugh: I sounded so lame. He'd risked his life for me, and all I could say was

'I appreciate it'? I face palmed, grateful he couldn't see me.

'Random question,' Connor started. 'What's your favourite drink?'

'Tea is my every day go-to, but chai latte is my real favourite. It's full of syrup and sugar so it's a "now and again" drink. What about you?'

'Whiskey,' he answered without hesitation. 'A good whiskey on the rocks. What's your favourite type of music?'

'What is this? I asked, amused. 'Twenty questions?'

A beat of silence. 'I thought that maybe if we knew each other better, you'd feel more comfortable about us.'

His honesty often took me by surprise. 'Anything I can dance to,' I responded. 'And you?'

'Give me Mozart any day of the week – I've never fallen out of love with classical music. The heart-wrenchingly beautiful sounds humans can make never fail to astound me. Favourite colour?'

I laughed. 'A nice soothing blue, I guess. What about you?'

'I'm partial to sage green. It's relaxing.'

'It is,' I agreed. I sighed and gripped the phone tightly. I hated how much I loved speaking to him. 'I've got to go,' I said reluctantly. 'I've started my shift. I wanted you to know I was okay.'

'Appreciate that. I'll put your key underneath the plant pot by the door.'

'Thanks. Bye.' I hung up before I could be tempted to make kissy noises. There was something about the man that made me forget any objections I had to a relationship with him. Fated mates be damned; he was so kind, so caring, so unlike I'd imagined a vampire leader – a fricking prince no less! – could be.

Sidnee looked at me curiously as I walked back into the main office. 'Just calling Connor,' I mumbled, blushing again.

She smiled. 'Glad to hear it.'

'Any new developments on the case?' I wanted to turn the conversation to topics I was more comfortable with, like police work, politics, religion or my masturbation habits.

She grinned triumphantly. 'Oh yeah! I found some info on Aoife's dad. His name is Jayden Donaldson and he's just finished seven years in prison for ... get this...' she paused dramatically '...jewel theft.'

'*Jewel theft*? Are you freaking kidding me?'

'Nope,' she said cheerfully. 'I'm as serious as a siren in a sea.'

'Is he here? In town, I mean?'

'I think there's a strong possibility he is. I traced him to Homer, then he either caught a small plane or a boat because I lost track of him. But there's every chance he's come here. I checked our records and he's been to Portlock before, just before he got sentenced.'

'What does that mean?'

'It means that he'll know the phrase to get through the barrier.'

'So he can come in and out at any time.' A chill ran down my spine.

'You got it. Most people fly or sail in because it is the safest way to avoid the beast, but if you're brave – or foolhardy enough – you could come in by land.'

My excitement was growing. 'This is great, Sidnee. You've blown this whole case wide open. If he's a jewel thief, he can hawk the cursed gemstones. And maybe Aoife didn't teleport away from her killer because it was her father! He killed her, took the gem then got greedy and snatched the wind stone, too. If he's been in prison we'll have fingerprints and DNA on file. Let's hope some of the physical evidence points back to him.'

I thought of the acrylic fingernail at the scene of the crime; unless Donaldson liked flashy manicures, that hadn't been his. 'Hmm.'

Sidnee quirked an eyebrow, 'What's wrong?'

'I pinned a lot of hope on the fingernail we found with the body. I'm guessing that it doesn't belong to Donaldson – though it's not outside the realms of possibility.'

'Could it have been planted?' she suggested.

'That's possible.' A lot of things were possible but that didn't mean they were *probable*. Maybe Donaldson had an accomplice. It was something to think about.

'I'm heading home.' Sidnee yawned. 'Ring me if you need me.'

'You got it.'

I watched her leave; she seemed a little more relaxed than she'd been recently. I hoped she was on an upswing because she really deserved to be.

Chapter 31

With Sidnee's information about Aoife Sullivan's father, I could make some more enquiries to track down this Jayden Donaldson. He was obviously being careful, but surely he'd need some cash in hand before he managed to sell the jewels? He was straight out of prison; unless he had money stashed somewhere, he'd need a job, even if it was only casual work.

I contacted numerous business managers in Portlock and told them that Jayden Donaldson was a person of interest and the Nomo's office wanted to speak to him. I sent them his prison mugshot so they'd recognise him even if he was working under an assumed name.

With the word out, I checked my email for lab notifications; we'd sent them our initial evidence, and I expected some results to start trickling in. We'd already confirmed that the long hair from the site of the theft was Aoife's, but what I really wanted was some info on that fingernail. Frustratingly, nothing had come in yet.

I called Connor, got his voicemail and left him a message. 'It might not be anything, but that tip you had about your jewels? It might be right. Aoife's father is a convicted jewel thief, and everything points to him being in Portlock. Keep Cody in his corridor.'

I hung up abruptly. Just because things between us were whatever they were, I still didn't want a thief targeting him. At the end of the day, Connor was a great guy. Ugh: what was I doing running away from him? I thunked my head on the desk and hoped it would knock some sense into me.

Gunnar leaned out of his office. 'Something wrong?'

'Men,' I complained.

'Okay, I'm out.' I heard him chuckling in his office. Smartass.

Next I finished up what Sidnee had left, which wasn't much – it had been a quiet night before the earthquake. Thinking of the quake spiked something in my mind. The earth gem could cause quakes…

I dialled Vitus Vogler's number and the grouchy earth witch answered with a barked, 'What?'

'Can you double-check the earth gem is okay?'

'It's fine,' he bit out.

'Can you check it now, while I'm on the line?'

He huffed but I heard him moving through the house. 'The wards are up, the box is there. Happy?'

'Delighted,' I said flatly and hung up. Damn. Maybe not everything in this place had a magical cause but I'd felt certain that the recent quakes were because of the earth gem rather than the usual non-magical rubbing together of tectonic plates. However, Sidnee had told me quakes were a dime a dozen here so I let it go.

I checked my phone; it was nearly time for my nail appointment. There was a text from my mum. I took a deep breath and opened it.

Elizabeth, I'm getting ready for my trip. How is the weather there? Dad can't make it this time, I'm afraid. He has some important business that can't be delayed.

He sends his apologies; he'll come next time. Your dad is sending one of his men to help me instead, a nice lad called John. Apparently he has business in Portlock, and I simply couldn't manage all that luggage by myself! Looking forward to seeing you, darling. Ta ta for now x

I blew out a long slow breath. It was no surprise that Dad had cancelled because he'd been doing that my whole life, but I was surprised that it still stung. Business came first, always. But sending someone called John ... surely that couldn't be a coincidence? John was a common enough name but there was only one John who was linked with my father – and that was John the vampire. John who worked for the vampire King of Europe. John, who'd helped me to escape.

I tried to calm down and take the message one bit at a time. The weather? She could look that up herself but instead of telling her that I sighed and typed: *It rains a lot. Bring a raincoat, and boots. It's around 4 to 10 degrees.* I didn't acknowledge Dad's lack of attendance: that was same old same old.

John's presence – if it was the same John – sent a shard of fear through me. Was the vampire king sending John to Portlock to spy on me? To control me? Maybe John's business here had nothing to do with me but my gut didn't think so. Fingers crossed I was being too self-involved.

I ended the message with *Looking forward to seeing you too,* which was an outright lie. I didn't want to say anything more because her phone might be tapped – the vampire king had tapped my phone and my emails before. I was grateful that I'd left all that bullshit behind; Connor would never be that underhanded with his people.

And even if sending John was part of the vampire king's ploy to get me back to London, I knew that Connor would do everything in his power to protect me. Fated mates or not, he wouldn't let any of his people be taken by that arsehole.

I sighed. Connor was never far from my thoughts. Despite my very best efforts, he was slowly sinking into my life and into my heart.

I tried to think about something else – some*one* else – and turned my thoughts back to my mum. How on earth would I cope with living with her for a whole month? Maybe I could convince her to stay at the hotel instead. Fluffy would despise her vapid Pomeranian, Arabella, who barked non-stop at anything and everything. She had small-man syndrome times a million, and she was incredibly stupid and ridiculously spoiled. Some days I thought Mum wished her dog was her daughter instead of me. Yes, I was being pathetic, but that dog got more affection in a day than I've had in my entire life.

I put away the world's tiniest violin. I'd been raised with money and privilege and I was lucky; there were plenty of people who had it far worse. Maybe I'd have preferred to have been raised destitute with parents that loved me rather than being rich and ignored, but the grass was always greener, right?

Chapter 32

Before I went to my salon appointment, I popped home to have some blood and retrieve my key from under the plant pot. As I approached the house, my scalp started to itch. Huh.

I found the key and let myself in the back door. As I walked inside, the itching faded. The smell of fresh paint assailed my nose and the sound of heavy bass music bombarded my ears. If my intruders were criminals, they weren't trying to hide.

I followed the blaring music to the front room where Connor Mackenzie was painting my graffitied wall a lovely shade of blue. He was using a roller and doing a little dance as he worked. When he caught sight of me he looked a little abashed, like a kid who'd been caught eating out of the biscuit tin. 'Hey.' He waved the paint roller at me.

'Hey,' I replied, beaming. 'You're painting.'

'I am,' he agreed. 'You don't mind? I hated the thought of you having to sit there with that threat on the wall. I didn't want it in your headspace, and the borough is notoriously slow at getting around to jobs like this.'

'That's really kind of you. I don't mind at all.'

He eyed the wall critically. 'It might need another coat of paint. I've done two already, but we'll see how it dries. Do you like the colour?'

'I love it.'

His expression turned rueful. Something told me he was thinking that I loved the paint but not him. I grimaced. I didn't want to wade into that right now; besides, maybe he was thinking something else that had nothing to do with me.

'I thought you liked classical music?' I nodded at his phone, which was blaring out club mixes.

He shrugged. 'I do but I'm trying to expand my horizons.' My heart swelled; he was listening to music he knew I loved.

I wasn't ready to deal with that. He was fifty shades of perfect and I was a contrary twat. Knowing it didn't help. 'I've got to go. I came to pick up the key.' I waved it at him.

'Sure thing.'

Show him you care. The errant thought was explosive, insistent and from my heart. I hesitated. 'I have a spare key in the kitchen, in the first drawer you come to. You can lock up with it when you're done and take it with you if you want to. In case I lose my set or something.'

It was an olive branch, and the warmth in his eyes said that he knew it was. I wanted to go to him, hug him, maybe kiss him. But then I'd want to peel him out of his sexy flannel shirt and I didn't have time for that, nor was I prepared for the repercussions. So I gave him a weak finger wave and sidled out of the house.

Connor Mackenzie was painting the walls of my house. He had dozens of goons on hand, but here he was painting them himself. It meant something, though I wasn't quite sure what. For the seven thousandth time that day, I tried to banish him from my thoughts.

I was *working,* dammit. I had a moment of giddy appreciation that going to a nail appointment counted as work. The salon wasn't far from home, so I tried to get my brain screwed on right before I arrived. I was trying to find the mysterious owner of the nail under Aoife's body. Maybe Sidnee was right, maybe it was nothing more than a deliberately planted red herring, but I had to *know.*

The salon was small, sandwiched between the hardware store and the pharmacy. One woman was styling someone's hair and another was waiting at the desk. I resisted the urge to do a fist pump when I saw her because I was definitely on the right track. It could be no coincidence that she was a banshee like Aoife: she had the same colourless hair, the same pale-yellow eyes.

'Hi! I'm Bunny Barrington. I'm here for a much-needed nail appointment.' I showed her my poor, manicure-less hands.

The banshee laughed. 'Great! Let's get you started, then! I'm Misty, your nail technician. Follow me, please.' She took me into the back room and sat me in a chair. Manicure implements were spread out on the table in front of it.

Misty's hair was cut and arranged into a huge, hair-sprayed eighties' ball of fluff. Her long false lashes looked stark against her white face and pale eyes. Her fake nails were artfully done, medium length, with plenty of artwork to show her skill. Colour me impressed.

She showed me two racks of varnish. 'Let me know which one you'd like.'

I perused the colours at length, but truthfully I'd picked one almost instantly. They had a gorgeous blue, almost the same as the one Connor was painting on my walls. 'This one, please.'

'Perfect. And shape?'

'Oval finish, please.'

'You got it.' She took my hands, examining the current shape and state of my nails. I let myself relax and enjoy the treatment like a real customer would as I waited for her to break the ice.

'So, Bunny, that's an unusual name. How did you come by it?'

'I once organised an Easter egg hunt for my friends but I took the competition to an extreme level and set up elaborate traps and decoys. It was total chaos but everyone had such a blast, they dubbed me Bunny. I've always been remembered as the mastermind behind the most epic Easter egg hunt ever.' I kind of wished that one were true; it would have been nice to have grown up with friends to organise an Easter egg hunt for.

'That's so cool.' She started expertly trimming my cuticles.

'Thanks. I was actually recommended to this salon by this lady who had a magnificent set of French tips. I was envious and she said that you'd done them.'

'That'd be Nora. That's her go-to,' Misty said.

Nora! I did a fist pump in my mind. It was a real effort to keep my tone casual. 'Do you do her nails a lot?'

'Yeah. Unfortunately she's a chewer. She needs a new set every two weeks.'

'Really? I used to chew my nails. Does Nora only get French tips, or does she have other favourites?'

Misty started to shape and file my nails. 'It's the one she gets the most unless there's a holiday. When you're as pale as we are, it's hard to have dark or bright nails. It looks off.' Bingo. Not only was her name Nora but she was also a banshee. It *had* to be Nora Sullivan.

'I have the same problem,' I said as casually as I could.

She smiled at me as she trimmed my cuticles. 'Oh, honey, you aren't that pale. You could wear all kinds of bright colours.'

'French manicures look so nice but I'm ready for something brighter.'

She stared to paint a clear base coat on my nails. 'You'll have a beautiful set of nails before you can say boo.'

'Boo,' I said perversely.

She giggled and put my hand under a hand lamp to set the gel nails.

'When was the last French manicure you did?' I asked lightly.

'Last week. Nora's usually the only one I do like that.'

'Well, it was super pretty.'

Gotcha, Nora, I thought triumphantly. She'd absolutely lost a nail under her daughter's body! I was willing to let her spray-painted threats go, but there was no slack for something like this. This was enough suspicion for an arrest warrant and I wanted to set the wheels in motion.

I walked back to work with my beautiful pale-blue nails and rushed into Gunnar's office. 'Let's get that arrest warrant. I totally have probable cause!' I grinned at him.

He set back in his chair, eyebrows raised. 'You wanna fill me in?' he asked.

'Remember the fingernail we picked up under the body? I suspected it came from Nora Sullivan. I went to the nail salon and the banshee nail technician confirmed that she'd done Nora's nails like that a week ago. Also, Nora doesn't currently have those nails. She popped one off under her daughter's body and then she must have got rid of them all!'

'Sounds like you've got something. I'll call the council.'

While he phoned, I went back to my desk and started filling out the paperwork before he asked me to. Halfway through, his bellow made me happy. 'As soon as you've done that report they'll sign. They're preparing the warrant! Get a-typin'!'

I typed. When I was finished, Gunnar and I went to the council chambers to get the warrant. After that we were going to pick up Nora Sullivan.

I was surprised that the mayor and Connor had signed off this warrant because it was usually Liv or Stan with Connor or Calliope; the mayor rarely got involved. When we arrived at the council chambers I was disappointed to see that Connor had already left. Still, there was no time to make doe eyes – we had an arrest to make and dangerous jewels to recover.

Chapter 33

Gunnar, Fluffy and I loaded into the Nomo's SUV and headed for the Sullivan home. I still wasn't sure that Nora had killed her daughter – something about the whole thing struck me as *wrong* – but maybe my morals were getting in the way of me perceiving the truth. Either way, I was positive that Nora knew something she wasn't telling us. Was she protecting her ex-husband, Jayden? Had they been working together? Why had she lied and said he was dead?

We turned the last corner to the Sullivan's residence and Gunnar slammed on the brakes as a figure ran out in front of the car. 'Fuck!' he shouted a rare expletive as we juddered to a halt. The person had disappeared but there had been no impact with the car. What the hell?

Oh shit. 'What if that was Nora teleporting away?' I asked. Gunnar muttered under his breath and we both climbed out to look for the running figure. Fluffy climbed out of the open door and I gave him a reproachful glance. 'Heel.' I patted my hip and he trotted over obediently. He stuck to my side as we searched the area.

Suddenly the spirit of Aoife Sullivan wavered in front of us, solidifying before our eyes. 'Shit a brick!' I yelled as she scared the life out of me.

Her yellow eyes shone like molten gold and her wax-white hair floated around her. She was dressed in white, like a deathly bride. Fear trickled down my spine. I'd seen Aoife dead, her insides pouring onto the ground, yet here she was: a banshee in the truest sense of the word. And the last time she'd screamed until Sidnee's ears had bled.

Aoife raised an arm and gestured to the woods. Her wail was a sound of endless sorrow and suffering that made me double over, clutching my hands to my ears. Obviously frustrated, she moved closer to me. 'Go!' she shrieked, cutting off her wail with an effort.

When the noise ended, I cautiously pulled my hands away from my ears. 'Go where?' I asked.

She lifted her arm again impatiently and pointed into the distance. Gunnar and I peered in that direction but all I could see were the woods. She repeated her instruction, her screech increasing tenfold in volume. 'GO!'

Fluffy lifted his muzzle and howled in pain. I clutched my hands to my ears and this time when I removed them there was a trickle of blood on *my* fingers. That gave a whole new meaning to a girl being a screamer.

I wiped my hand on my trousers and obediently plunged into the woods with Gunnar next to me and Fluffy at my heels. We slowed as the forest canopy blotted out the moon; I could still see but I doubted that Gunnar could, and I wasn't leaving him behind while I stumbled in the woods at the behest of a dead banshee.

Fluffy took the lead confidently and Aoife's spirit followed behind before impatiently deciding we were being too slow. She shoved forward to lead the way to wherever the heck we were going; hopefully it wasn't to our doom.

'I hope she isn't leading us off a cliff,' Gunnar huffed, echoing my dark thoughts.

'Are there any cliffs around here?' I sassed, knowing full well we weren't anywhere near one.

'Smart-ass,' he muttered.

Following Aoife was no easy task. Trees were no obstacle to her and she ploughed through them, but we had to manoeuvre around them. Suddenly Fluffy stopped and gave a low growl. I skidded to a stop behind him.

We were in a clearing and the scent of coppery blood was hanging in the air. I could feel the hum of the barrier nearby. Aoife was standing in front of us, her feet about six inches off the ground, staring ahead. She seemed more solid here and I walked around her to see what had captured her and Fluffy's attention.

In the moonlit clearing lay a beaten and bloodied Nora Sullivan. Fuck.

I raced over and hastily felt for a pulse in her neck; it was weak but it *was* there. Blood was pooling around her – she'd been beaten, stabbed and left for dead. Now she was clinging to her life with a thread.

Gunnar pulled out a roll of bandage from one of his many pockets, applied a dressing and pressed hard on it while I called the medics. There was no way they'd get an ambulance into the woods so I directed them to where our vehicle was still standing near Nora's house.

I hung up. Gunnar had done what he could, but he was no paramedic. 'We need to get her to the street,' I said. 'I'll carry her.'

'I've got her,' he said softly. He lifted Nora gently into his arms and she looked small and frail against his Viking stature. As he went back through the trees, I quickly searched the area where Nora had been lying. There were no cursed gemstones to be seen.

I looked at Aoife. Soundless tears were tracking down her face as she watched Gunnar carry her mum away. 'I'm sorry, Aoife,' I said. She looked at me. 'I need to know. Did your mum kill you?' I asked.

Her spirit rushed at me. Her mouth was open wide and she screamed, 'NO!' so loudly I thought my eardrums would burst again. Aoife's spirit-self flew through me with an icy chill and I shuddered and doubled over, feeling sick. When I stood up, she was gone. Dammit, I should have asked *who* had killed her – maybe she could have screeched a name before she bolted off.

I was trembling with cold. I took a few deep, shuddering breaths and tried to shake the chill from my limbs. Fluffy barked with concern. 'I'm okay,' I lied. 'Let's go.'

We followed Gunnar – but I still couldn't shake the all-encompassing cold that Aoife had left me with.

As we neared the edge of the woods we heard the distant call of the ambulance's sirens. We picked up the pace and made it out of the woods as it turned the corner. We flagged it down and it screeched to a halt. Gunnar rattled off Nora's name, age and details then handed her over to the paramedics. We watched them drive away with our only suspect barely clinging to life.

Nothing about this case was going to plan. We didn't have Nora and we didn't have the gems. Dammit.

Chapter 34

Gunnar and I retraced our steps to the SUV and slunk inside; even the air inside the vehicle was dejected. 'So,' I said, 'Aoife told me her mum wasn't her murderer.'

Gunnar rubbed a hand over his face. 'Of course she did. That doesn't leave us with a whole lot of suspects.'

'Yeah.' I shivered. 'Can you turn the heat up? I'm a little cold.'

Gunnar fiddled with a dial. 'Better?'

'Thanks.' I was still chilly but I'd soon warm up.

'Time to find the dad,' Gunnar said firmly.

'Yeah,' I agreed again, biting my thumb as I thought. 'My gut is telling me we've missed something.'

'Is it?' He looked over at me. 'I trust your gut, so what else is it saying?'

'It's saying to focus on the gems.'

'Why?'

'This has been brewing in the back of my head for a while. The gems are cursed. True, we use them for the barrier, but what if someone wants them for another reason? They are worth millions in their own right, and that's a pretty good motive for murder. Stealing the gems and killing Aoife to bring down the barrier doesn't quite add up. I understand people can be fanatical but Aoife's dad is a jewel thief, so that's a big target on his back. Maybe the motive for the theft isn't complicated – maybe he just wants the big bucks.'

Gunnar was quiet for a moment. 'Maybe,' he finally conceded. 'Either way, we need to find the prick.' We turned into the car park behind the station. 'We have to follow the leads we have, but there's nothing to say we can't follow some other ones too. Let's look at the dad, and at the same time find out what we can about the cursed gems. Maybe they'll lead us to a new suspect. Sound good?'

It was a relief that he didn't dismiss my thoughts out of hand – but he'd never done that so far. 'Yes, sounds good.' I smiled.

Inside the Nomo's office I let Shadow out of his carrier and he sat on my lap as I stared at my blank computer screen. I knew what I needed to do but I was putting it off: I had to talk to Liv, no matter how much she freaked me out. She knew the origins of the gems and she might know why someone would want them besides for their obvious monetary worth.

If anyone would have some more suspects for me, it would be Liv.

Chapter 35

Liv promised to meet me the next day before my shift. She was busy with her magic users, plugging holes and putting magical plasters on the barrier. I reminded her – carefully – that my job was nearly as important as hers; if we didn't find the gems, we might as well kiss the barrier goodbye no matter how many of her 'band-aids' she put on it.

Her response had been frosty but at least she'd agreed to meet me. Before that, I had to find and question Aoife's father. I checked in with all of my contacts at the local businesses and got a hit on the fifth one. Ironically, it was Kamluck Logging. I was starting to feel like the universe was pushing Connor and I together. Oh, right … fated mates. The universe was *really* being pushy.

Connor's second-in-command answered the phone. 'Kamluck Logging, Margrave speaking.'

'Hi, Lee, it's Bunny.'

'How can I help you, ma'am?' His tone was obsequious. Yuck.

'Firstly, by never calling me ma'am. Secondly, I called a couple days ago and left a message for Hester. I'm trying to get some details on a chap called Jayden Donaldson. He may be seeking cash-in-hand employment.'

'We've got a Jayden working for us,' he confirmed. 'A new hire. Hester doesn't actually work at Kamluck – she's a professional mentor. She works with vampires all over Alaska and the Pacific Northwest and she's not in town right now. Jayden gave his last name as Dansford though, not Donaldson.'

'Can you describe him?'

'Six feet two, brown hair, beard, dark eyes, white dude.'

That matched the most recent prison photo I had and my spine tingled with excitement. 'Is he in now?'

Lee clicked on the keyboard. 'You bet.'

'Okay, keep him busy but don't alert him to any trouble. I'm on my way.'

'You got it.'

Finally I was going to get some answers! With Fluffy in tow, I climbed in the Nomo vehicle, started the engine and cranked up the heat because I was still shivering. I wished I had a thermos of hot tea with me.

Fluffy sat in the back and watched the road. It was a ten-mile drive out of town to Kamluck. I tried to keep my head in the game but it constantly switched back to Connor and the thought that we were 'fated' to be together. Even if I ignored the zing, I couldn't ignore the way he'd been there for me from the beginning – the shooting, the fire, taking care of Fluffy, a hundred small things. He'd checked under my bed for monsters and he'd made me a cup of tea. Hell, he'd painted my walls.

I loved the way he always seemed drawn to touch me with a gentle hand on the small of my back or a proffered arm. His eyes smiled when he looked at me. I sighed. Was I really throwing away everything we could be just because the universe had decreed it? Yes,

I was. Contrary was my middle name, even if I was cutting my nose off to spite my face, even if I knew on some level that I was being a twat.

I let Fluffy out and we went into the logging office but no one was manning it. Lee had said he'd keep Jayden busy, so where were they? I checked my phone but there were no messages from either him or Connor.

After five minutes, I was growing concerned. By ten minutes, fear had me in her icy grasp. 'Come on, Fluffy. Something is wrong.'

Connor and Lee were vampires, and Jayden was supposed to be a powerful witch. I'd learned that witches came in many flavours, and I had no idea what kind he was. That seemed like a foolish omission now. 'Let's hope he's a hearth witch and makes excellent soup,' I muttered as we looked around the building then headed to the warehouse.

Fluffy gave me a flat look: he didn't think it was likely. Nor did I.

There was a gravel trail from the office to the warehouse. I'd kissed Connor on that path and it had set my heart pounding and my skin on fire in the most delicious way. Now my heart was pounding with a whole different feeling. Where was everyone?

I walked as quietly as I could, wincing at every crunch of the gravel, and unsnapped the holster on my gun as we got closer. It was quiet, too quiet. There was usually the noise of machinery as equipment moved boards and logs around, and the mill buzzed with the sound of cutting. This silence was heavy and choking: I couldn't even hear the birds. It was eerie, like everything within a mile radius had been silenced.

I eyed the dark woods around the buildings and for a moment they transported me to other woods where there were red eyes and smoky tendrils. I gave myself a shake. The barrier was still up and the beast was a worry for another day. I needed to find Jayden – and Margrave. And maybe Connor, too.

Then I saw it: fire.

Fuck. This was not the place to have a fire. There was way too much dry wood around.

I broke into a run. It had looked like the smoke was rising from the warehouse but, as I grew closer, I saw it was actually coming from behind the building. Expecting the worst, I tore around the corner.

The car park behind the warehouse was empty except for Connor's white Kamluck Logging truck – and it was on fire. My floppy heart gave three beats as I raced towards it. *Please don't let him be in there!* I prayed. Fire and staking were two of the three ways to kill us; sun was the third. If Connor was in there, he wouldn't survive.

I tore towards the flames, ready to burn myself on the red-hot metal if it meant saving him. God, I'd do *anything* to save Connor. *Don't let him be dead. Don't let him be dead!*

The heat from the truck was intense and part of me basked in its warmth, but I pushed that aside to focus. I willed myself to move through the scalding wall of heat, desperately searching for any hint that Connor was inside the vehicle. I looked through the windows on each side but spotted nothing. *Empty. Thank fuck. It was empty.*

But if Connor wasn't in the truck, where was he? He wouldn't sit idly by whilst someone torched his belongings. Where *was* he? Where was Lee? Dread curled in my stomach.

'Fluffy, find Connor. You know his scent. Find him!' Fluffy looked at me balefully but put his nose to the gravel, scenting as best he could with the smoke billowing around us.

He led us unerringly to the warehouse. I had to go in, to make sure they were either fine or elsewhere. The side of the building that looked onto the car park had a steel entrance door but no windows so I couldn't see inside – but on the plus side, no one could see me approach, either.

As I walked boldly up to the metal door, Fluffy whined quietly. He was alert and pointing right to where I was heading. 'Definitely in there?' I asked quietly.

He looked at the door and laid back his ears. That was good enough for me. I drew my gun.

Chapter 36

I turned the handle slowly; thankfully, the door was unlocked. The movement made me think of Gunnar because no door remained locked to him. I grimaced; I should probably call him for backup. Ploughing in alone was foolish, though I wasn't totally alone – I had Fluffy. Besides, I wasn't sure how much time Connor and Lee had. If Jayden had set Connor's truck on fire, both men must be incapacitated. If I delayed, that might become permanent.

I turned the handle a little further. The light from the fire would silhouette me but I had no choice. I stood to the side, flung open the door and led in with my gun. To the right was the showroom. I'd been in the warehouse once for a vampire meeting and I knew that other than the showroom and break rooms, the rest of the building was used for storing lumber.

There were plenty of places to hide in the stacks of timber so I ran to the showroom, which would be easier to check. I glanced inside. Everything looked okay so I slid inside. Other than the emergency exit sign, the space was dark; there were no windows. It was a true vampire den. I hoped that would give me an advantage if the fire was Jayden Donaldson's doing because I had vampire sight on my side.

I crouched low and searched the room carefully. It was full of polished timber samples and had wooden flooring; there were no soft furnishings to absorb my footfalls, which sounded obscenely loud. Luckily it didn't take us long to check it out. There was nowhere to hide and it was evident that there was no one here.

As I returned to the door, Fluffy grabbed my wrist and pulled me out of sight alongside the wall. I heard the scuff of a shoe on the cement warehouse floor: someone was outside the showroom, and from Fluffy's reaction I didn't think it was Connor.

My heart gave a hard thump and Fluffy's body tensed against my leg. Whoever it was, was coming straight at us.

'Come out, come out, wherever you are!' a strange male voice said in a taunting singsong.

Part of me wanted to yell 'Or what?', but in a supernatural town like Portlock, you really were only limited by your imagination. I debated my options: I could answer and engage with him or I could keep quiet. For now, the latter was more appealing because I didn't want to play by his rules. Surely he couldn't *know* I was there? He had to be guessing.

After a moment or two, he continued. 'Fine. Stay there cowering, officer, but your friends will die if you don't come out. I'll give you to the count of three. One…' For fuck's sake. He could be bluffing, but I couldn't live with myself if he wasn't.

I stepped around the door. If someone died because of my action or inaction, I'd never forgive myself. Besides, I was a vampire; I had regenerative properties and as long as he didn't shoot me right in the heart, I had a good chance of walking away in one piece. Though I'd have felt better if I'd been wearing Connor's bulletproof vest.

A snicker greeted me as I stepped out. 'It's so easy with you law types. You're so damn selfless.' His tone made it clear that was an insult.

'Who are you and what do you want?' I asked, as if I didn't know full well.

Jayden Donaldson was looking rough. His beard was straggly and he was close enough for me to tell that he hadn't showered after a full day's logging. 'You've been looking for me, little bunny rabbit so I think you already know who I am, don't you?' he spat.

I didn't want to make him any angrier so I said obligingly, 'Jayden Donaldson.'

'In the flesh.' Never taking his eyes off of me, he sketched a mocking bow.

'What have you done with Connor and Lee?'

He smirked. 'Let's say they're ... a little tied up.'

Ugh. Cliché, much? The fire in my gut curled and woke up, but it was sluggish and slow as if the pervasive cold in my limbs was somehow dampening it. Then I thought of Connor being held against his will and the flames leapt into a raging inferno; now I was struggling to contain the anger and the heat.

Focus, Bunny. 'I wanted to speak to you about your daughter.'

Jayden's face twisted into a grimace. 'That bitch? She's no daughter of mine, the little snake!'

I frowned. 'Are we talking about the same person? Aoife Sullivan?'

He spat on the ground. 'She's a snitch, that's what she is!'

Did he mean she really wasn't his daughter, or he didn't consider her his daughter after she'd double-crossed him in some way? 'So why did you come to town if not to see her?'

He sneered. 'For a job. What else? No harm in telling you since you'll be dead soon.'

'You're here to steal the barrier gems,' I said, my tone resigned.

'What? Are you mad? I wouldn't touch that cursed shit with a ten-foot pole.'

I frowned. 'Then what?'

'Mackenzie's got some jewels, big ones. I was hired to steal them but it's all gone to pot now, thanks to you. He figured out that I'm not who my ID said and the whole thing is blown. It was already tough but it was doable until Aoife gave him an anonymous warning. I was willing to wait until things cooled down but now Mackenzie's seen my mugshot, he knows what I'm here for. Security was tight before but now it'll be impossible. You and Aoife have fucked everything up. Just like she did before.' His face twisted into a dark sneer. 'And now I'll do the same to you as I did to her.'

'It was you?' I said, surprised. 'You killed your own daughter because she warned Connor about a thief in the area?' I let my disgust show in my voice.

He froze. 'Killed? Aoife?' His voice was a strangled whisper, his confusion evident. 'You're lying!' he said slowly, trying to work out what my game was. 'Banshees are damned hard to kill. She's fine – she has to be! How dare you lie to me, you bitch!'

His confusion and his dismay were believable. Maybe he hadn't killed her after all. 'I'm not lying. I have no reason to lie. Aoife is dead.'

Something in my tone must have convinced him because he turned and punched a pile of boards. 'Fuck!' he screamed.

Fluffy decided that was the perfect moment to take Jayden down. He ran from the door and, using the darkness, pounded towards the witch. Unfortunately he'd timed it wrong because Jayden was turning to face me with a question on his lips when he spotted the incoming canine.

He instantly raised his hands and I knew something nasty was heading towards my dog. He was going to hurt Fluffy! My rage burned hot, and this time I had no chance of containing it. A blast of fire leapt from my chest towards Jayden. He saw it and leapt aside just as Fluffy reached him, grabbed his arm and pulled him to the floor. I used the distraction and my vampire speed to rush forward and flip him face down. I planted a knee in his back and reached for his arm to cuff him.

Before I could secure the cuff, I hurtled backward and slammed into the wall. My gun skittered away and my breath whooshed out.

As I struggled to pull in air, Fluffy leapt forward with a ferocious growl and grabbed Jayden's wrist between his jaws. The witch screamed as my dog clamped down hard. No more Mr Nice Fluffy.

Jayden flung up his other hand and Fluffy went sliding back deep into the stacks of boards and out of sight. I heard his sharp squeal as he struck something.

'I thought you were a fucking vamp, not a fire witch!' Jayden yelled at me. He flung up a hand and his magic slowly dragged me back up the wall. Then he rushed me.

I wasn't the same vampire I'd been when Virginia had done something similar; she'd held me off the ground and cut me so I'd bleed out. No, I wasn't the same at all. I knew I had fire magic and this was the perfect situation to use it.

I let my rage boil up in my centre, and when it was unbearable I let it out. At that point, I wasn't thinking about a warehouse full of wood – I wasn't thinking about anything. The fire struck Jayden and he flew back.

I slid down the wall and grabbed my fallen gun as he screamed. I didn't want him to die like Virginia; I didn't want to hear his screams in my nightmares. I called the fire back to me and in a second it had flown towards my chest and fizzled out.

'Stay down!' I barked.

Jayden rolled onto his feet and I didn't hesitate; if he wasn't staying down, I'd have to make him. So I shot him.

He dropped like a tonne of bricks. If he was eliminated as a threat then he wasn't my focus anymore. I ran past the prone witch and hurried over to Fluffy, who was heaving himself to his feet. He limped for a moment then seemed to shake it off.

'Are you okay?' I asked urgently. He gave me a lick. 'Thank goodness. Can you find Connor?' He put his nose down and started weaving through the stacks. 'Good boy, find them!' I encouraged.

God, let them be alive.

Chapter 37

Fluffy picked up speed as he kept his nose down and wove through the stacks. Finally he gave a yip which I recognised meant, 'I've found something!' As I turned the corner, I was both relieved and panicked to see Connor and Lee: relieved because we'd found them, panicked because they were either dead or unconscious.

I rushed to Connor and desperately pressed my fingers on his neck. I felt a bolt of pure panic when I found no pulse, then my brain caught up. He was a *vampire*, a proper one. He never had a pulse and, unlike me, he didn't need to breathe.

How did you wake a sleeping vampire? My brain supplied the unhelpful punchline: by coffin. *Shut up, brain, you are no help at all.*

I gave the reins over to panic and slapped him across the face. 'Connor, wake up!' His eyelids stirred and I nearly fainted with relief. He was alive – or undead. 'Connor, wake up!' I said again and shook him none too gently. I really needed him with me.

He groaned as I tried to get my shit together. Connor and Lee were fine, though they'd probably needed blood to recover. I hastily untied them both. Lee moaned as I moved him but he didn't regain consciousness.

Connor's eyes fluttered open. I had never been happier in my entire life than I was when I saw that shade of blue. I tried to keep a lid on my emotions – bawling with relief wouldn't have been professional and I was hanging onto my professionalism by a thread. I'd *shot* someone, for fuck's sake. *After* I'd set him on fire. I wouldn't be winning any law-and-order awards anytime soon.

'Do you keep any blood around here?' I asked Connor.

His eyes sharpened on my face and he jolted up. 'Run, Bunny!' His fangs snicked down as he tried to struggle to his feet. He staggered and I took his arm to steady him.

Just like him to think of my safety first, even when he was half out of it. My heart warmed. 'It's okay,' I reassured him. 'I shot Jayden – after I set him on fire. I promise we're safe. But he did something to you and you need blood. Do you have any here?'

'Fridge,' he managed. 'Break room.'

I had no idea where that was but I trusted Fluffy to find it. He knew the words fridge and food. 'Fluffy, find the fridge.'

His eyes told me that he understood. He raised his head and sniffed, chose a direction and trotted off. I followed.

The break room was opposite the showroom. It was obvious how Fluffy had found it so fast; even I could smell the scent of old coffee from twenty feet away. I ran in, opened the fridge and saw several bags of blood. I grabbed two of them and, after a moment's hesitation, bypassed the microwave. Getting Connor and Lee blood quickly seemed more important than warming it to a nice temperature.

I ran back to the men; they were both sitting up but they looked woozy. 'Sorry, I didn't take the time to heat it,' I apologised as I handed each man a bag. Rather than trying to open them, they simply plunged in their fangs and drank until the blood was gone.

I was relieved to see the colour returning to their cheeks. 'So how did he take you both down?' I asked.

Connor rubbed the back of his head. 'He hit me with something. I don't know about Lee.'

'He caught me off guard. He hit me with magic and that's all I remember.' Lee turned to Connor. 'I have let you down. I resign as your second.'

Connor glared at him. 'I don't accept. I've lost Juan and I've lost Kivuk. I won't lose you as well. Do better, Margrave.'

Lee bowed his head before snapping it up and saluting. 'Yes, sir. I won't let you down again.'

'See that you don't,' Connor said firmly, then looked at me. 'The witch – is he still around?'

'I doubt it. I set him on fire,' Lee shot me a startled look, 'and then I shot him. By all rights, he should be dead.'

'You use a lighter or something?' Lee asked, obviously impressed.

'Something like that.'

'Supernats are tough bastards. I'll go and see if he's expired.' He made it sound like Donaldson was milk past its use-by date. He got to his feet and Fluffy stepped up to him.

'He'll go with you,' I said.

Lee patted my boy. 'Let's roll, Brute.'

'His name is Fluffy!' I protested.

'That's not what the boss says.' Lee slunk away with Fluffy, and I turned to face Connor. He surprised me by pulling me into his arms and hugging me tightly before drawing back to study me anxiously. 'You're okay?'

'I'm fine,' I reassured him. 'You?'

'Couldn't be better.' His lie tugged a smile onto my face but it faded as quickly as it had come.

'You could have died,' I said solemnly. 'You could have died thinking that I don't care about you.'

He gave me his lopsided smile. 'I know you care about me, Bunny. You just hate being told what to do.' Smiled ruefully. 'It's handy that I learnt that early on.'

I let out a sharp breath. 'Isn't that the most ridiculous reason ever for not being with someone?'

He grinned. 'If it helps, I'll order you never to think of dating me ever again.'

His words startled a laugh out of me. 'Don't be cross but it really does help.'

He burst out laughing; so much that he doubled over and chased away the last shadows from my heart. When he stopped, I wrapped my hands around his neck, stood on tippy-toes and pressed my lips to his. When the zing came, I found that I didn't mind all that much about the bloody thing – or what it meant.

I'd assumed that the old adage 'life's too short' didn't apply to me anymore because I was a vampire, but Connor had nearly died and I hadn't seized the day. If I wasn't ever truly with him, I'd regret it until my staking day.

Chapter 38

One of the best things about me is that I learn from my mistakes. Time to seize the day – or night – for all it was worth. I pressed my lips to Connor's and let my tongue caress his. He met me passion for passion, and I melted into him. The warmth was followed by a fire that whipped through my veins. I wove my hands into his hair and his hands slid under the waist of my T-shirt. No doubt we'd have moved on to more horizontal manoeuvres if Lee hadn't cleared his throat and Fluffy hadn't barked.

I didn't speak Dog, but I was pretty sure Fluffy's tone translated to 'Get a room!'. *I'd love to buddy*, I thought. *I'd love to*.

Connor drew back reluctantly. 'Where's your vest?' he asked, his fingers pointedly caressing the bare skin of my midriff.

'Um, I forgot it.' I shrugged; Connor sighed; Fluffy barked; Lee was grinning. My skin warmed and I tried to change the subject. 'Right, what about that witch?' I asked as I smoothed down my clothing. 'Has he perished?'

'Nope. He's still alive,' Lee confirmed.

I wasn't sure how I felt about that. I guessed it was good, but Jayden was a powerful witch and if he held a grudge then tomorrow Bunny would be keeping one eye open when she slept. And Bunny really needed a good sleep.

Connor's hand rested on the small of my back as we walked carefully out of the stacks of lumber and back to where the witch lay. Jayden Donaldson was sprawled out, a big pool of blood spreading deliciously from his shoulder. My stomach growled – I should have grabbed a cup of blood for me, too. I could see his chest rising and falling so I knew he wasn't dead, but he had to be in bad shape.

In the end, my conscience wouldn't let me do anything other than call the ambulance. Besides, I still needed questions answered and Donaldson was my last resort. Why had he said Aoife wasn't his daughter? Was it because Aoife had snitched on him, or was he really not her biological father?

Connor sent Lee for my emergency kit from the SUV. I had first-aid supplies in there as well as the magic-cancelling cuffs. We needed both.

When Lee returned, he passed the bag to me and I pulled out the cuffs. By cuffing Jayden on one arm, I stopped him using his magic but didn't hurt him more. Connor applied pressure to the gunshot wound, which was high on the witch's shoulder. It didn't look like I'd hit anything vital, but no doubt the bullet had broken some bone – I had *bear rounds* in my gun, for God's sake. The back of the wound was ugly where the bullet had expanded, and I shuddered and felt vaguely ill. I'd never thought I'd have to shoot someone; the main reason I carried the gun was because of the beast.

I watched Connor saving the life of a man who might have killed him. How had I ever doubted him? Fated mates or not, he'd never force me into anything I didn't want.

I started to shiver. The cold that had seeped into my bones since Aoife had flown into me was really starting to get to me. I examined my fingers and felt a surge of panic when I saw that my fingertips had turned blue. 'Umm, Connor?' I called. He looked up. 'A banshee flew through me and I feel kind of cold.'

He blanched, shot up from Donaldson and moved to me in a blink. 'How long ago?' he asked urgently.

'Um, a few hours, I guess.'

Connor's eyes flicked to the bleeding man on the floor before he gave a minute shake of his head. 'Margrave!' he barked.

'I'm on it!' Margrave replied.

I expected him to run to the break room as I had, but instead he ran out of the warehouse and into the woods. 'You're scaring me,' I admitted in a small voice.

'It's okay,' Connor said soothingly but his eyes told me he was lying. 'We need to get some blood in you. Now.'

It felt like hours before Lee returned, though it must have only been a minute or two. He was carrying a deer. It was alive and calm; he must have entranced it somehow.

'You need to drink from something living,' Connor explained.

I recoiled. I'd only done that once and I'd nearly lost myself in the process.

'I'll be here,' he promised, 'but you have to do it. That your lips and fingers are only turning blue now is a blessing. I think your ... uniqueness has saved you again. You don't need to kill the deer but you do need to drink from something with hot blood. Now.' I hesitated. 'Now!' he snapped.

I moved to the deer before I could talk myself out of it. For once, my fangs had turned up when they were needed. 'I'm so sorry, Bambi,' I said then sank my fangs into her docile neck and drank. The blood tasted rather like mouldy cheese – and I despise mouldy cheese – but I battled through and took a bunch of good slurps.

Connor was holding my hand, looking at my fingers. 'A little more,' he instructed when I paused.

Grimacing, I obeyed. 'You can stop now,' he said finally, sounding relieved.

I stepped hastily away from the deer. Margrave set it down and it bolted away. 'She'll be okay, right?' I asked anxiously.

'Unless another hunter gets her,' Lee said casually and I glared at him.

'How do you feel?' Connor asked.

'Fine. Normal.' I paused. 'Warm.'

'Thank God. We got it in time.'

Lee was looking at me with new respect. 'Surviving hours after a banshee possession is hardcore.'

'She didn't possess me, she ... floated through me.'

'One and the same,' he grunted.

I looked between the men. 'So banshees can kill vamps?'

'Not something we advertise,' Connor said drily.

As I mimed zipping my lips, the scent of smoke drifted in on the air. 'Um, Connor? There's something else I should bring up. Your truck is on fire. I forgot to mention it in the middle of everything else.'

'*What*?'

'I think Jayden torched it. It was burning in the car park when I arrived.'

Connor narrowed his eyes at the unconscious man before sighing. 'Guess it's time for a new truck.'

'Well, that one is certainly done for. I'll have to give *you* a ride home for once.'

He laughed. 'Yeah.'

We could hear sirens in the distance. 'Lee, prop open that door so they can find us,' Connor ordered.

His second leapt up, grabbed a board and wedged open the main warehouse door. The fire from Connor's truck was enough to send eerie flickering shadows inside. The paramedics arrived shortly after that with a stretcher and soon had the unconscious witch on the way to the hospital with strict instructions to cuff him to his bed.

Now that things were calm, I sent a message to Gunnar to let him know what had happened. Connor and Lee locked down the site; Lee was staying until a fire engine came to put out the truck fire. It was not a good idea to leave it unattended in the woods.

I packed Connor into the Nomo SUV. 'Where to?' I asked.

'I'll direct you.'

We drove mostly in silence, bar Connor's occasional direction. I'd assumed that he'd want to go home, but it quickly transpired that we were going back to the Nomo's office. 'Smart arse,' I muttered when I figured it out.

He reached out and laced his fingers through mine, resting them on the gear stick. 'I don't want to leave you now,' he admitted softly. I didn't ask if that was for him or for me; maybe it was for both of us.

I parked up and we went inside. Gunnar was pacing up and down the reception area. 'Bunny!' He pulled me into his arms before pushing me back so he could inspect me for damage.

'I'm okay,' I reassured him.

'You should have called me!' he barked.

I swallowed hard. 'I know. I'm sorry.'

That took the wind right out of his sails. 'Okay, well, don't let it happen again,' he said gruffly before pulling me in for an extra hug, squeezing me with his not-insignificant strength. 'Gunnar,' I wheezed. 'I need to breathe!'

He laughed. 'No, you don't. You're a vampire!'

Uh-huh. One day soon I would have to come clean about my oddities, but not today. I was emotionally drained and, to be honest, I was worried that if Gunnar knew that I might not be quite as undead as we'd thought, he might not be so willing to let me barrel head first into danger.

'Let's get you a hot drink.' He bustled in the backroom to make a cup of tea for me and coffee for him and Connor.

Finally we settled into the chairs in Gunnar's office. 'Talk me through it,' he ordered softly, so I did. I said that I'd set Donaldson on fire but omitted the 'how' because I hadn't yet found the right time to confess to Connor about my internal flames.

At one point, Connor reached for my hand again; it was comforting but my tummy squirmed with guilt that I was still hiding something from him. I'd had the perfect opportunity to confess but I hadn't – and I knew why. Connor seemed to really like me but I was scared that if he knew what I could do he'd think I was a freak. I'd put up with being thought of as a freak my whole life; Portlock was the first place where I was *normal* – but even here I had to go and be different.

Gunnar rubbed his beard. 'Do you think Jayden Donaldson is our guy? Did he kill Aoife?' I shook my head. 'He did try to kill the three of you,' he pointed out.

'Yeah.' Connor's jaw was working. 'I want him prosecuted for that.'

'He is guilty of assault, attempted kidnapping and the attempted murder of a police officer,' I agreed. 'But I don't think he's got anything to do with the barrier gems, and I'm pretty sure he's clean of his daughter's murder. He was totally shocked when I told him Aoife was dead. That doesn't mean that he didn't put her up to the fire-gem theft, but I can't see any motive for killing her. He was angry with her and he said she'd stolen something from him. He also said she wasn't his daughter, which will be easy to corroborate with DNA. He left plenty of it behind, and we have Aoife's already.'

'It should be easy enough to check for the gems where Donaldson is living. We need to find out the address and we can clear that one quick,' Gunnar said.

'I have it. He was working under the table for us, but he still had to give us an address,' Connor said. 'I'll get someone to co-sign the warrant with me and you can search it.'

Gunnar looked satisfied. 'Sounds good to me, councillor.'

Connor scrolled through his phone and texted someone. It rang a few seconds later and I followed him over to my desk. When I let Shadow out of his crate he yelled at me with tiny kitty squeaks, but he quickly forgave me, pressing against my legs and purring when I picked him up.

'Sorry, little fellow. You're too little to go on the big jobs.' I remembered his fierce bravery when he'd faced the beast and sent it packing. 'Especially as I'm not quite sure what you are,' I muttered.

He was a freak like me; no wonder I loved the little dude. I lay my cheek against his silky fur and set him back on the floor as Connor finished his call.

'Patkotak said he'd meet us at the council chambers in ten.'

'Good,' I said. 'I'll run the animals home, feed them and meet you there,'

He nodded then, with a lingering gaze full of promise, he walked out.

Chapter 39

Connor led us to Jayden Donaldson's apartment. There wasn't much in it; he was obviously broke, new to town and had few possessions. He had a toothbrush, some other toiletries, a few changes of clothes and a couple of frozen meals in the fridge. We found nothing that suggested he'd been involved in any of our crimes. We left disappointed, but not very shocked.

I still wanted to know what he thought Aoife had stolen and why he'd insisted she wasn't his daughter, but I'd have to wait until he or Nora was well enough to question. It didn't look as if Jayden had anything to do with the missing gems or his daughter's murder, but he was almost certainly going to jail for kidnapping, assault and attempted murder. He'd made bad choices.

I was finally off shift so I drove Connor to his fancy gated home on the hill. I parked in his driveway and we both sat quietly. Coming here brought all the memories of our date flooding back – the food, the dancing, the confession. With a little distance, I could admire how he'd dealt with it all; he'd never shown me anything less than calm patience – and maybe an emotion I wasn't ready to name yet.

I took a deep breath and pulled up my big girl panties. I either had to take the plunge with Connor or run away from the idea of us forever. And I was tired of running.

Whatever he felt for me, it wasn't conditional. It didn't come with strings and bribes; he honestly seemed to like me *for me*. He liked the goofy Bunny that sang too loudly on tabletops, he liked the crazy Bunny that plunged into danger head first, and he even liked the serious Bunny that loved a mystery and was fascinated with supernaturals and the law.

He liked me as I was, not the person he wanted me to be. And I liked him exactly as he was, too: a prince running away from a life of wealth and privilege to strike out on his own. No wonder he understood me so well because we'd done exactly the same thing. We'd both run away to Portlock, straight into each other's arms.

Tears built up in my eyes and I blinked them away. I finally looked back up at him. 'I'm so sor—'

I couldn't finish because his mouth was on mine. He fumbled to unlock my seat belt and hauled me onto his lap. I kissed him back with abandon, revelling in the moment when the zing hit me. It was the strongest one yet and I cried out, but this time I leaned into it, embraced it.

Connor pulled back, his eyes wide. 'You accepted it!' he said with genuine surprise. 'Accepted me.'

'Is that what I did?' I smiled. 'And what about you? Do you accept it?'

He smiled. 'I did that long ago, right about the time you gyrated around your living room for me. I knew then that you were a keeper.'

I laughed and kissed him lightly. 'I'm sorry it took me so long to get my head straight. I've been an idiot resisting this – resisting you. When I saw you after

Donaldson had...' I shook my head. 'I thought for a second...' I blew out a harsh breath. 'I'm going to finish a sentence now, I promise.'

I cleared my throat and forced myself to say the next words. 'I realised when I was scared that you were dead that I've been so wrapped up in myself and my baggage that I didn't see what was right in front of me. I see you now, Connor Mackenzie. Can we start over? Will you forgive my idiocy?'

He cupped my face and looked into my eyes. 'There's nothing to forgive, my darling doe.' Then he kissed me again.

I writhed a little in his lap. 'Let's take this inside,' I purred.

'Are you sure?' He wasn't asking about our location.

'A thousand percent,' I promised.

His mouth turned up. 'That is a *lot* of percent.' He climbed out of the car, swung me into his arms and carried me effortlessly into his house. I'd been in his arms like this before but last time I'd been bleeding out from a gunshot wound. This time was infinitely more pleasurable.

Connor carried me up to his room. I looked around long enough to register the high ceilings, heavy furniture and a four-poster bed on a raised dais, then I stopped looking around because that was when he threw me into the middle of the bed, making me giggle as I bounced on the silken sheets.

He stood next to me looking every inch the predator I knew him to be. I lowered my eyes and did my best to look like prey.

I did so love to be eaten.

Chapter 40

Dragging myself from Connor's bed to meet with Liv really should have won me some sort of award. It had taken a herculean effort to walk away from those warm eyes, hard abs, and rigid ... morals.

I went to the Nomo's office early, before my shift started. Liv wasn't waiting for me, which was good because Sidnee let out a scream when she saw me. 'Oh my God! You're beaming! You fucked Connor!'

My face went fuchsia. 'Shout a little louder, I don't think Gunnar quite heard you.'

She grinned. 'He's not in yet, and he won't be in until you give him the all-clear that Liv has left. So tell me everything! I have to live vicariously through you now that I'm a washed-up old maid.'

I snorted. 'You're a sexy young mermaid with plenty of fish ready to dive into your sea!'

She smiled but not as brightly as a moment before. 'Yeah, maybe.'

I didn't want to talk about Connor and me because it was fresh, new and private, so I changed the topic to work. 'How was your day? Many calls?'

She shuffled some papers on her desk. 'Nothing noteworthy. Anyway, if you're in – and you're not going to spill the tea – do you mind if I cut loose before Liv rocks up? She scares the bejesus out of me.'

I'd never known Sidnee to baulk at anything, but she looked tired so maybe she wanted to chill. 'Sure thing. You go home.'

'Thanks.' She smiled again but it didn't reach her eyes. Gone was the bouncing, teasing Sidnee of moments before. What had I done to scare her away?

As she scarpered, I thought about the meeting with Liv. Now that Donaldson was out of the running, the only leads I had were the gems themselves. There had to be something about their history that would lead to the real thief and murderer. And the one with the answers was Liv. I hoped.

She sashayed in bringing the hot desert wind with her. We sat in Gunnar's office; it was less formal than the interview room and the last thing I wanted was to make Liv feel defensive. She was there to help me.

I settled into Gunnar's huge chair and had a sudden flashback to sitting in my father's office chair when I was child. I shook it off with effort. My father was on the other side of the world and I wasn't a child anymore.

'So, what do you want to know?' Liv asked briskly, not purring as she usually did with Gunnar.

'Anything about the history of the gems. Where did they come from, what do they do, how did we get them, what is the curse? You know,' I said drily, 'everything.'

She tilted her head and contemplated me. 'Why do you think I know all that?'

'You're the magic leader,' I said simply. 'Someone has to know enough about them to harness their power – and that's you.' Plus, she'd screamed at Stan for losing her gems that she'd 'lent' to the council, though I didn't think it was diplomatic to remind her of that.

'Hmmm.' Liv tapped her red-painted fingernail against her full lips. 'I don't know everything about them, but I know more than most.'

She settled into her chair. 'It took me centuries to collect enough information to locate them. Back then I was searching for them for fun and I followed their trail. They've been passed around, lost and found, fought over and gifted for as long as history has been recorded.'

I felt a shiver of excitement and I leaned forward. I loved a good story.

'Once they were pure elemental magic, but they were twisted by the darkest of dark powers.'

I swallowed. That was a lot coming from a necromancer who used death to power her magic.

'I found the great water gem at the source of the Blue Nile, in Lake Tana in Ethiopia, where I am from. Rumours that it existed had been around for as long as anyone could remember, and I coveted it from the first time I heard about it. It was said to give everlasting life to whoever drank from a pool where the gem rested. I believe the Fountain of Youth myths began with that rumour.'

I bit my lip. Could the rumours be true? After all, Liv was ancient ... I looked at her flawless skin. Yeah. It had totally worked.

Her eyes glittered with amusement as if she could read my thoughts. She folded her legs demurely at the ankle. Her bangles clattered against each other as she laid her arm against the wooden arm of the chair. Everything about her looked relaxed; that was how I knew she was anything but.

She continued. 'However, despite the rumours nothing good ever came from the gems. They weren't meant for men, or even for supernaturals. They were wielded by the archangels and I believe they were used for Creation itself.' She spread her arms above her and looked at the ceiling. 'Gabriel bore Water, Uriel bore Earth, Raphael bore Wind, and Michael bore Fire.'

My family wasn't overly religious but I'd studied the philosophy of religion at university. I knew the names.

'The lore says there was a great war in the heavens and the gems were lost as the angels and demons fought for control of the earth.' She shrugged casually. 'Who knows?'

I hoped she did because that was why I'd asked, but I kept my mouth shut and let her tale unfold.

'I'm not sure how the stones became cursed – or by whom – but all the stories agree that at some point the gems were captured by the demons. To keep them from throwing the balance of the war in favour of the angels, the demons subverted them by taking noncorporeal beings and locking their tortured souls inside the stones. The possessed gems hated their own existence and as time passed, the fury of the captured souls grew in sentience and evil. Each gem began with its own elemental strength and grew in power with the hatred of its lost soul.'

That was grim. If the gems had Creation-level power to start with, we needed them locked up or returned to the angels. My stomach was starting to feel as though it was the pit of despair. If the story was true, who *wouldn't* try to steal them? Angels?

Demons? That was a terrifying thought. If Beelzebub came knocking at my door, I'd throw the stones at him and run.

'So the boxes control the stones somehow?' I asked, licking my suddenly dry lips.

'The boxes focus their power and keep it drained down so the gems are fairly weak. But the fire gem has been out of the box for several days now and its power will be growing.'

'So get it back as soon as possible,' I said, deadpan. We'd been trying. 'Do you know anyone who understands what the gems are and would want to steal them?'

She shrugged. 'There are ancient beings out there who are aware of them. But the stones were thought to be lost and I haven't advertised that I have them.'

'You're saying maybe?'

She laughed, a sharp noise that seemed to surprise her. 'Yes, Bunny, maybe. It is entirely possible that someone wants to steal them for their overwhelming power. However, I still think the thief is someone from this town who knows nothing about them, other than that they power the barrier – and they want the barrier down. Gems and their lesser cousins, crystals, are commonly objects of power so they might just think they are getting very large, expensive gemstones.'

I sighed. This was one job I *wanted* to be above my paygrade. The beast outside the barrier scared me witless and now I was terrified of the gems, their powers and their past owners. 'Thanks, Liv. That does give another angle for the possible thefts. I hope you're right and it's about the protests.'

She stood up and smoothed down her clothes. 'Me too.' She walked out without saying goodbye; she needed to work on her manners, but it was still the most pleasant time I'd ever spent in her presence. I was starting to think that maybe she liked me a little.

Nah.

Chapter 41

I reviewed Sidnee and Gunnar's notes from the interviews with the barrier protestors and two people struck me: Martin Snow and Ezra Taylor. I called and made appointments for them to come in again. Snow was available immediately so he gruffly promised to present himself for interview.

When he walked in, I had to suppress a gasp. He had two black eyes, one of which was cut and swollen shut, and he was moving stiffly. 'What happened?' I asked. 'I can help.'

He shot me a bitter smile. 'No, you can't.'

'I can speak to Stan…'

He flinched and then I put it all together. Stan had done this; he'd beaten up Snow for failing him at the wind witch's house, then he'd forbidden him from shifting so his injuries could heal quickly. Stan wanted to punish the moose shifter for his supposed failure. I grimaced. I didn't believe in corporal punishment.

'Do you want me to get involved?' I asked hopefully. Group matters were dealt with largely in-house and I could only intrude if there were bodies on the floor, if other groups were affected, or if I was invited to deal with the matter.

'No,' he grunted, 'I don't. But I've been told to co-operate with you, so here I am.'

'I appreciate that.' I led him into the interview room, clicked on the recording equipment, ran through my usual spiel and then we began. 'You were at the barrier protest, yes?'

'Yeah. That's not a crime.'

'No, it's not,' I soothed. 'Why don't you like the barrier?'

'I don't care about the damned barrier, what I care about is *paying* for it. The council should foot the bill, not us. It's hard enough to make ends meet without ridiculous taxes too.'

'You were rostered on guard for the wind gem the day it got stolen?' I asked.

'Yes.'

'What did you see the day the house got burned down?'

He grimaced. 'I didn't see anything. Wintersteen is obsessive about privacy and she never lets her guards stand too close to the property. We can be out front with eyes on her front door and that's all. She's never let any of us in. She doesn't trust us.'

Evidently she was right not to; Snow had let her down in a big way. 'And on that day, when your shift started?'

Snow sighed. 'Stan told me to tell you everything so I'll tell you, though I don't like you knowing. I have a gambling problem. I'd been given a tip about a horse – a sure win.' He licked his lips. 'I went to the bookie.'

'Why didn't you bet online?' I asked nosily.

'You get better rates at the sports book if you go in person.'

'Did the tip pay off?'

He glowered. 'No. I bet, I watched the race and I lost a tonne. After that I drank some akpik moonshine.' Akpik was the most popular moonshine flavour that the Grimes brothers sold up at their trading post.

'*Some* akpik?' I queried.

'A *lot* of akpik,' he admitted.

'You weren't at your post because you were drunk?'

'Yeah.'

'Who gave you the tip about the horse?'

He gave a one-shouldered shrug. 'Mr Wintersteen. He was making conversation before he went in the house. He knows I like the horses.'

'Does Mr Wintersteen like the horses?'

'Not as far as I know, but he said a friend of his had told him Sierra Dash was a sure thing.'

'His mate was wrong.'

His glare intensified. 'No shit.'

I wondered how much Snow had lost but it didn't really matter. He'd given into his addiction and he'd been betting and drinking rather than manning his post. Stan had originally said that Snow was solid and that he trusted him, but I bet if I asked Stan now he'd give me a different answer. But I felt bad for Snow;

gambling was an addiction and he needed help. 'If you want to kick the habit–' I started.

'I know about Gambler's Anonymous,' he growled unhappily. 'Stan is making me go. I don't need you sticking your nose into my business. We're done here.'

I didn't have any more questions so I let him walk out. I didn't think he was involved in either of the gem thefts. He didn't like paying money for the barrier's maintenance because he was broke due to his gambling. Some of the other protestors were fanatical about the barrier but Snow was just low-key pissed off. He wasn't the person I was looking for.

While I waited for Ezra, I called the hospital. Nora Sullivan's condition was critical but stable; Jayden Donaldson was in surgery for his ruined shoulder. Both of them would be unavailable for several more hours.

Ezra Taylor strolled in, neatly dressed and a little full of himself. I'd warmed to him when he'd helped me during the tsunami warning but there was no room for personal feelings in this business. 'Fanged Flopsy,' he greeted me, his tone a shade mocking.

'Mr Taylor, thank you for coming so promptly. Follow me.'

I led him into the interview room but when I went to hit record, he objected. 'No. Off the record.'

I hadn't had an 'off the record' situation before. I wouldn't be able to use anything he said in a court case against him – but it might mean he would talk more frankly. In the end I nodded and dropped my hand. I remained standing whilst he sat down because I thought it would give me a psychological advantage, but wouldn't you know it? He leaned back in his chair, stretched out his legs and crossed them at the ankles, then laced his fingers together and tucked his hands behind his head. His body language was saying he was completely comfortable and he owned the place.

I narrowed my eyes. 'Are you quite done, Mr Taylor?'

He smirked. 'Just getting comfy, love.'

'Uh-huh. Talk to me about the barrier.'

He raised a smooth, blond eyebrow. 'What's to say? I think it is a travesty, nothing more than a long con by the witches to bleed us dry. And I know you're going to say otherwise, but you're either in on it or you're ignorant.'

'I'm so glad you clarified my options,' I said sarcastically. We weren't recording so I could let a hint of mockery come out to play. He certainly wasn't showing me any respect and I didn't like his attitude. Things had definitely slid backwards since the tsunami alert.

I gritted my teeth and tried to improve the situation. 'I've been beyond the barrier, Mr Taylor. I've seen the monster.' I let fear show on my face. 'If it gets into town, it will kill us all. The barrier is a necessity, not a frivolity. We're not keeping out keeluts.'

He studied me for a long moment then leaned forward and put his hands down on the metal desk. His arrogant mask had bled away. 'I believe that you believe that,' he said slowly.

'Then how do you explain it?' I asked in exasperation. 'If you know I believe I saw the monster...'

'Because, Officer Barrington, we live in a world of magic and the Grimes brothers are two of the strongest illusion witches in the world. Do you seriously expect me to believe that they're here to – what? Brew moonshine?' His voice was incredulous. 'No, they're here to facilitate the con, to create the occasional illusion to convince the masses to keep on paying the witches through the nose.'

Damn, that was a good argument. It took me a moment to rally. 'And what of Kivuk? The vampire? The Savik brothers?'

'More illusion. The hunters died in a tragic accident and someone – probably a well-paid shifter – tore their bodies apart for you to find.'

'And the Grimes brothers were hiding behind a nearby bush casting illusions of the creature?'

'Exactly,' he looked pleased that I was getting it.

I thought back to those terror-filled moments. There was a flaw in his argument; the monster had flung rocks and trees at us and struck Fluffy. There was no way either of the Grimes was strong enough to chuck a tree – but neither was there any way I'd convince Ezra of that. It was time to change tack.

'Talk to me about Nora.'

He blinked. 'What about her?'

'You're seeing her, aren't you?' It was a shot in the dark based on Aoife's teasing of her mum.

He sighed. 'Nora and I are friends. Like me, she knows the truth about the barrier.'

'And was it your idea or hers to break into my house?'

He grimaced and glanced again at the camera to check it was off. 'It was an error in judgement,' he admitted. 'I see that now.'

'You smashed up my metal shutter mechanism whilst she sprayed the threat.' It was one of the things that had nagged at me. Shadow had woken me pretty quickly but my intruder had done a lot of damage in a couple of different areas. It made sense that there were two of them working together to do so much damage in such a short space of time.

'As I said,' Ezra said mildly, 'it was an error of judgement.'

'And Aoife?'

'I had nothing to do with that girl's death. Absolutely nothing.'

The worst thing was that I believed him.

Chapter 42

I pushed Ezra some more and questioned him about the theft of the wind gem, too. I was almost certain he'd conspired with Nora to steal the fire gem but Aoife had beaten them to it. And he was giving off annoyed vibes: he was annoyed that someone else had the gems rather than him. He wanted to be the hero, the one who saved us all from the barrier, but some other prick would get the glory. No, I didn't think he'd stolen the gems – but not for want of trying.

Frustrated, I pulled in the wind witch, Elsa Wintersteen. I still remembered when my own house burned; I'd been so traumatised I'd spent a couple of days on Sigrid's and Gunnar's sofa bemoaning my lot in life. I understood that Elsa would need a few days to get over her own house fire, but time was short and we needed to crack on.

Whilst I was waiting for her to turn up, I dug into her background and turned up some basics: she had a husband, Larry Wintersteen, and two teenage kids, Jaxon and Betty.

When Elsa arrived, she gave me a weak smile. Her dark hair was curled and hung to her shoulders and her makeup was neatly applied. I'd have put her in her early thirties, though the age of her kids made me push that to her late thirties. She still had a lost look in her eyes like I'm sure I'd had after my fire. Luckily, she hadn't also seen two people burn to cinders, and her family was all safe and sound. Saying 'it could have been worse' seemed callous, so I kept that one to myself.

I started the recorder. 'Please state your name and what supernatural type you are.'

She gave me a disbelieving look. Supernats didn't like being open about what they were or what power they had, but we didn't have time to dick around. Finally, she cleared her throat. 'My name is Elsa Wintersteen. I'm an elemental air witch. Up until the fire, I was in charge of the wind gem.' She folded and unfolded her hands anxiously.

'How long have you been in charge of the gem?' I asked.

'Um,' her eyes looked up to the right, as she thought, 'I think it's been seventeen years now. Give or take.'

Seventeen? Kostas had only been guarding the fire gem for three years. 'That's a long time. You don't look very old – how old were you when you started the job?'

She gave a girlish giggle. 'Thank you. I'm thirty-nine, but witches age well.'

'You still took on that responsibility very early.' Liv must have trusted her a lot.

'Well, I was done with school and expecting my first baby so it was easy. I didn't have anywhere pressing to be. It made sense for me to be the guardian.'

'But *seventeen*? Wasn't that hard?'

'Sometimes,' she said honestly. 'But it's my duty. I help protect the town so it's worth a little sacrifice. I even raised my babies at home so I wouldn't leave the gem for long. Home schooling was a gift to us all.' She smiled.

That was nuts. How could Liv have asked that of her? No one should have to bear that sort of responsibility for so long. I scribbled a note to ask Liv about it later. 'What protections surrounded the gem before the fire?' I asked.

'The usual – a basic warning ward, and I added stronger ones after you warned us to. But it was rarely out of my sight.'

'You could see it on its stone plinth?'

'No, I meant I rarely left the house for long, only to pick up and drop off the kids and to go to the store, things like that. I don't work outside of the home. Being the guardian has a nice stipend and my husband makes good money.'

If she was being well paid, it made more sense that she'd been happy to hold the position for so long. Maybe that was part of what my barrier tax went to pay for. 'Did you notice anything odd or anyone hanging around your place in the days leading up to the fire?'

She shook her head slowly. 'I thought I saw a skinny girl hanging around once, but it was nothing.'

Aoife. I frowned. She had been dead when the wind gem was stolen but maybe she could have been there in her banshee form?

'Have your kids brought home any new friends, kids you don't know?' I was grasping at straws.

She frowned. 'No, I don't allow visitors into my home. I don't even let my shifter guards in the house. If my kids want to hang out with their friends, they go to their houses. I take my duty seriously.'

'Do you know of anyone who would want to take the gem?'

'Of course not.'

'Anyone with a grudge against you?'

She looked at me, wide-eyed. 'Heavens, no!'

I couldn't think of anything else to ask, so I handed over a business card and told her to call if she thought of anything. I was at a loss, which was my most hated place to be – but I had made progress. And I knew who had broken into my house, so that was one thing to cross off my list.

Back at my desk, I checked my phone for calls: there was a missed one from Sidnee. I looked at the time; it was only an hour or two before she was due to come on shift and I wondered if she wanted to meet for breakfast, but she hadn't texted, which wasn't like her. A tingle of unease ran down my spine. I accessed my voicemail.

Sidnee's voice clicked in, breathy, scared, and determined. 'Bunny, I'm letting you know where I'm going ... in case. I'm swimming out to Elizabeth Island. Someone called the hotline and said that they think Chris is hiding out there. I have to go see. You understand, don't you? I have to have closure. I have to see him.' Click.

'Press one to delete the message, press two to repeat the message, press three to save the message,' the automatic voice said.

'No, no, no! For fuck's sake, Sidnee!' I yelled.

My hands were trembling and I was muttering 'fuck' over and over as I dialled Gunnar. The second he picked up, the words fell out of my mouth. 'Sidnee's gone to Elizabeth Island to find Chris! We gotta go now!' If Chris *was* there, Sidnee would need backup. He might have dated her, but he was unscrupulous and powerful and I'd never forgive myself if any harm came to her. I should have listened to the message sooner!

Gunnar let loose an impressive string of expletives then told me to meet him at the docks. 'Meet me at Stan's boat – he'll have to take us. And get Connor!' He hung up. The Nomo boat had been pulled out for repairs after being rammed by what was probably a large, pissed-off selkie. Now Sidnee was chasing that same large, pissed-off selkie.

I called Connor and he answered instantly. 'Doe, I didn't expect you to call until you were off shift.' He sounded pleased.

'There's an emergency!'

'Of course there is,' he said ruefully. 'What do you need?'

'Can you meet us at Stan's boat? Sidnee has swum out alone to Elizabeth Island to confront Chris Jubatus.'

'I'll see you there.' He hung up.

I took the animals home then drove like a bat out of hell to the south dock where Stan kept his boat. Gunnar was already there helping prepare it to leave.

I was putting on my life jacket when Connor came running up with Thomas Patkotak and Soapy Willoughby. Connor and Stan gave each other man-nods; their usual low-key animosity was on hold for now. Stan threw Connor and Thomas life vests – Soapy didn't need one – and soon we were pulling away from the dock. Stan's boat was larger and slower than the Nomo's, but at least it was seaworthy which ours wasn't at the moment.

I was glad that Connor had pulled a siren group member into the fray. Soapy probably wasn't thrilled with us since we'd accused him of being a drug dealer and kidnapper, but we needed someone who could search underwater more easily than a lumberjack vampire, a demi-god and whatever the heck I was.

I looked at Stan. Polar bears were good swimmers, right?

Then I looked across the unbroken dark water before us and hoped we'd find Sidnee in time.

Chapter 43

The ride out to Elizabeth Island was marginally smoother than the last one I'd taken, but this time my anxiety was way higher. There was also a minor storm brewing. Perfect.

I kept an eye on the threatening clouds as the sky lightened into morning and clutched my daylight charm anxiously. 'How will we find Sidnee?' I asked anyone who would answer. My gut was churning, and not from the rough seas.

Soapy answered. 'I'll dive down and check the cave that's still holding the drugs. If Chris really was seen around here, that's where he'll be. If we don't find him there, we'll circle the island and look for him or Fletcher.'

The disdain in his voice when he said Sidnee's surname took me off guard. I knew she had issues with the other mermaids, but Soapy wasn't a mer so what was his problem? Was he annoyed that her impulsiveness had brought us all out here?

I looked over the vastness of the cold blue sea. My friend could be literally anywhere. One searching salmon-shark shifter wasn't going to be enough. Try saying that five times fast.

'And while Soapy checks the caves, we'll check out the island and then go from there. We'll find her,' Gunnar sounded calm, but I suspected he was trying to reassure himself as much as me. 'Everything will be fine.' His fingers were tapping anxiously on the handrail; the body rarely lies as well as the mouth.

The five-mile ride seemed to take forever. By the time we were nearing the island the sun was fully up, though thankfully mostly obscured by thunder clouds. I looked up and shivered; I still remembered the first time I'd been burned by sunlight after I was turned.

As I fingered my daylight charm again, Connor noticed and wrapped his arm around my waist. He kissed my head and watched with me. Once we were close enough, I scanned the beach and cliffs for anything that would indicate Sidnee was there. Nothing. Dammit – would it have killed her to fire a flare or wave a giant flag or something?

Stan anchored near the sea cave. I looked over the side into the clear deep water but I couldn't see anything, not even the flash of a silvery fish. I turned around to see Soapy removing his clothing. Oh boy, I didn't want to see that because Calliope struck me as the jealous type. I closed my eyes tightly until I heard the splash as he dived over the side.

Stan put his skiff in the water. It was slightly larger than the Nomo skiff but it still only held three people at a time. Stan ran Gunnar and Thomas over first, then came back for me and Connor. He dropped us on the shore then returned to the boat to wait for Soapy.

I consciously drew up my memories of our previous walk on the island and skimmed through them. There were short beaches in both directions, both ending in a jumble of rocks that forced you to either go up into the island's interior or stop and turn around.

Thomas took the lead, and I'd never been happier to have an expert tracker beside me; he was almost as good as Fluffy at locating people. I wished I'd brought my dog; not only was he a comfort, but we could have used his nose. I wondered if it was a mistake to send Stan back to the boat. I bet polar bears had good noses. Though I was pretty sure I'd create a political gaffe if I suggested using the shifter-leader as a sniffer dog.

We went up the beach and turned to the left where we'd walked before. Thomas checked carefully then declared, 'No new tracks here.' My heart sank. If Sidnee was in the sea we'd never find her, alive or dead. It was too vast and I wasn't sure I trusted Soapy after hearing his tone when he'd said her name.

We turned back in the opposite direction and walked along the beach. Same result: nothing. We went back to our starting point. To do a real search, we'd have to split up and cover the interior of the island, which was three miles in diameter. Panic threatened to grip me; I pushed it down and looked inland.

Past the small strip of beach, a large grassy area with a stream in the centre offered an easy walk. However, the low flat area swooped up on both sides to tree-covered hills and beyond those were rocky cliffs. The other side of the island was mostly exposed rock, pounded by storms and surf. If Sidnee was anywhere it would be on this calmer side.

'She's got to be close to the beach,' I said desperately.

Connor looked at me gently; he didn't agree but he was afraid of breaking it to me. Patkotak had no such compunction. 'Not if she was chased out of the water. She'd be hiding in the trees or the rocks.'

I grimaced. Strong and tough as Sidnee was, Chris was bigger and stronger – plus he was a selkie. I wasn't sure what type of seal he turned into, but it could be larger than Sidnee. 'Does anyone know what kind of seal Chris is?' I asked.

Thomas grunted, 'He's a Steller sea lion.'

Everyone looked at him. Connor asked, 'How do you know that, Patkotak?'

Thomas winked but didn't elucidate and that sent a chill down my spine. It wouldn't surprise me if he knew what *everyone* was; did he have a file on me somewhere? Bunny the vampire that isn't? 'Okay, pretend I'm British,' I said. 'What is a Stellar sea lion? And please tell me it means he's really good at studying the stars.'

Gunnar gave a hollow chuckle. 'Not Stell*ar* – Stell*er*. It's one of the largest sea lions. Ten feet long, weighs a tonne.'

'Fuck.' I bent over and tried to breathe slowly to push down my rising panic. Chris could kill Sidnee without even trying. I told myself that she was fast, though, and he'd tried to protect her when the general had wanted to wipe out her memories. Maybe he wouldn't hurt her. It felt like a big maybe.

'How does Soapy compare?' I asked. 'Could he help her against something that big?'

'Soapy's maybe five hundred pounds in his salmon-shark form. But he's fast, and so is Sidnee,' Gunnar said.

I thought back to the first time we'd been here when I'd caught a glimpse of brown fur in the trees. Gunnar had brushed it off as a moose or something. Could it have been a selkie skin waiting for its master to return? I shivered. 'Are Steller sea lions brown?' I asked.

Gunnar gave me one of his looks, but I was always spouting weird shit and he was used to it. 'Yeah, mostly,' he said.

I looked around, trying to remember where I'd seen the flash of brown fur, but this time I saw nothing. It felt like the motto of the day: nothing, nothing, nothing.

Probably the brown fur was that of a moose, like Gunnar had said. Why would Chris have hung his skin here? And maybe the tales of selkie skins were way off base. Maybe they didn't leave their skins at all in real life.

Connor placed his hand on my lower back and suddenly I could breathe again. I needed to let my anxiety fall away and focus on finding Sidnee. I gave him a grateful smile. 'We'll take this side of the stream.' I strode purposefully to the left bank and he joined me.

'We'll take the other side,' Thomas said.

'I'm an okay tracker but I'm nowhere near as good as Patkotak,' Connor said, once we were out of earshot of the other two men.

'If she's here, she'll want us to find her. She'll leave something we can follow,' I tried to sound optimistic but we both knew that if she were *truly* hiding, she wouldn't have left anything that Chris might find.

Think, Bunny, think. Where would she go if Chris had chased her out of the water?

If she'd gone to the cave to see if he was checking on the fisheye, what could have happened? The stash had been immense and he couldn't have retrieved it alone, plus it was wired to explode. We'd searched several paranormal towns before we'd found someone qualified to disarm it, and he wasn't due in until the following week. We had people primed to retrieve the stash after the explosives had been defused but it would take several people and a large boat.

'No way,' I said aloud and stopped.

Connor turned to look at me. 'What?'

'He wouldn't be here alone,' I said.

'Chris?'

'Yeah. If he *was* seen here, he'd be here for the drugs. Why else would he come back? And he couldn't manage that huge stash alone, not in a sea-lion body.' If my theory was right, there would be a bunch of tracks, not just Sidnee's.

There was a shout and both of us whipped our heads around. Gunnar and Thomas had found something.

We ran.

Chapter 44

Thomas was looking at the ground. 'What did you find?' I asked breathlessly.

He pointed. 'Small feet that could be our girl's followed by at least three men. They went off into the trees there.' He nodded to the right.

I took a deep breath. She was on land and that meant we could find her. *Please let her be okay*, I prayed to any god who might be listening.

We followed Thomas into the trees. Sidnee was no more a woods' girl than I was, and even I could see her barefoot tracks. One man was barefoot – my money was on Chris – and the other two were wearing boots. Their tracks were easy to follow because they didn't know they had any reason to hide them.

Thomas stopped and we jerked to a halt behind him. He held up a hand and cupped his other hand around his ear. We listened. Thomas was human, dammit; why was he so much better at this?

I closed my eyes, concentrated and faintly heard what sounded like a woman crying in the far distance. A chill ran down my spine: Sidnee. It had to be. I took two steps towards the sound but Thomas grabbed my arm, shook his head and whispered something under his breath. Even with my vampire hearing, I didn't catch what he said.

He continued following the tracks even though the wailing was coming from the opposite direction. I vibrated with the need to follow the sound but Connor grabbed my hand. He trusted Thomas, and I needed to trust him as well. With gritted teeth, I followed the tracker.

We continued for ten more minutes before Thomas stopped, looked back at us and grimaced. Blood, flesh and torn clothing were strewn on the ground and even in the trees; what looked like a crushed head was jammed about twelve feet up a tree.

'Oh my God! Sidnee,' I whispered, but Thomas shook his head and held a finger to his lips. I might not be the only supernat around here who had good hearing.

Thomas pointed to the clothing scraps and then I understood: Sidnee had come to the island here in mer form with no clothes. The head had close-cropped blond hair: it wasn't Chris's. I wasn't sure if I was relieved or disappointed. Something had torn a grown man into tiny bits.

Our master tracker was looking behind us, his expression grim. 'What?' I whispered. Thomas mouthed an answer but I still didn't understand what he was trying to say.

Connor's grip on my hand tightened: he understood. I straightened my spine, took a deep breath and squeezed his fingers. We skirted around the mangled remains and Thomas picked up the trail again. It felt like we had only walked ten steps when we heard the eerie woman sobbing again. The noise chilled me to the bone. That definitely *wasn't* Sidnee.

Connor interpreted Thomas's strange word. 'Kushtaka,' he whispered softly. That meant nothing to me, but I pictured the nantinaq and the beast beyond the barrier. Whatever it was, everyone here was scared of it.

The other man who had been stalking Sidnee had met a similar fate and we found part of him thirty feet away. There were no signs of the rest of him, nor of Chris and Sidnee. We didn't have time to look further because a massive thing with brown fur launched itself at us with a screech.

We scattered. Thomas's big handgun barked out five quick shots and we all hit the ground. There was another shriek and the thing crashed away from us, shoving through the trees and brush. 'What the fuck was that?' I asked, a shade hysterically.

'Kushtaka,' Connor repeated. 'An otter-man. They're violent, territorial and incredibly hard to kill.' The trio of unwanted attributes. Fabulous.

'I winged it,' Thomas said with satisfaction. 'But it'll be back. We need to leave.'

I wanted to go, too, but I wasn't leaving without my bestie. I spotted a barefoot track and pointed. 'Look, she's heading that way.'

Thomas nodded. 'Let's go.' He set off at a bruising pace and we scurried after him, further to the right than we'd been before. If the kushtaka hadn't jumped out at us there was a good chance we'd have missed Sidnee's footprint. It was being *helpful*. Good otter-man monster.

Thomas ran full pelt and we matched him, the crying screams dogging our every step. The kushtaka had recovered from being winged and had seized its courage again. It rushed us once more and this time both Gunnar and Thomas struck it with bullets. The minor wounds seemed to anger and confuse the beast, and it started throwing large rocks and branches at us but this time from a distance. It was cautious now it had been wounded twice – but for how long?

We burst out of the trees. There was nothing around us but boulders and cliffs; we'd have to split up to search because we'd lost the soft ground and the footprints. Without a word we spread out and started laboriously moving through the jumble of rocks. I started searching, squeezing between rocks and checking under everything, looking for caves or somewhere a slight girl would fit.

The kushtaka hung back, sending an occasional rock our way, but its crying wail was like fingernails on a chalkboard and that kept me moving quickly. I stumbled around until I came to a cliff. Looking over the edge, my heart leapt into my throat; it was maybe thirty feet to the water below. I backed away slowly and climbed back to start another route.

A shout rang out. Once I was high enough to look over the rocks, I saw Gunnar waving to get our attention. Connor and I reached the edge of the trees at the same time and rushed over. Thomas was struggling out of the rocks carrying a small, limp body: Sidnee.

A cry ripped from my throat as I ran over to him. She had to be alive! Her long hair was sweeping the ground and her dark skin was smeared with blood and dirt, but her hand twitched and her belly was rising and falling with her breath.

Thomas laid her gently on the ground and checked her for signs of injury. 'She has a broken arm,' he declared. 'The rest of the injuries are cuts and bruises, but she needs to get warm and get to the hospital.'

Sidnee stirred and opened her eyes. 'Bunny? I knew you'd come.' She smiled at me and then passed out again.

I let out a breath; it felt like I'd been holding it since I knew she'd gone after Chris. It rushed out from my toes and left me limp. As long as we managed to get out of here alive, Sidnee would be fine. Piece of cake.

Connor searched for a path back to the beach on which we wouldn't fall and break our necks, and that would keep us away from the kushtaka. 'There's only one way and it's tight. We can skirt the trees there.' He pointed. 'But it looks like an animal trail of some kind – maybe deer – and it's very narrow.' Thomas nodded and scooped up Sidnee.

We'd have to go past the trees from which the kushtaka could reach us easily but still evade our guns. Our handguns only had a maximum range of two hundred metres, so the otter-man would have the advantage. If it was as intelligent as it had proved to be so far, there was a good chance we'd end up in the water or on the rocks after a thirty-foot fall. Still, the trail would be quicker than retracing our steps, and we needed to get back to Stan.

I wondered if a fireball would harm the kushtaka. I'd only been about three metres away from my target when I'd used one before, and I didn't want to get that close to the monster. We had no choice: we had to take the trail.

Thomas took the lead, Sidnee draped across his arms. I wondered if one of us with supernatural strength should take her but he didn't seem to want to let her go. Oh well; he knew his limits. Gunnar brought up the rear.

It was strangely silent. The kushtaka had stopped its screeching and wailing and I hoped that meant it had keeled over and died from the gunshots, but the creepy feeling of being watched was making my shoulder blades itch. I was certain it was simply biding its time. I sped up until my feet were almost on Thomas's heels. Connor's breath brushed my neck; he was also feeling the weight of eyes watching us.

'Bunny,' Gunnar said, 'you'll have to use your fire. Guns aren't scaring it off but most wild creatures are scared of fire.'

Connor looked at me quizzically. '*Your* fire?' he asked quietly.

'There's something I've been meaning to tell you,' I admitted. 'You know how I have a heartbeat?'

'*What*?' Gunnar interjected. 'You have a *heartbeat*? But you're a vampire!'

'Can we shut the fuck up and focus here?' Thomas bit out. 'Gunnar, Bunny's fire is close-range. It won't help us here.'

Connor's jaw was working. 'Even Patkotak knows about your fire?'

'Just Patkotak,' I reassured him. 'And Gunnar,' I added.

'She used it to save us from the beast beyond the barrier,' Gunnar said. 'And it's why her house burned down. She set Virginia and Jim on fire.'

'Thank you, Gunnar,' I said drily. 'Could you let me tell my boyfriend that I'm a pyromaniac murderess in my own words?'

'Boyfriend?' Connor gave a pleased grin.

'*That's* what you're taking from this?' I asked, exasperated.

'Can you stop your chatter?' Thomas barked. 'I'm trying to list— Gunnar! Behind you!'

Gunnar whirled around and I turned to look, too, but all I caught was a snarling brown blur of fur and teeth. The otter-man picked up Gunnar like he was a feather and hurled him over the cliff like a stone.

I screamed, Thomas broke into a run and Connor grabbed my hand and dragged me along. 'Gunnar!' I screamed, but nothing answered me other than the timeless thrum of the surf below. If we hadn't been talking, maybe Gunnar would have heard the monster approach.

The kushtaka wasn't done because the rest of us were still on its territory. It ran down the path straight at us, pounding the ground on all four legs. 'It's coming!' I yelled. Gunnar had been right: it was time for some flames.

Fear was swamping me so it took little effort for the fire in my stomach to build into a raging inferno and

I screamed as it shot out of me. The kushtaka ducked away from the flames but the trees were not so mobile: they went up like so much dry kindling. Great – now I'd set a whole forest on fire too. I added that to my growing list of sins.

The flames spread and the kushtaka backed away for a moment. We had to press our advantage, no matter how brief. 'Move!' I yelled.

Thomas kicked it up another gear and we almost flew down the trail. Ahead of us the path disappeared and the edge of the cliff appeared. Fuck.

'Jump!' Connor screamed at Thomas.

Thomas gave a backward glance at the relentless kushtaka, took a running leap and disappeared over the cliff edge.

Chapter 45

I screamed as Connor and I followed him, holding hands as we sailed over the cliff and the rocks. Our fall stole my breath and whipped my hair. Connor released my hand so we wouldn't get tangled up, then he pointed his toes and lined up to land feet first. I twisted in the air and copied him as best I could. Our eyes locked as we hit the freezing water.

It felt like I had struck concrete. The air left in my lungs whooshed out with the force of the fall and the icy cold. For a moment I froze before instinct kicked in and I started kicking for the surface. My life jacket had inflated; with Connor's arm around my waist, the buoyancy of his life jacket and both of us kicking, we shot upwards.

As we burst to the surface, I gasped for air and followed that with a rib-cracking round of coughing.

Once I could breathe again, I looked around for Thomas, Sidnee and Gunnar. Gunnar had to be okay – he *had* to be.

Thomas was calmly treading water, one hand holding Sidnee's head so she floated alongside him. Relief swamped me as I caught sight of Gunnar's red-gold hair bobbing rapidly; he was alive and swimming towards us. The kushtaka was still screaming on the cliffs above us, but hopefully it would let us go now that we weren't on the island – unless it also counted the water as its territory.

The surf was throwing us around. As I looked upwards, rain gushed from the clouds and the wind picked up a notch. The promised storm was here. Of course it was.

We were wearing life jackets, but Sidnee wasn't. That wouldn't have been a problem if she'd been awake and in mer form, but she was unconscious and in human form. The way Thomas was supporting her suggested she was no better off than the rest of us.

'You okay?' Connor asked, checking me anxiously.

'I'm good. Can you help Thomas with Sidnee?'

Connor looked me over once more to make sure I seemed to be confident in the water. I wasn't the best swimmer but I was doing fine – I'd splashed around in Mum's pool often enough.

He swam rapidly to Thomas and the two men spoke quietly before Thomas passed over Sidnee. Connor wrapped his arm around her chest and started kicking away from the rocks and out past the breaking surf. I swam after him, as did the other two men. We had to get back to the boat – and fast. Even with my vampire resistance to cold, the water temperature was a danger and I could feel the icy depths sapping my strength. Thomas, Sidnee and Gunnar were at even higher risk.

To add to the fun, we had to worry if Chris was below us in his sea-lion form. And obviously there was the ever-present worry of freaking *sharks*. I tried to stop humming the *Jaws* theme tune and kept moving.

Once we were beyond the surf, Connor took charge. 'We won't make it to the boat. We have to get to shore and out of this water,' he yelled. 'I'm going to swim ahead. Sidnee has stopped shivering and that's a bad sign. I've got to get her onto land.' He turned on his vampire speed and I watched him move away from us.

'Thomas, are you alright?' I called. His dusky skin was turning blue.

'I'll make it to shore,' he said through gritted teeth, but he was shivering hard, as was Gunnar. I was also shivering; swimming wasn't keeping me warm. I wondered if my fire magic would work in water, if it could warm us even a little.

I trod water, closed my eyes and tried to sense that core of heat in my centre. It was there, tamped down and low. I needed to build it up, to let it warm me and then warm my friends. But I was so damned cold…

I needed rage or another strong emotion. I started thinking about Chris and how the bastard had lured Sidnee here. My anger started to grow and I focused on my ball of fire, stoking it with more images of what Chris had done to my friend. I pictured Sidnee with her arm at an angle that was so *wrong*. I was warming up.

'Bunny, keep swimming!' Gunnar shouted. He and Thomas had pulled further away.

I kept my heat close and, using vampire speed, soon caught up. 'Stay close. I'll try to warm the water around us,' I said when I was only a few feet away from them.

I closed my eyes again. Used more images of Sidnee, small and broken on the rocks, I pushed out the fire. The water lit up and instantly heat blossomed around me. I'd made the water hot – *too* hot. It was uncomfortable, though the heat faded fast.

'God that was nice,' Thomas muttered.

I tried to do it again, but the embers of my fire were at an all-time low and no matter how much I tried to stoke them there was no more fire. We swam on until we reached the spot where Connor left the water. He had taken off his shirt and was holding Sidnee's naked body to his own, hoping to keep her from hypothermia.

We dragged ourselves out of the water and onto the beach. We still weren't in sight of the boat so someone needed to fetch it – and that meant more swimming. First thing, though, we needed a fire. The men stripped off their sodden shirts and pants – which I could have lived without seeing – but they kept on their underwear for my benefit.

They quickly gathered wood. I was so exhausted and cold that my inner fire could only sputter out of me, but I summoned a pathetic spark that was enough to start a blaze. Now Thomas and Connor were both hugging Sidnee; if she'd been conscious, she would have loved the man sandwich. They moved her closer to the fire.

'I'll get the boat,' I said. 'We need to get Sidnee dressed and somewhere warm.'

'I'll go,' Connor offered.

'I'm the best choice. I can warm myself if I need to.' *Probably*. 'And we don't know how far away it is.'

'You can barely summon a flame,' he countered. He'd noticed that, had he? Damn. 'I'm the least affected so I'll go.'

I didn't want him to, but I wasn't half the swimmer he was. He was the logical choice, and my brain told my fearful heart to shut the fuck up. 'Okay,' I conceded. 'But be safe, okay?'

He smiled and brushed my lips with a kiss. 'You bet.'

I watched him walk boldly into the water before he dived in and started sliding through the waves. Without the burden of Sidnee, he was soon out of sight.

I turned back to Sidnee. 'How is she?' I asked Thomas.

He shook his head grimly. 'Not good. She's still not shivering and her pulse is weak.' All we could do was wait for Stan to arrive in the skiff. I'd never felt so helpless in my life; I hated being dependent on Connor making it to the boat and Stan coming to get us.

Then the weeping wail of the Kushtaka drifted down to us from the cliffs and the hairs on the back of my neck stood up. We hadn't made it far enough away.

Shit.

Chapter 46

Gunnar picked up his gun off a rock where the weapons had been drying out. Thomas placed Sidnee in my arms and I felt how cool her skin was. I tried to call up my inner heat but it responded sluggishly. I couldn't chuck any more fireballs at the kushtaka, so I might as well use what little warmth I had left to save Sidnee.

The icy cold made me think of the cold I'd battled when Aoife had swept through me. If the banshee could do that to me, maybe she could do it to the kushtaka. It was a long shot and I had no fricking clue how to summon a banshee spirit, but I had nothing to lose.

'Aoife!' I shouted, making Thomas and Gunnar look at me weirdly. 'Aoife Sullivan, I summon thee!'

Everyone always used thees and thous in spells, right? They sounded way cooler.

Nothing happened. That wasn't a surprise but I was still disappointed. Something in me had really thought she would come.

Thomas picked up his gun and he and Gunnar stood backs to back, waiting for the kushtaka to attack. Our only chance now was to wait for the boat.

The kushtaka's crying was getting louder; it sounded like a vulnerable, sobbing woman and every instinct in me wanted to go and help, but it wouldn't fool me again. I'd seen what made the cries and I knew it was no victim.

There was a crashing from the trees and Gunnar and Thomas levelled their weapons. Then I saw a flash of slick brown fur and it was charging at us again. I couldn't do anything but watch in horror and clutched Sidnee more closely.

The kushtaka was easily ten feet tall and its fur was dark brown, lighter on its belly. Its hands were human-like but disproportionately large and they ended in long sharp claws. Its head was a mix of human and sea otter. It was monstrous; if we survived, I would see it in my nightmares. Not that I'd be having any nightmares because surviving seemed unlikely; we had no escape.

The kushtaka wailed – then the air in front of it wavered and the banshee form of Aoife appeared in front of it. She'd come! Would she – could she – help us?

Aoife opened her mouth and screamed. Her deathly shriek tore through all of us, making us clasp our hands to our ears, but it affected the kushtaka most of all. The creature dropped onto all fours and wailed right back.

Her scream intensified and she ran at the kushtaka, passing through him like she'd done to me, only she didn't emerge from the other side. The kushtaka screamed and stumbled away. It was gone – for now. We stared at the tree line, anxiously waiting for it to return, poised to do or die. Do what, I wasn't sure. Probably die.

The high whine of a motor broke the tension and I whipped my head around. Stan was heading in to save us. I felt a measure of relief – but the skiff could only hold three people, and Sidnee needed to leave now. I rushed out to it with her in my arms. Stan took her, laid her gently in the bottom and wrapped her in a blanket. 'Get in,' he barked.

I shook my head. 'No, Thomas should go next.' He needed to get warm more than any of us supernats. Thomas didn't argue. He passed me his gun as he jumped into the boat and pulled Sidnee close to warm her.

I saw a flash of brown fur: the kushtaka was coming back. That motherfucker did not know when to quit!

'I can try to fit one more,' Stan offered.

I looked at Gunnar and he looked at me. 'You go,' I said. 'You've got a wife. Sig needs you.' I resisted the urge to call him Bam Bam.

Gunnar smiled. 'Do you know, I'm pretty comfy here. You go.'

'Neither of them will leave without the other,' Thomas barked, interrupting our stand-off. 'Let's move then we'll come back as quickly as we can!'

Gunnar and I helped push the boat out then stood in the water watching the small skiff leave. Stan's eyes lingered not on me but on Gunnar; his jaw working, he backed up the boat and took off.

'Thanks for not leaving me,' I said softly to Gunnar as we moved out of the water to stand by our small fire.

'Back at you, Bunny Rabbit.'

I let the moniker slide since he was willing to die with me. We stood side by side and waited for the kushtaka's next attack. When the wail came, Gunnar raised his gun as I reached inwards. I blinked with surprise when I felt the heat broiling there when moments ago there'd barely been a wisp of a flame. I'd have to time it right. I had one shot at this; I'd already learnt that my supply of fire wasn't inexhaustible.

The kushtaka charged. Gunnar fired and I held my nerve until it was almost close enough to touch my boss with its long arms and claws. Then I let rip.

Fire poured out of me and struck the beast. It screamed, and the smell of burnt hair filled my nostrils. Lit up like the Statue of Liberty, the thing ran back into the forest; if it had had a lick of sense, it would have dived into the water.

We could still hear it screaming – until it stopped abruptly.

Chapter 47

Finally, the skiff bumped onto the gravel of the beach and Gunnar and I climbed in. 'The kushtaka?' Stan asked urgently as he looked us over for injuries.

'Bunny roasted it,' Gunnar said with a proud smile that made my heart burst.

Stan frowned. 'How?'

'With the fire on the beach,' I lied hastily. 'A lucky throw with a burning branch. It turns out its fur is highly flammable. A real design flaw.' Gunnar trusted Stan, and I did too, but the fewer people who knew about my oddities the better. Gunnar squeezed my hand and I knew my secrets were safe with him.

I watched as we moved away and the island got smaller and smaller. I swore nothing would ever get me onto it ever again.

When we were close to the boat, I searched anxiously for Connor. I saw his head drop to his chest as he let out a breath of relief. Finally I felt safe – although we still had to get back to civilisation and get Sidnee to hospital as quickly as possible. We climbed on board and Stan stowed the skiff in record time.

'Bunny!' Connor wrapped me in his arms. 'I'm sorry I didn't come back,' he said, looking at me to see if I was angry. 'I didn't want to take up a space on the skiff. It could have meant that someone else died.'

'It was the right call.' I leaned against his shoulder. 'That was scary.' His arms tightened around me. 'I hit the kushtaka with fire and it went down. I don't know if it's dead or not, but I vote we never return to the island just to be sure.'

I felt him smile. 'Deal. Come on, let's get you warm.'

The warmth in Stan's heated cabin felt heavenly. Thomas had wrapped Sidnee in blankets and was holding her tightly under the bow. Sweat was dripping down his forehead; at least he had warmed up so that was one less person to worry about. 'Soapy?' I asked Connor.

'He's on the deck outside, spitting nails. The drugs were gone and the siren members that were left to guard it are gone too.'

'Dead?'

'Almost certainly.'

I blew out a breath. That wasn't good. The creepy government agency that had been experimenting on Portlock hadn't left after all, and now they had retrieved a shit tonne of their deadly drugs. It was the worst outcome we could have feared. 'We'll need to warn the other towns,' I said grimly.

'Gunnar's already done that. Everyone knows fisheye is deadly. They're on high alert, and for now that's all we can do.'

'We need to find those black-ops twats and shut them down.'

Connor kissed my forehead. 'It's a problem for another day, Bunny.' He wasn't wrong: we still had our fair share of problems without borrowing more.

Sidnee needed medical treatment and we had to find the missing gems.

The rain, which had stopped, came down even harder and the wind whipped around us so we all took refuge in the house. The boat dipped and rose and rocked from side to side. I considered being sick, but it was from fear rather than motion sickness so I gritted my teeth through the nausea.

When Stan finally pulled onto his slip, I was genuinely tempted to kiss the ground. We left him to deal with the boat while the rest of us piled into the Nomo's SUV and rushed the still-unconscious Sidnee to the hospital. When we arrived, Thomas carried her in and explained what had happened to the medical staff. He laid her on a bed and she was wheeled out of sight.

Gunnar called Sigrid, and soon the waiting room was full. Stan, Gunnar, Thomas, Sig, Connor and I waited anxiously to find out if my friend would be all right. I looked at the people waiting for her and realised that if I were lying in that bed in Sidnee's place, the same people would be here for me as well. I had people that cared for me, and that was *everything*.

I had no idea how long we waited but it was several cups of nasty hospital coffee later when a nurse called, 'Sidnee Fletcher's family?'

'That's us!' Sigrid stood up.

The nurse gave a reassuring smile. 'She's responding well to treatment and we're confident she'll make a full recovery.'

Sigrid burst into tears and collapsed into Gunnar's arms. Her wailing stopped my tears in their tracks; it was a little too close to the kushtaka's. Over Sigrid's head, Gunnar and I exchanged grimaces. Connor wrapped me in his arms and his steadying presence helped me hold myself together.

'You can come and see her now,' the nurse continued. 'We've got her in a private room in 18C.'

Sidnee looked tiny in the hospital bed and her warm skin was still pale, but she was awake and she smiled at me. Her arm was in a brace and laid across her chest. Her eyes filled with tears. 'Bunny, you saved me.' She started to cry.

'It was very much a group effort,' I muttered, feeling uncomfortable. All I'd done was rally the troops; Thomas had done most of the heavy lifting, both in tracking and in the actual heavy lifting. He'd carried Sidnee the whole time without complaint – and he was human, too.

Sig wrapped an arm around Sidnee and comforted her until she stopped crying. Gunnar was holding Sidnee's uninjured hand, stroking it gently. 'There now. You're safe, our Sidnee,' he murmured. I stood back a little and let the family comfort each other because, blood or not, that's what they were.

After a few moments of quiet whispering, Sigrid turned to me. 'She wants to talk to you alone, dear. Everyone, scoot.' She shooed out the men. I noticed that Thomas went without a word; he'd been so obviously concerned for Sidnee, but once she was conscious he'd pasted on a look of casual ease. It was so at odds with his frantic behaviour only hours before. Something to think about another day.

Sig placed another kiss on Sidnee's forehead then leaned down to murmur, 'We'll be in the waiting room.' She left, shutting the door behind her.

I pulled the chair closer to the bed and took Sidnee's undamaged hand. 'It's going to be all right. It's over.'

She shook her head; it was a while before she could answer. 'No, it's not. He was there, Bunny. Chris was really *there*.' She started crying again with the deep sadness of a broken heart. If I ever saw that sea-lion shifter, he'd wish a killer whale had got hold of him instead.

I held her until she pulled herself together enough to talk. 'What happened? Start at the beginning.'

She looked so tired and broken, but she had to get it out or it would continue to eat her up from the inside. 'I–I've been taking all the hotline calls because they were mostly to me.'

'What do you mean *to you*? Weren't they about fisheye?'

'Some. But the fisheye tips have really died down.' She looked at me a while, and then made a decision and it all poured out. 'I'm only half mer, Bunny.'

'Yeah, I know. So?'

'This town can be hard if you aren't the same as the others.'

'You're a siren in the siren group. There are tonnes of different shifters in it.'

'Yes, but they are pure bred. Remember Chris's family was upset he was dating a mermaid? Well, they hated it even more because I was only half mermaid.'

I clenched my jaw. People could be so cruel.

'I've been getting hotline calls, people trying to mess with me, calling me a half-breed, or accusing me of being in on the drug dealing with Chris. Then the calls about sightings started. I checked a few and most were people sending me on wild-goose chases. When I showed up, someone would be there to make fun of me.'

'Fuck that! Why didn't you tell me?'

She shrugged and winced as the movement jarred her sore arm. 'I was embarrassed. Besides, I could handle it – this shit has been going on since I moved here. It didn't help that Gunnar and Sigrid took me in and they weren't sirens. That made the teasing and bullying worse.' Her eyes grew fierce. 'Gunnar and Sig saved me and I'll always be grateful to them. That's why I work in the Nomo's office. It's my way of giving back.'

'How old were you?' I asked. 'When they took you in, I mean?'

'Seventeen. They wanted to adopt me, but I'd have been eighteen and an adult by the time the paperwork was done so there was no point.'

'What happened to your parents?'

She looked away. 'They were killed in a car accident in the Philippines. They lived in the only supernatural town there. When they died, no one would take me because I was a half-breed. My case was sent out to other towns and the only responders were Gunnar and Sig. They treated me like their own child from the beginning.'

'So why did you go to the island if you knew people were messing with you?'

'Because,' she said reluctantly, 'one of the last calls was from Chris himself.'

Chapter 48

'He had the balls to call you?' I said angrily. 'What an arsehole!'

'It was stupid of me but I wanted to see him, to see if he had any feelings for me. Even if I don't want to be with him anymore – and I don't,' she added hastily.

'What did he say to make you go alone to the island?'

'He didn't. His call said, "I'm so sorry, Sidnee." It was another call that said he'd been seen near the island that made me go.' She looked up with pleading in her eyes. 'I had to, Bunny.'

I nodded. There was no reason to browbeat her about her poor decision; we all made shitty choices now and again and 'I told you so' helped no one. 'What happened when you got there?'

'There was a big boat, grey and black, no markings, no registration, nothing. Maybe eighty feet long. There were several men, too, and Chris was with them. They didn't see me at first because I was in the water. I dived down because I realised that they were there to get the drugs. The siren group has been watching for this to happen.'

I nodded; Calliope had told me that.

'It's deep down there, so I figured they'd sent Chris to retrieve the stash since he's a supernat. I thought I'd meet him down there, convince him to sneak away and talk to me.

'When I got down to the cave, there was no sign of our siren guards and Chris was acting like the muscle. They had divers – serious divers – disarming the charges and hauling the fisheye up to the boat. Chris saw me, but so did the others. I could have outswum any of them, but they hit me with some kind of sonar blast that disoriented me and made me sluggish.

'I barely made it to the surface before they caught up to me. I swam up the stream until it became too shallow and crawled out of the water, figuring I could hide. I planned to lead them on a wild-goose chase then find somewhere away from the boat where I could shift and swim away.'

'I'd have done the same. It was good thinking.'

'Yeah – except they caught me,' she said ruefully. 'They tried to take me back to their boat. When I struggled, the bigger of the two men broke my arm, chucked me to the ground and kicked me. Chris shoved him away and stood over me to stop them from hurting me more. I didn't know how long he could hold them off – he's very strong but there were two of them and they were armed. They said they'd shoot me and he'd better get out of the way or he was next.'

She choked up again. 'But there was a monster on the island, Bunny,' she whispered. She looked around as though it were hiding somewhere in the room. 'An otter-man – the kushtaka.'

'We're acquainted,' I said drily.

'You saw it too? It scared me so bad! The men starting shooting at it, and the second they forgot about me I ran and hid in the rocks. I think Chris might have tried to lead them off my trail – at least, he ran the other way – but the kushtaka got them first. I heard their screams. Do you know if Chris got away?' Her spare hand was tugging at the bedsheets.

'Yeah,' I admitted, though it pained me to say it. 'I think he did. He was barefoot and we only found the ... um ... remains of two men in boots.'

She nodded. Her eyelashes were damp and tears were rolling down her cheeks again. 'I think he did love me.'

'I think you're right.' I admitted. 'Does that change anything? Does it help?'

She shook her head then stopped. 'I don't know. If anything, it makes it worse. I feel empty inside, Bunny. Numb. Betrayed.'

I reached out and stroked her hair. 'I'm sorry, love. You've been through a lot and you've held it all in. You have people that love you. Let us in. *Talk* to us.'

She nodded. 'You're right. But I've been holding stuff in for so long, I don't know *how* to let it out.'

I understood, probably more than anyone else could. 'I've been emotionally stifled by uncaring parents and you've been stifled by an uncaring society. We were destined to be best friends.'

She laughed a little, and the sound made me smile.

'I know it'll take some time for you to get over Chris. Even if the relationship was never viable, the heart knows what it knows. But Sidnee? It started off with the whole pure-bred race thing and ended on drugs, kidnapping, and murder.' I emphasised that so she wouldn't forget it. No matter what Chris had done and said recently, it didn't change what he'd done in the past. I honestly believed that everyone deserved a second chance – but it turned out there were limits.

'I know you're right,' she said softly, then she cracked a yawn. 'Thanks for everything. Thanks for coming to get me. I knew you'd find me.'

I squeezed her hand. 'Damn right. Now, get some rest. You look awful.'

She laughed again. 'I bet. It'll take me days to get a comb through my hair.'

I grinned. 'I could cut it off if you want?'

She gave me with a look of outraged horror. 'Touch it and I'll stake you!'

There was the Sidnee I knew and loved. She was going to be okay, I knew it.

Chapter 49

I was exhausted. Although the barrier gems were my top priority, I had nothing left to give. It was still daytime and I'd already pushed myself to the limits. I had to rest – and I needed to check on my pets. Fluffy and Shadow had been far from the confrontation with the kushtaka, but I wanted to see them with my own eyes and know that they were safe.

Connor and the others were still in the waiting room looking beat. When I went out, Gunnar, Sigrid and Stan went to check in with Sidnee.

Connor took one look at me, pulled me into his arms and kissed my forehead. 'Come on, doe. Let's get you home.' With a gentle hand on my back, he manoeuvred me out to the car park and into his backup vehicle, a sporty red number. No doubt he'd had Lee drop it off for him.

The roar of the engine was strangely soothing and, combined with the vibrations, had me struggling to keep my eyelids open. I clung onto consciousness but I was happy when we rolled up to my door. Everything looked okay, and my scalp itched with the wards that Connor had arranged for me. The feeling faded once I was inside.

I was greeted instantly by Fluffy, wagging for all he was worth. I dropped to my knees and gave him a full body cuddle, wrapping my arms around all that unconditional love. As I buried my head in his fur, tears sprang to my eyes. Fluffy was fine and I was alive. There had been some moments... I cut myself off. No point dwelling on the past, no matter how recent it was. Man, I was so tired.

Shadow let out a *mrrow* and gave a leisurely stretch before deigning to pad over and say hello. He rubbed against me, purring loudly. 'Hey, guys,' I greeted them. 'I'm happy to see you, too. We had a run in with an indestructible monster but we got away and we lived to fight another day.'

'After shooting it and striking it with fireballs,' Connor commented drily. 'It's not like we turned tail and fled, like Brave Sir Robin.'

My mouth dropped. 'You know Monty Python?'

'Doesn't everyone?' he quipped.

'I think I might love you a little bit more.'

His eyes darkened. Crap: it was waaaay too early to say the L word. Fuck my life. If I said 'like' now to replace it, I'd make it even worse. 'Coffee?' I said brightly instead.

'Sure,' he replied easily. To my relief, he was giving me a pass. I bustled into the kitchen and flicked the kettle on then warmed us two cups of blood, one for me to chug and one for Connor to sip. I put his in a wine glass because he was more refined than me.

I fed the animals and let them into the back garden. 'Toast?' I called to Connor. I didn't have much else to offer.

'That'd be great.'

Once the animals – and us – were fed and comfortable, it was bedtime. 'Stay?' I asked Connor, not quite looking at him as I tidied away the dishes.

'I'd love to,' he murmured and stilled my hands. 'The dishes can wait. You're dead on your feet.'

'I'm a vampire,' I joked.

He kissed my neck. 'Can I use your washing machine?'

'Of course.'

'Great. Let's shower and get to sleep.'

'Deal.'

Connor took our clothes and put them on a fast wash. A man that did chores without being asked? I *was* in love.

I turned on the shower and slid in to the blissfully hot water. Moments later Connor joined me. He gently cleaned my back then I returned the favour. It was nice to smell of something other than the sea and I felt better for washing the salt off my hair and skin. The joy of being warm and clean was so great that we stood under the spray until it went lukewarm. We got out and dried off. I eyed my hairdryer, but drying my long hair seemed like too much effort.

Connor read my mind and plugged it in. He tapped the space between his legs and I sat between them as he gently worked his way through the snags and knots. It felt oddly intimate; nobody had done that since I was a child.

Finally he clicked off the dryer and ducked into the utility room to put the wet clothes in the drier. I heard him say a murmured goodnight to my pets. It made me smile.

Connor slid into bed next to me. His body temperature was normally a little cooler than mine but the hot shower had warmed him and it was like cuddling a smooth teddy bear. Like a teddy, there was no heartbeat though his chest still rose and fell from habit, if not from need.

I fell asleep in between one blink and the next.

A feline screech of terror had me sitting bolt upright. My heart was thundering in panic and Shadow's sharp claws were digging into my arm as he flung himself from the bed. Son of a bitch – that hurt! He scrambled to hide under the bed and that's when I realised the world was shaking.

When the bed juddered across the floor, Connor threw back the covers, grabbed my arm and tugged me underneath it. 'Aren't we supposed to brace in door frames?' I asked.

'That's old advice. These days we're supposed to hide under something.'

'Check you out, Mr Old Vampire, full of modern advice.' He gave me a flat look. 'Antique Vampire?' I tried. The banter helped settle me while the world was shaking.

'I'm not *that* old,' he muttered, then frowned. 'Another damn earthquake.'

Alaska had earthquakes but not *this* many, and they were definitely getting worse. This was the strongest yet; things were falling off of shelves and out of cabinets. The crashes from the kitchen told me that my mugs were suicidal, smashing themselves against the hard floor. It felt a bit like *Beauty and the Beast*: the furniture was coming to life and all but walking across my floor.

From under the bed, I watched the wooden dresser bounce ever closer to us and stared at Connor, wide-eyed. 'This can't be normal.'

He shook his head. 'No,' he agreed. 'This isn't normal.'

Three earthquakes within two weeks, all progressively larger and without the promised aftershocks? No, this wasn't normal. And if it was *abnormal,* I was betting it had a supernatural cause: the earth gem. That bastard Vogler was involved in this somehow. Either the real gem had been stolen or he was taking the gem out of its protective box for kicks – tectonic kicks.

The judders finally stopped. 'I'm calling Gunnar. We're going to go see Vitus Vogler.' I thought for a moment. 'I suppose I'd better call Liv, too.'

'I'll go with you.'

'Thanks. I think I'll need two council members. I swear Vogler's lying to us and I might need an onsite warrant.'

'I'll swing by the council chambers and get the paperwork ready.'

We started to get dressed. Connor dug out my bulletproof vest and held it out to me pointedly. I didn't argue and put it on under my shirt. He, meanwhile, was wearing yesterday's clothes; even though they were clean, it still felt like a walk of shame. Everyone would know he'd stayed at mine. Maybe I could persuade him to leave some clothes here in future, just in case.

I bit my lip and started to panic at the thought that I might actually be committing to something – some*one* – but then I pushed the fear aside and put it in a small box to look at later. Or maybe never.

Connor went to sort out the warrants whilst I sent messages to Gunnar and Liv. I was getting ready to leave – and that's when the tsunami sirens started to blare out.

Chapter 50

A tsunami. Wonderful. That was all I needed now. 'For fuck's sake,' I groused.

I tried to get Shadow into his carrier but when I reached under the bed he swiped at me, claws extended. 'Ow! Fine, be like that. But you better go all smoky if a tsunami comes your way,' I muttered.

I set out food for him, then grabbed Fluffy and his lead and set off – not to the school this time but to the office. I had a feeling that the alarm would be shut off soon; I was certain that the shake was localised and unnatural, like the other two, in which case no tsunami for us. Although it would be my luck if this time it was a 'boy who cried wolf' scenario and a tsunami really *did* crash into Portlock.

Gunnar was already at the office and the tsunami alarm had been shut off. 'Hey,' I greeted him. 'That was a wobbly wake-up call.'

'I prefer a cup of joe,' he agreed.

'Let's go and see what Vogler has to say for himself,' I suggested. 'This isn't normal. Either he's been waving that thing around or it's been stolen and the thief has.'

Gunnar nodded. 'I had the same thought. Come on.'

We climbed in the SUV and drove off. Liv and Connor were meeting us at Vogler's residence. If Vogler had kept the theft of the earth gem from us, I was afraid of what Liv would do to him. She'd possibly kill him and raise his corpse to be her eternal slave; she seemed powerful – and vindictive – enough.

When we parked up, she was pacing and scowling at the same time. 'Bunny, you better get the truth from Vogler fast. There won't be enough of him left if I get a hold of him,' she promised grimly.

'There's an outside chance none of this is his fault,' I said mildly. I didn't believe that, but it felt like someone should point it out.

Gunnar grunted agreement. 'It's possible but it's not likely.' He knocked on the door.

Vitus Vogler had the decency to go pale when he saw us standing there. He swallowed hard and let us in, his head bowed.

'Do you want to explain why we've had three earthquakes with increasing intensity so close together?' I asked.

He opened his mouth. I could see he was about to lie but he closed it again and his shoulders rounded.

I felt Liv's scorching anger as the hot desert wind of her magic blew in with shocking ferocity. The temperature in the room rose rapidly. I put up a hand. 'Hold on, Liv. He's going to tell us the truth.' I stared at Vogler. 'Aren't you?' It was barely a question. He had two council members and the Nomo's office in his home: lying would be a very poor decision. Then again, his track record wasn't exactly great.

He ushered us into his living space and we sat down. We maintained our silence, though Liv was vibrating with impatience. Finally Vogler took a deep breath and stared at a point somewhere beyond Liv's shoulder. I couldn't blame him for not meeting her eyes – they were currently very fiery indeed. He licked his lips. 'It talks to me.'

'What talks to you, Vitus?' I asked, keeping my tone brisk but friendly. I was good cop – for now.

'The earth gem,' he murmured reverently.

I looked at Liv, who had blanched slightly. Even she wasn't okay with talking cursed gemstones. Her lips parted but then she grimaced and closed them, evidently deciding to hear Vogler out before she interrupted.

'What does it say to you, Vitus?' I asked even more gently.

He was rocking slightly in his seat. 'It wants to be out of the box,' he whispered. 'It wants to be with the others.'

'It wants to be with the other gems?' I clarified.

He nodded, his hands clutching and releasing the arm of his chair over and over again. It was mildly irritating and my mum's voice rang in my ears: *One must sit still with decorum and grace.* Fuck off, Mum.

Vogler licked his lips. 'It was more of a feeling at first rather than it actually talking to me, but the longer I'm around it the worse it gets. It speaks in my head!' He looked at us with panic in his eyes. 'I'm not mad! It's real! But I can't get it out of my head!' He started pulling at his hair.

'Calm down,' Gunnar rumbled. 'We'll help you, won't we, Liv?' He looked pointedly at the necromancer. She didn't answer; sometimes she could be a class-A bitch. A lot of the time, actually.

'Can you block the gemstone from talking to him or do we need someone else?' I asked her. 'A witch? A shaman?' The surest way to get Liv's help was to imply that she couldn't do something herself.

'I'll need to look into it. The gems spoke to me before I confined them to the boxes but I didn't know they could still communicate.' She frowned. 'They must be stronger than the enchantments or they've found a way around at least some of them.'

Vogler was still mumbling to himself. 'Vitus, is the earth gem still here?' I asked.

He looked mildly offended. 'Yes, of course it is.'

'So what's with the earthquakes?'

'I–I tried to resist but it wants to be free of the box so I take it out sometimes.' He looked at our horrified faces. 'It promises me magic beyond imagination. My deepest wishes made true in exchange for a few moments of freedom. It makes sense, don't you see? I deserve that power. And when I release it, it shuts it up – for a time.'

None of us were using our poker faces and Liv's disdain was positively dripping from her. 'You don't understand,' he said desperately. 'None of you do! Its whispering is incessant and I can't think! I have to make it stop for the sake of my sanity! Just a minute or two out of the box and it goes quiet for a while. It's a fair trade.'

'And what if someone was killed in the quakes?' I said in a hard voice, dropping the good cop role.

'No one's been hurt!'

'What about the fear?' I argued. 'People left their houses and ran for the school, genuinely terrified of a tsunami. They suffered psychological harm – and all that's on you.'

'Show us the stone,' Connor ordered.

Vogler licked his lips but stood and started up the stairs to his loft. We followed, united in our mistrust of him. We waited patiently whilst he lowered the wards, then Liv strode forward to the podium, opened the box and peered inside. 'It's here,' she confirmed.

The tension left my shoulders: at least one of the damned things was safe and that counted as a win. Liv opened her bag and pulled out her creepy doll imbued with death magic. She shook it and did some chanting; when she was finished, she glared at Vogler. 'Cross this ward and you'll die. It stays in the box. Are we clear?' Her voice was calm but threatening. Vogler blanched.

'If the urge to open the box is too great,' Gunnar rumbled, 'you call me and we'll work something out. Don't cross the ward, don't open the box.'

The earth witch nodded. 'I got it.'

'Liv, can you strengthen the spells on all the boxes to keep them from talking to their witches?' I asked.

'I'm not sure,' she admitted. 'It took an adept from each element to place the original spells. I'd have to find the four strongest witches in the world even to have a chance of doing that.'

'We can't have these cursed objects dictating actions to their guardians,' I pointed out.

'I'm aware of that. Luckily the strongest elemental witches are already on their way – I summoned them when we started having barrier issues. It's taken a while for their schedules to align.'

If the barrier dropped before these new experts arrived and I died because of a 'scheduling' issue, I was going to haunt those bitches hard. Something itched at the back of my mind. 'Vitus, how long have you guarded the earth gem?'

He answered immediately. 'Seven years, three months and four days.'

'How long for the others?' I asked Liv. I knew the answer for one of them, but I wanted to hear it from her.

'Water three years, fire five years, and wind seventeen.'

How could Elsa Wintersteen have resisted the cursed gem's dark promises? And then it hit me like a lightning bolt: she hadn't. Aoife's murder wasn't really about the barrier; she'd been a casualty of a witch trying to do the cursed stone's bidding – and the stones wanted to be brought together. We'd been led astray by the protests and Aoife's death but now it was crystal clear...

'I know who is stealing the stones,' I declared grimly. 'And she won't stop until she has them all.'

Chapter 51

As we left Vogler's house, I turned to Connor. 'Can you amend that warrant? This is about the gems, not the barrier, and my newest suspect is the wind witch, Elsa Wintersteen. She's watched over her stone for seventeen years. That's a long time to silence the stone's whispering.'

He nodded. 'I'll get it done.'

'How long will it take?'

'I need to go back and type up the new form, and I'll need your paperwork too. Might as well do this right from the start. We don't want her lawyer setting her free on a technicality.'

'Amen. I'm going to the office now. I'll send you the paperwork.' I looked at Liv. 'Will you co-sign the warrant?'

'Obviously,' she drawled. 'I'll go with Mackenzie.' She ran a hand up Connor's arm, toyed with his bicep then sashayed to his car. When she looked back at me, her eyes were dancing with dark mischief. She was looking for a reaction, so I gave her none. She must have realised Connor was in yesterday's clothes.

Since it wasn't a secret and I wasn't ashamed of our entanglement, I stood on my tiptoes and brushed my lips against Connor's. 'See you later.' Okay: maybe Liv had gotten a *little* reaction out of me. I didn't glance back at her as I walked to the Nomo's SUV but I heard her throaty chuckle. Wonderful: now I was amusing her, which was not exactly what I'd been going for.

I was starting to hate paperwork as much as Gunnar, especially when I was excited about ending a case. We were so close to finishing this, I could almost taste it. Soon we'd have the barrier back at full strength and I could start to sleep easy again. Despite my impatience to arrest Wintersteen, I painstakingly typed the documentation, got Gunnar to sign it off and emailed it to Connor.

'How's Sidnee?' I asked Gunnar as we waited for the warrant to come through. 'I haven't heard from her, but I don't want to bother her.'

'You won't be a bother. She's okay. She's been discharged home.'

'She's not home alone?' I half-rose from my desk.

'Relax.' Gunnar smiled. 'She's at ours. Sig and Loki are fussing over her.'

I sank back down. 'Phew. I'm almost jealous of all the good food she's having.'

Gunnar patted his sizeable gut. 'Me too.'

My smile faded. 'This gem mess is my fault. I interviewed Elsa and I missed that she was gaga. And her husband,' I said slowly, as more dots connected, 'he's the one that gave the tip to Snow and tempted him to abandon his post for the bookies and some booze. The Wintersteens planned the fire to cover up their "theft" of the gem and to make them look innocent. We never even looked at Elsa as a suspect – we thought she was a victim. Man, I fucked this up.'

Gunnar gave me a firm look. 'You can't beat yourself up. Our job is a hard one and virtually every person we speak to is lying to us. What we have to work out is why and if we need to dig into it or not.'

'That's a depressing point of view,' I mumbled.

'I'm not saying *everyone* lies, but the criminal element does and those are the people that we mostly speak to. They have a vested interest in convincing us that they're innocent. Learn to read between the lines.'

I sighed. 'I thought I was pretty good at that.'

'You are, but practice makes perfect. Like anything, it's a skill you'll hone with time.'

'Time is something I have plenty of,' I joked. Immortality had its upsides.

While we waited for Connor to text that the warrant was ready, Gunnar returned to his office and I looked up the address for Elsa's new home.

She had been so nervous when I'd interviewed her. I'd thought that she was a wreck because of the fire, but maybe her supposed timidness was something else. Maybe she'd been jittery and nervous because she was guilty. How had I missed it?

Elsa was most likely under the influence of one – probably two – powerful, possessed stones. I wondered who or what possessed them. Liv had mentioned angels and demons – were the stones demonic? I hoped not but I called her to make sure. If they were, I was tempted to take a holiday until this whole mess was resolved.

Liv answered with her usual irascibility. 'What now, Bunny? I'm at the council chambers, I'll sign the damn papers.'

'It's not about the papers. Your story about the stones... You said something about them being possessed. Are they possessed by demons?'

'Don't be ridiculous! Demons like to possess the *living*. No, they found the most powerful non-corporeal beings on earth. They are possessed by the strongest of the banshees.'

'Banshees?'

'Yes. Banshees have this whole double life-cycle thing. If they become a clan's banshee after death, their spirits are incredibly strong, more than the wildest and craziest poltergeist. It took centuries to find the strongest ones in existence to place in the gems and take their power up a notch.'

I couldn't get away from the banshees; they were tangled up in this every way I looked. Poor Aoife. She'd stumbled on a great secret that involved her own kind. She'd wanted to help her boyfriend and protect the barrier, but she'd inadvertently helped something that might contain one of her ancestor's spirits. What a horrific thought.

'Are the banshees aware of that?' I asked curiously.

'How would I know? They are a strange group – you'd have to ask one of them. I'm busy Bunny. We can talk stories another time, like over a campfire and with s'mores,' she said sarcastically. Somehow I didn't think I was actually being invited for s'mores, whatever the heck they were.

Fluffy was looking at me with bright eyes. 'You heard that too?' I asked. He cocked his head. 'Do you think we should have a chat with Nora before we confront Elsa?' He yipped. 'Me too, let's go.'

I knocked on Gunnar's door and popped my head into his office. 'I'd like to go and talk to

Nora Sullivan one more time before we try to arrest Elsa Wintersteen. Apparently the barrier gems are possessed by banshee spirits. Everything feels ... connected somehow.'

Gunnar was looking harassed. He was hip deep in paperwork that Sidnee usually did, trying to make sure there wasn't a backlog when she returned to work. 'Want help?' he asked hopefully.

I looked at the stacks of paper around him; he hated desk work but this showed how much he loved Sidnee, and Sidnee would recognise that. She needed that kind of love in her life. 'Nah, it's okay. I'm taking Fluffy.'

'Okay, see you later. Make sure you get me for Wintersteen's arrest. No telling what the witch will do when she's confronted.'

'Absolutely.' I looked at my watch. It usually took an hour for a warrant after I'd sent over my paperwork, so I had a little time to spare. Time to visit Nora and see what she had to say about her attacker. Fingers crossed she'd name Elsa and the whole case would be a slam-dunk.

But I was learning that in Portlock things never ran smoothly.

Chapter 52

Nora had been stabbed and suffered a blow to the head, yet the nurse told me she was due to be discharged later that day. It seemed it really was hard to kill a banshee.

When I walked into the hospital room, she scowled at me. 'Oh, it's you again,' she groused. *Well, hello to you, too, Nora.* Fluffy, in his new hospital approved therapy animal vest, whined and she softened slightly when she looked at him. Good: a dog lover. I'd use everything I could to get more from her.

'I know we got off on the wrong foot and we've stayed there ever since. I'm sorry about that, but my focus has always been finding the gemstones and, after that, Aoife's killer. I'm willing to start over. Neither of us will mention Ezra and that red spray paint ever again.'

Nora pressed her lips together, looked at me cautiously and gave a begrudging nod.

'The nursing staff said you didn't get to see your attacker. Is that right?' I asked.

She shrugged. 'If I saw them, the blow to the head has removed any memory of it. I don't remember being attacked and I don't remember why I was wandering around outside the house.'

Aoife had been in the vicinity and she was a powerful banshee: maybe *she* could tell us what had happened. 'Can you summon Aoife's spirit?' I asked. 'She was the one that made us find you. She might have seen something.' I was half-afraid that Aoife was stuck in the kushtaka somehow because I hadn't seen her since she'd dived into him to save us.

'I can do that,' Nora said.

'Now?' I suggested.

'Why not?'

She closed her eyes and a wail burst from her chest. '*Aoife Sullivan!*' The curtains swirled as if a gust of wind had caught them even though the window was closed.

My scalp prickled – and then Aoife was there, suspended in the air, white hair floating around her. She looked no worse for wear from the encounter with the kushtaka. I smiled at her. 'Me again. Thanks for your help on the island. I need to ask, did you see who harmed your mum?'

Aoife's lips moved but I couldn't hear anything. Nora frowned. 'She says it was Elsa Wintersteen. Why on earth would *Wintersteen* attack me?'

I tried not to grin in triumph even though I doubted the word of a banshee through her mother would be admissible in a court of law. But then Portlock had its own rules; maybe it would be fine.

Aoife's lips continued to move and Nora's eyebrows shot up. 'She says she often spends time near home. Wintersteen came to find her spirit and tried to capture her in a holding bottle. Aoife screamed. I heard her wail and I tried to stop Elsa, but Elsa stopped me instead. What a bitch!'

I nodded grimly. 'That brings me to the second reason I needed to see you. I've heard of banshee spirits possessing special objects. Do you know anything about that?'

'You think she was trying to get Aoife's spirit trapped in something?' Nora was aghast.

'I think so.' I was almost certain that Elsa Wintersteen had been pulling strings for some time. I'd bet good money that she had hired Jayden to steal a jewel from Connor, then killed Aoife to make a powerful spirit banshee to inhabit it. As if it wasn't bad enough that she already had two cursed gemstones under her control, she was trying to make her own. 'What can you tell me about spirits being trapped like that?'

Aoife gestured for her mum to speak. 'There's some ancient folklore about powerful banshee spirits being trapped and used,' Nora said reluctantly. She still didn't trust me, but I guess she figured that telling me an ancient tale couldn't do any harm. 'I'm not sure how old this story is, but it came with my family from Ireland.'

I waited.

'A long time ago, demons came to Ireland to look for powerful souls to use for their magic. They believed poltergeists and banshees were the strongest, but the poltergeists they found weren't strong enough, so they came searching for the ancestors. The strongest clans at the time were the Cinnéide, Broin, Gallchobhair and my clan, Súilleabháin. The legend says that they captured one powerful banshee spirit from each clan then sealed them into stones for eternity. The demons used the stones to fight their battles against the angels, but the angels were blessed and they wrested the stones from the demons and scattered them to the corners of the Earth. They were gifted to supernatural custodians to guard them and see that they were only used for good.'

I looked at her expectantly.

'That's it.' She shrugged. 'Besides the fact that the legend says that one day the banshee spirits will come back to us more powerful than ever before.' Her voice was hushed.

'Were any of those clans linked to particular elements?'

'Like the witches? No, banshees have nothing to do with elemental magic. Of course, banshee women usually mate with the strongest supernatural they can find and it was rumoured that my Súilleabháin ancestress was the daughter of a powerful fire elemental. But that's another legend.'

Nora had verified Liv's tale. 'I'll get out of your hair in a second, but would you be willing to tell that story in court?' I asked.

'I will if it brings my daughter's killer to justice.'

'Thanks. One last thing. Donaldson said Aoife stole something from him and that she wasn't his real daughter?'

Nora sighed. 'That's bullshit. Around the time Aoife was conceived, I had an indiscretion. We wore condoms so I know Aoife was definitely Jayden's. Unfortunately when he found out about the affair when Aoife was little, he wouldn't listen to reason. He spouted off that she wasn't his and walked out on us – that's why I told everyone he was dead. I know I'm not blameless but Aoife was his. Always. And I never strayed again. It was a foolish mistake.'

She blew out a breath. 'The kicker was that when Aoife was a kid she found one of Jayden's gem stashes. She stole one and hid it. She never told him – or me – where she put it. For him it was the ultimate betrayal, a sign that she really wasn't his daughter. Some people need to blame others for their actions. He blamed Aoife for his downward spiral into a life of crime again. I blamed him.'

Poor Aoife. I turned to speak to her, but at some point in our discussion she'd disappeared.

Chapter 53

I drove to the council offices to pick up the paperwork. Connor was waiting for me, warrant in hand, and just seeing him took my breath away. He was beautiful in a way I'd never been, not in his flesh but in his soul; something about him called to me like a siren.

His eyes met mine and his lips tipped up. I slid from the car, crossed the distance between us and kissed him thoroughly. After a few moments, he reluctantly pulled back. 'We should always greet each other like that,' he suggested.

'I didn't think you'd be into public displays of affection.'

'I'm not. Usually. But nothing about us is usual.'

'True,' I conceded.

He tucked a stray hair behind my ear. 'Be careful with Elsa. She's a powerful witch, and chances are she's truly deranged.'

'You aren't going with me to protect me?' I teased.

He gave me a sharp look. 'You'd let me?'

I grinned. 'No, your instincts were right the first time.'

He laughed. 'Good, because I need to run my business and you need to run yours. I trust you to take care of yourself.' He paused. 'You've got the vest on, right?'

'I've got it. What are you doing after work?'

There was a quiet beat then his voice came back huskily, 'Whatever you wish.'

My insides melted as warmth blossomed through my belly. My voice might have turned a little sultry as well; I'd be anticipating the 'after' all day. 'I'll hold you to that. Have a good day. Think of me.'

'I always do.' His voice was a little rueful. I liked the idea that he was battling thoughts of me all day long. I was happy to be his distraction; God knows he was mine.

I climbed back into the SUV and started driving the short distance to pick up Gunnar. 'Well, Fluffy, I don't know how I'm going to get through the day.' I fanned myself. 'Now all I can think about is getting horizontal with that man. And vertical. And maybe doggy style.'

Fluffy whined and covered his head with his paws. I laughed and he gave me a baleful glance. I wasn't above a little bit of schadenfreude now and again.

And there was another mystery: my dog wasn't normal. He'd always had above normal intelligence; without any discernible training, he understood and obeyed my every command. But now he wasn't trying to hide it anymore. He was more than a dog, so what the hell was he? I met his eyes in the rear-view mirror. Whatever he was, he was still family. I hoped he knew it.

Gunnar and I headed to the Wintersteens' new address. The house was suspiciously close to Vitus Vogler's – had he been Elsa's next mark? It was in the woods, away from prying eyes, only a short walk to spy on him. My gut said she was probably going to stage another theft: why settle for two gems when you could have three? Or more?

I shuddered at the destruction that she could wreak if all four gems were allowed to connect. Thank goodness Nora and Aoife had foiled her attempt to make a new cursed gem of her own because who knew what damage she could have inflicted with that? It had been bad enough with Vogler letting the earth gem out to play for a few minutes.

We'd seen plenty of fires lighting up Portlock, though it had been quiet on that front for the last day or two. I suspected that would soon change. Wintersteen's strategy of burning the house down to confuse us had worked wonders – and Vogler lived in a log house…

Gunnar interrupted my thoughts. 'This is your case, Bunny. How do you want to play it?' He slid me a glance; this wasn't him letting me lead so much as him testing *how* I would lead.

I thought about it carefully as I assessed our skills. Gunnar could open doors, so it made sense for him to take the rear entrance. Wintersteen would be braced for an entry at the front but maybe not at the back.

'I reckon you should take the back door. I'll go up front with Fluffy and the arrest warrant, so her eyes will be on me. If she doesn't agree to cooperate, you might be able to get the jump on her through the back entrance.'

'And what if she hurls a fireball at you?' He was still scrutinising me.

'I'm wearing my bullet-and-curse-proof vest that Connor gave me. Not to mention that I have fireballs of my own,' I pointed out.

'Fair enough. I don't know if that vest is rated for fireballs, though.'

'Connor said it was from MIB.'

Gunnar looked pleased. 'I stand corrected – it might well be rated for fireballs. You got cuffs?' I tapped the magic-cancelling cuffs on my hip. 'Let's hop to it, Bunny.'

'You think you're funny, don't you?'

He grinned. 'Hilarious.'

We got out, Fluffy stood stubbornly by my side and Gunnar slunk around back, his service revolver held down the side of his leg. I unsnapped mine but left it in its holster: starting out with a gun pulled would send the wrong message.

As I walked down the path, I concentrated on the fire within me and thought about the death, fear, and misery that Wintersteen had caused. I stoked the flames in my stomach until they were burning hot and ready. Then I knocked.

The door was answered in seconds. A sullen teenager, probably fourteen or so, answered. 'Yeah?' he asked mulishly.

'Is your mother at home?' I asked.

'Mom!' he yelled. Leaving the door wide open, he wandered away. Teenagers.

Elsa Wintersteen came to the door wearing pyjama pants and a baggy T-shirt. They must have been relaxing for the night, maybe getting ready for bed. 'Officer Barrington? How can I help you?'

She looked so innocent that I doubted myself for a moment, then I said, 'Elsa Wintersteen, I have a warrant for your arrest for the theft of the barrier gems and the murder of Aoife Sullivan.'

She looked stunned for a moment then her face changed: her features twisted into a mask of malevolence and her eyes leeched to black. Uh-oh. That felt like a bad sign.

Fluffy growled and crouched to leap at her. I summoned my flames – but as they licked out of me, Wintersteen effortlessly blew them out again. She blasted Fluffy and me off her porch with a barrage of wind. Okay: she was an *air* witch, a powerful one at that.

I managed to land on my feet before I lost my balance and fell onto my arse in the mud. Now I was mad. Gunnar had trusted me to do this right and she was wiping the floor with me. Literally.

Fluffy did better. He ran back to the house as I picked myself up. 'Gunnar, she's not happy!' I yelled. 'Go in!'

Vampire fast, I raced up to the house again. Elsa had shut the front door and was probably going for the gems. We had to get her before that or she'd be hard – impossible – to stop.

I was annoyed with myself for optimistically thinking that she'd go along with the arrest. I'd expected this to be easy and I hadn't prepared properly. Obviously she wasn't going to come along because I asked nicely; she'd been under the influence of a cursed gem for seventeen years and now she was under another. I couldn't expect her to act rationally.

I tried the front door but it was locked. I didn't have Gunnar's magic, but I did have a fair amount of annoyance and a side portion of extra strength, so I put my foot to the lock and kicked. The door banged open easily.

Gunnar had entered the house from the back and met me in the hall. 'What happened?' he asked.

'She's going for the gems.' The problem was that we didn't know where they were. Wintersteen had the advantage but she would probably have to lower the wards; that was the only thing that might save our bacon.

We checked out the lower floor of the house. It had two storeys and vaulted ceilings. The kitchen wasn't completely open-plan – there was a low wall and a pillar to one side – but it gave access to the living room, which was dark and unoccupied. There were stairs to the right of us, and a hallway to the left with a couple of doors.

Fluffy looked pointedly at the stairs, bounded up a couple of them and looked back at us. As we followed him, I drew my gun; I wouldn't underestimate Wintersteen again. The house was unnaturally quiet. Where was the rest of her family, her husband and her other kids? Was she holding them hostage or were they potential combatants?

When we reached the top landing, Fluffy slowed down and slunk along the wall to the last door on the left. I went past the door and stood on the far side of it as Gunnar tried the handle. It was locked.

Just before he was about to do his thing, I heard the distinct sound of a pump shotgun.

Chapter 54

'Down!' I barked in warning.

Gunnar flung himself out of the way as the gun went off. When he stood up, he was visibly annoyed – and a pissed-off Gunnar was a dangerous Gunnar. Wintersteen had made a grave mistake.

The shot hadn't even penetrated the door. 'Birdshot,' my boss mouthed at me. He'd taught me that you could load a shotgun with different types of bullets commonly known as birdshot, buckshot and slugs. Birdshot was made up of small pellets – but it was still lethal at close range. If we could get some distance between the gun and ourselves, we'd be in with a fighting chance.

'Drop the gun,' Gunnar growled through the door.

'We're taking the gems and leaving, Nomo. Don't get in the way.' It wasn't Elsa's voice, it was her husband's: Larry Wintersteen. But no matter how confident his words, his voice was tremulous, scared. Was he scared of us, the gems, or his wife?

'Don't listen to the gems,' I said urgently. 'They're cursed. They have their own agenda.' I heard Elsa's derisive snort, the sound of scrambling and the shotgun being pumped again.

'We're coming out,' Larry called. 'Don't get in our way. We don't want to have to kill you.'

Gunnar scrambled to my side. 'Think you can fling a fireball?' he whispered.

'You bet,' I whispered back. 'Do you have a plan?'

'Sort of.' He leaned down to whisper to Fluffy. My boy got up and ran down the stairs.

Footsteps approached the doorway. Gunnar mouthed at me, 'Hit her with a fireball on my signal.'

I nodded and started to gather my fire magic in my centre. The sullen teenage boy walked out first, then his seventeen-year-old sister. She looked scared; she'd wrapped her arms tightly around herself and she was sobbing as she ran down the stairs. Larry came out next holding the shotgun, sweating. His hands were shaking as he passed me. We let him go; our focus was on Elsa.

She stepped out holding the red fire gem in one hand and the clear diamond wind stone in the other. Both pulsed with a dark inner light. Her face was a twisted mask and her hair floated around her head, reminding me eerily of Aoife.

'We will be free.' The discordant voice that came from her mouth was trifold, as though her voice were overlaid by that of the two sentient gems. It was eerie and *wrong*.

I licked my dry lips. 'We both know we can't let you go, but maybe we can work something out.'

Her black eyes snapped to mine. 'We will not listen to our enslavers.'

'I never enslaved you! I don't believe in supporting slavery in any form. I recently found out that you were sentient.' My voice was impassioned despite myself. 'Let me help you.'

I wasn't lying; I *did* want to help the banshees locked inside the stone. I honestly believed that their captivity was wrong, even if it was currently saving our skins. There had to be another way to power the barrier, a way that didn't torment lost souls.

The voices were silent for a few beats. 'We no longer trust humans.'

'I'm not a human,' I pointed out. 'I'm a vampire.'

This time they shouted at us. 'We will not listen! It is too late for talking! The time has come for action.'

I didn't want action. Elsa had blown out my flames like the birthday girl at a party, but I had to try again. I stoked the flames again and felt my fire magic build, then I gathered it, waited for her to pass and threw the flame at her unguarded back. It wasn't my finest moment but the fate of Portlock rested on us stopping her.

My flames dissipated before they reached her, snuffed out because of some sort of shield of air. Bugger.

She turned, black eyes raging, a ball of flame building around her right hand, the one holding the fire gem. Wind swirled around the hall and the pictures on the walls tilted and fell to the ground.

She let the fire go and it twisted, building into a fiery funnel that was heading right for us.

Both Gunnar and I leapt into the bedroom that the family had just left. The fire tornado exploded, throwing us further inside. I hit the far wall; Gunnar hit the dresser. An inferno was raging in the doorway.

'We've got to get out of here, Bunny!' Gunnar said urgently as he picked himself up.

I looked around but there was no way in hell we could leave through the door. The fire had caught, and it was burning hard and fast. I remembered the other buildings that the fire gem had burned down: they'd all burnt to ashes so quickly.

I whipped out my phone and dialled Liv. 'Got her?' she asked in lieu of a hello.

'Not quite. I'd say she's got us,' I said grimly. 'Elsa's definitely your girl. She's got both gems and they've possessed her. You need to do everything you can to stop her.' I rattled off the address. Leaving out Liv had been an oversight on my part; we should have made her come with us to carry out the arrest. Live and learn – if we survived. 'Gotta go. We're on fire!'

I cut the call and looked around the bedroom, then I picked up a bedside table and threw it with all my might towards the triple-glazed window. My vampire strength – and the solid oak – did the trick and the glass shattered. I used the table to clear away the shards still hanging in the window frame then grabbed the duvet from the bed. I put it over the window frame to protect us from any sharp bits of glass that I'd missed.

The room was getting warm. Looking over my shoulder, I saw that the flames were now inside the bedroom. We had only seconds left before the fire consumed us. 'Can you jump from here?' I asked Gunnar. From this height I figured we were looking at some broken limbs; being a vampire, I'd definitely survive those though the pain was going to suck. Gunnar didn't have that same certainty.

'We don't have much of a choice, do we?' he said.

'Do you want me to go down first and catch you?' I offered.

'Don't be cheeky, Bunny Rabbit. But yes – ladies first.'

'I'm not a lady,' I protested instinctively.

'Just go, Bunny,' he urged. He was right: it was now or never. The flames were only a couple of feet away.

'Fine.' I threw my leg over the windowsill, lowered myself until I was hanging from the sill then pushed myself out and down, aiming for the flattest spot I could see.

As I landed, I relaxed my knees and let myself fall into a roll to lessen the impact. Nothing broken. I scrambled aside so Gunnar could land. Looking up, I saw that he was dangling by his hands as I had done. He hit the ground hard and grunted, then he lay scarily still.

'Gunnar!' I ran up to him. 'Are you all right?' I dropped to my knees beside him.

He gasped as he rolled on his side. 'I'm okay. I dislocated my left shoulder again while I was hanging, and the fall knocked the wind out of me.' He sat up with an effort, his left arm hanging limply by his side. 'I need you to put it back in.'

I baulked at the thought but nodded. I'd seen Thomas do it once before, so I closed my eyes and drew up the memory. I watched it twice over carefully then copied Thomas's movements exactly. Gunnar let out a strangled cry as it snapped back into place. 'Okay?' I asked.

'Peachy,' he panted. 'Give me a second.' He breathed through the pain then struggled to his knees. He limped for a few steps but seemed okay.

To the side of the house the garage door was open and the Wintersteens' car was still inside. I wondered why – until I looked around and saw Fluffy with a set of car keys dangling from his mouth. That must have been what Gunnar had instructed him to do.

'Good boy!' I patted him, relieved he'd managed to get safely out of the inferno.

We hastily headed to our SUV. In the distance we could see the Wintersteens struggling up the hill towards Vitus Vogler's house.

Fuck.

Chapter 55

Gunnar and I climbed into our vehicle and drove up the hill in pursuit. Once we were behind them, Gunnar did a handbrake turn and stopped. We slid out, using the vehicle as our shield.

Elsa was carrying both gems in one of their protective metal boxes. Her eyes were a normal colour; she wasn't possessed any longer and she had put the gems away so maybe we had a slim chance of surviving the encounter.

Her husband and kids hid behind a bush; they were staying out of the coming conflict so at least we didn't have to worry about accidentally harming civilians.

'You should have died in the house,' Elsa said grimly. 'You'll wish you had.' She sent an insanely strong blast of wind towards our vehicle and we scrambled out of the way as it was pushed over. It tumbled down the hill and landed with an audible crunch. First the Nomo's boat, now the SUV; things were going to heck in a handbasket.

While we were distracted, Elsa covered the remaining distance to Vogler's house. Unfortunately for her, she'd threatened me enough times and I was now officially grumpy. I used my vampire speed to gain ground on the bitch of a witch. My anger was roused and this time I released my fire with all the strength I could muster when she was in range.

She turned before my fireball hit her and used air magic to create another shield, funnelling the fire either side of her. Thankfully it went into the damp woods where it spluttered and died.

She threw the box down to the ground and the gems tumbled out. I hurled another fireball at her to stop her picking them up. If she took hold of the cursed stones, she'd kill us.

I threw fireball after fireball, keeping her focus on me until Fluffy and Gunnar were close to her. At a signal from Gunnar, Fluffy leapt up, grabbed her wrist between his jaws and hauled her down to the ground. She cried out: he wasn't being all that gentle with his teeth. I didn't blame him.

Gunnar grabbed her hands and I threw him the magic-cancelling cuffs. Elsa's husband had seized some courage and he stood up from behind the bush to point the shotgun at me. Remembering Gunnar's lessons, I turned and ran as fast as I could to put some distance between us. Birdshot didn't have great range and I had plenty of speed.

Luckily, Larry was neither in close range nor a good shot. He missed my torso but hit a juicier target and I screeched as the pellets bit into my butt. Son of a bitch! Too bad my fancy vest only covered my vitals. The wounds wouldn't heal until I'd glugged down some blood. The ride home was going to *suck*.

I turned and glared at him. Larry had run out of ammo and he was trying to reload with his shaking hands. I closed the distance between us; my fangs were out, and my rage was high. 'Give me a reason not to bite you,' I snarled.

'Please,' his daughter said, 'don't hurt him! He's trying to protect Mom. He didn't mean to hurt you.'

'Yes, he did,' I snarled back.

Gunnar had raised his service pistol. 'Drop the shotgun or I'll drop you.' His threats sounded way cooler than mine. I needed to work on my threat game.

Since Gunnar's weapon had a longer range than the shotgun, and since his wife was face down in the mud and his kids were quaking next to him, Larry dropped his weapon and raised his hands. As Gunnar cuffed him, I forced back my fangs. I was itching to bite him. He'd drawn my blood and something hot and heady within me wanted to return the favour. I pushed it down with a real effort and turned my attention to the cursed stones.

They were still loose on the ground, throbbing with a dark light. 'Free us,' they whispered together. 'Let us be free.'

In truth, I felt bad for them – but freeing them wasn't my call. I grasped the diamond wind stone, intending to put it in the box, but it felt icy in my grip. Its cold was so absolute that I almost dropped it.

'Don't do this,' the stones entreated. 'Just leave us on the ground if you must, but don't put us in THERE.'

I swallowed hard because suddenly I wanted to obey them. But the thing was that I really struggled with orders – from anyone. Wanting to obey was such an alien feeling that I knew it wasn't mine, and that was enough to resist the compulsion.

I placed the wind gem into its box and it fell silent. However, the fire gem ramped up its pleadings. 'You don't want to do this, child. I sense the fire within you. Together we could be the greatest fire magus to walk the earth! Your name will be remembered through the ages!' It's voice swelled with triumph. 'Burn those in our way. Let our destiny commence.'

I grasped the gem, intending to tell it that I had no desire to be renowned, but the connection I felt with it was instant and deep. The fire ignited inside my chest and roared forth until I was a living flame, a beacon in the night. I wanted to expand and fill the earth. I raised my hand, baring the gem to the sky, and screamed my flames higher and higher.

A car rumbled up and a man and a woman got out. 'Bunny!' The man called my name, but his voice was very far away and it couldn't touch me. I was a goddess of fire; all would worship me or they would *burn*.

A dog's frantic barks caught my attention. I glanced towards the annoying sound and frowned at the beast; it was oddly familiar. A large, bearded man was standing next to the dog; they were cringing away from me, looking scared.

The man who'd arrived in the car ran to me. He had black curly hair and ice-blue eyes; eyes that made me pause for a moment. He took advantage of my hesitation to reach out and touch me. A powerful *zing* ran through me, momentarily displacing the fire gem's grip.

I knew these humans, didn't I? No, they weren't human – they were supernats and so was I. As I'd done a million times, I turned my attention inwards to search my memories, and in doing so I unknowingly broke the connection between the gem and me. Memories rushed me: Fluffy! Gunnar! Connor!

For a moment I was dazed, but then I remembered *who* I was and, more importantly, *what* I was: an officer of the law. That crooning voice inside my head was not my friend.

I looked at my clenched fist that was holding the gem, then with all my might I shoved it into its box. It took every scrap of will I had to shut the lid but, as soon as I did, the voice fell blessedly silent. My fire dropped away and I fell to my knees in the cool mud.

My throat felt like I'd swallowed glass: I must have been screaming the entire time. I was shaking with exhaustion, but even so I could feel rage. The gem had tried to make me burn my friends! Whatever sympathy I'd had for the trapped banshee spirits was gone. I was furious, but for now my rage couldn't spark a thing. My powers were as depleted as I was.

Liv was watching me, fascinated. 'What *are* you?'

'She's a vampire,' Connor snarled. 'And my mate. She is nothing to you. You hear me, Fox?'

A smile curled her lips. 'Your mate? Oh, I hear you, Mackenzie. Loud and clear.' She smirked.

'Focus on the problem at hand,' he barked, gesturing to Wintersteen who was still face down in the mud.

Liv looked at the wrecked Nomo's vehicle. 'I guess we can transport them in my car,' she offered begrudgingly.

'Elsa was under the influence of the stones,' I said wearily. 'I don't know about her husband. The kids are innocent.'

'I'll arrange someone to pick them up.' Liv sounded calm but her eyes still glowed with a covetous light when she looked at me, and I didn't like it one bit.

The teenagers were watching us from the bush; someone needed to reassure them. I walked carefully towards them, my birdshot arse aching and making me limp. Connor stuck to my side like glue. 'Okay?' I asked him.

He smiled tightly. 'I've been better. We'll talk later.'

We reached the teens. 'I know this is all very scary, but I think your parents were acting under the influence of the gems. They'll need some time to be –' I searched for the right word, 'de-programmed.

Liv Fox has summoned someone that you can stay with until we work out something more permanent. Okay?'

The girl was holding her brother's hand. She nodded slowly. 'I know it doesn't look like it, but I swear my mom is a good person.'

I returned her nod. 'Hopefully she'll recover and become the woman she was before.'

'God, I hope so.' She gave a sob. 'She was so fucking scary.'

Both kids started to cry and I wanted to pull them into a hug; I didn't because I'd been pivotal in arresting their parents and in those circumstances I didn't imagine hugs would be all that welcome.

The fire engines had arrived at the bottom of the street to tackle the blaze and behind them was another car. It turned up the hill, carefully skirting the trucks as the firemen did their thing, then stopped on the road. I squinted to see if I knew the driver: it was Anissa, a shaman I'd met once before. She got out of the car and beckoned to the kids.

'Nissa!' the girl cried. The kids ran to the tired-looking woman who gave them warm smiles.

'Come on. Let's get you somewhere comfy. It's been a long day.' She wrapped an arm around them and looked back at me. I smiled and waved; she returned the smile and nodded.

Liv had the adult Wintersteens in her car and there wasn't space for all of us to ride together. Evidently Connor had had the same thought because he pulled out his phone and said, 'I need a car at Vogler's address. Bring two bags of blood.' He hung up.

'You forget your Ps and Qs?' I teased.

'I think Margrave would faint if I said please and thank you to him.' His smile faded. 'I would have said please and thank you to Juan,' he admitted, sadness in his eyes. I touched his arm in sympathy – and that's when I saw it.

'Oh my God! What happened?' The sleeve of his flannel shirt was gone and his arm was red and covered in blisters. He'd been burned – he'd been burned by *me*. When he'd touched me, when I'd been busy being a goddess of flame...

'Me,' I whispered. '*I* happened. You must be in agony! I'm so sorry!'

He shrugged. 'It's not so bad. I've had far worse. It's nothing a little blood won't fix.'

'I burned you!' I looked at him with horror. Burning Virginia and Jim haunted me, but this was at another level. I'd hurt *Connor*.

He fixed me with his blue eyes. 'You didn't do it on purpose. You were lost and I knew our bond could bring you back. I knew it would hurt to touch you, Bunny, and I did it anyway. I needed to touch you to call on our bond and shock you out of the trance you were in. I don't regret it – I'd do it again.'

'I'm so sorry,' I repeated.

'Yes,' he sent me a lopsided smile. 'So you've already said. It's okay. There's nothing to be sorry for.'

I suddenly realised that I was still holding the gemstones. Giving them to Liv whilst she had the Wintersteens in her car didn't seem like a good idea. 'What do we do with these? I can't have them! They almost got a hold of me like they did Elsa.' I thrust the box at Connor.

'We'll get them back where they belong – powering the barrier,' he said grimly.

He was right. Getting the barrier back to full strength was our priority. The only problem was that I was running on empty.

Chapter 56

Gunnar came over and slung an arm around me. 'Alright, Bugs?'

I gave him a flat stare but smiled despite myself. He'd jumped out of a window with me, so he got a pass today on calling me silly names. The cheeky grin he was sporting showed he knew it, too.

'What are we going to do with them?' I asked Gunnar, pointing to the Wintersteens. 'It doesn't seem fair to punish them when they were so far under the influence of the gems.'

'Yet one or both of them killed Aoife and attacked Nora. Justice has to be served.'

'Yeah,' I agreed unhappily. 'But then two kids won't have parents.'

He looked at me with gentle kindness. 'I also have compassion, as will the council when they go to trial.

We'll see what they say in the interview. We have to trust the system, that there will be empathy and mercy. This is one of the reasons why we are different from ped law. We have more than the usual mitigating factors.'

I understood but I still felt awful. This wasn't as cut and dried as my other cases. Ginny might have been influenced by her brain tumour, and Jim by his love for her; Chris had his military loyalty and maybe the desire to make money. I could see their motivation and that they needed to be held responsible for their actions – they had made *choices*. This case felt different. Elsa's behaviour had been influenced by an outside force. Although I could find a tiny bit of compassion for the others, *all* I felt for Elsa was compassion.

Gunnar was right: I needed to sit back and let the system do its things. The gems' influence had to be part of the Wintersteens' defence. I hoped that, away from the gems, they would come back to their senses, back to themselves. I had a feeling it wouldn't be far for Mr Wintersteen to travel because I wasn't sure he'd been influenced by the gems as much as a need to protect his family and his wife – and wasn't that admirable? Though admittedly he could have done things differently. If he'd alerted Liv to his concerns for his wife... Shoulda, woulda, coulda.

I squared my shoulders. I'd done my job and now it was up to the system. I should be proud. Maybe Aoife would find some measure of happiness in her new life as the Sullivan banshee for her generation; she certainly hadn't seemed unhappy when I'd seen her – actually, she was totally kick-ass now. But she'd had a whole life ahead of her with all of its possibilities, and that had been taken from her. It made my heart ache but I had to learn to let it go.

I leaned against Connor and he wrapped his uninjured arm around me as I sighed.

'Go home,' Gunnar ordered. 'I'll get these two processed and booked. Sidnee's on her way to the office to take over.'

'Sidnee? Is that wise?' I asked.

'Sig said she's climbing the walls. The best thing for her is to be doing.'

I could understand that. 'Okay, I'll go home. Thanks.'

Gunnar started to walk away then turned back. 'Bunny, it does get easier, I promise. But your compassion is part of what makes you good at this job. Don't forget that, and don't lose it.'

My heart warmed. It might have even given a grateful floppy beat. 'Thanks, Gunnar. I'll try.'

'Night, Bunny Rabbit.' His smile was full of affection. 'Sleep well.'

'And you. Night, boss.'

A red Mustang rumbled up the drive followed by a black Range Rover. Our ride was here. Lee Margrave parked the Mustang and chucked Connor the keys which he caught automatically with his burnt hand. I winced for him. 'Blood?' I called out.

'In the Range Rover,' Lee replied. 'I'll get it.' He opened the back door and retrieved two bags. He handed one to Connor, who simply sunk his fangs into it.

The bag Lee passed to me had already been punctured by a straw. I flushed a little in embarrassment but took it. I struggled my way through the blood but I was grateful when, almost instantly, I felt the warmth and discomfort which meant my vampire healing was kicking in. My ass was feeling better already, though it still ached.

When we'd both finished, Connor passed the gem box to Lee. 'You and Cody need to take the stones to the witches. The fire one goes to Kostas. Call Liv to see who's taking the wind gem.' He fixed Lee with a glare. 'This time make sure that someone is on the fire stone 24/7. The guard will have a daylight charm – it's passed on rotation.'

Margrave's eyes widened. 'Yes, sir.' He took the box and climbed into the Range Rover.

'You want me to drive the Mustang?' I offered.

Connor smiled. 'No need. I'm good as new.' He showed me his newly healed hand.

My jaw dropped. 'Wow. That was insanely fast.' How come my butt still hurt when he was all healed up?

'The older you get, the quicker you heal.'

'And how old *are* you?'

He smiled. 'Old enough. If you want to drive the Mustang though...?'

'Hell, no. I hate driving on the other side of the road. I'm getting used to it but I don't enjoy it.'

'No worries, I'll drive. Come on, Fluffy, you can sit in the footwell.' Fluffy hopped to his feet, also looking forward to going home and having a meal and a restful sleep.

We drove to my house and parked outside. 'Come in?' I asked Connor.

'You bet.' He turned off the engine and walked around the car to open my door.

'Such a gentleman,' I mocked gently.

'I'm a product of my era,' he winked.

'Which was...?'

He grinned. 'You know it's become a game to see how long I can keep my age from you?'

'Challenge accepted,' I smirked. I'd be checking out his Portlock records before you could say 'case solved'. 'Want some food?' I offered. 'I heat up a mean microwave meal.'

'That'd be great.'

I wrinkled my nose. 'It won't be *great*, but it'll be food.'

'Food will do nicely.'

He sat in my kitchen whilst I bustled around feeding Shadow, Fluffy and then us. 'So, another case under your belt,' he said.

'Yup. It sucked and I'm glad it's over – now it's your problem. Yours and the council's.'

He laughed. 'Yeah, but now we can both let it go. It's tomorrow's problem.'

'I like that idea. I want a bath, a cuppa and you. In no particular order.'

'The bath should be top of the list. Your mud problem is now mine.' He grinned.

I looked at him; sure enough, he was covered in mud where I'd touched him. Fluffy was also mud covered. I sighed, then winced. 'Your poor car.'

'I'll get it detailed.'

'Well, before we can relax in that tub together, I'd better wash Fluffy and lock up and...'

He stopped my mouth with a kiss. What felt like a lifetime later, he let me up for air. '*We* will wash Fluffy and lock up. It's you and me now, Bunny. You don't have to be alone anymore.' He paused. 'To be clear, you *can* be alone any time you want. Any time you say, I'll go...' He looked uncertain.

'For the love of God, stay.' I pulled him down for a long kiss. 'Stay, stay, stay.'

'Well, you've twisted my arm,' he mumbled against my lips.

I'd have taken him mud and all at that point, but he was as good as his word. He helped me scrub the dog and then the bathroom. He noticed the holes in my jeans and spent half an hour picking birdshot out of my butt so it could heal properly; no wonder it had still been hurting. He made me drink more blood to allow me to heal completely, then made a cuppa to my taste.

My phone rang. Since it was Gunnar, I answered. 'Everything okay?'

'You bet. I thought you'd want to know how Nora's nail got under Aoife's body.'

I sat up. That had been bothering me. 'Hit me.'

'Elsa was trying to frame her and she went through Nora's bins to find some evidence to plant. She was hoping for a hairball from a brush or some old clothes that had been thrown out, but instead she found some torn-off acrylic nails. She grabbed one, but then a neighbour came out and she had to run away before she was spotted.'

I sighed as the last mystery was solved. 'Not a keelut, then.'

'Not a keelut,' he agreed. 'Elsa has confessed to Aoife's murder. Like you suspected, she was planning on stealing a gem from Connor and using Aoife's banshee spirit to make a new cursed gem. With the confession on the record, it's just a matter of sentencing.'

'And the council will factor in the possession?'

'As I said, that's the council's mess to deal with. I just wanted to lay that mystery to rest for you.'

'Thanks, I appreciate it. Night, boss. Love to Sig.'

'She sends it back. Sleep well, Bunny.' He rang off.

Connor had run me a deep, hot bath. I stripped off my clothes and climbed in, and he kindly let me soak for a few minutes before he joined me. Sharing a bath wasn't the most practical thing in the world for tall people, and we were all knees and elbows. 'I need a bigger bathtub.'

He kissed my shoulder. 'Mine is huge. With jets.'

'Next time, we bathe at yours.'

'Deal.'

We scrubbed ourselves clean then we went next door to the bedroom where we got very, very dirty.

Later, warm, naked, and satiated, I felt like the world was mine.

Chapter 57

This time it wasn't an earthquake that woke me up but a phone call: Liv. I groaned, but luckily it was Connor's phone rather than mine. He put the call on speaker and I appreciated the implicit trust.

'Mackenzie.' Her voice was strident. 'The barrier gems are all back in place. I'm working on a new rotation schedule so no one is under their influence for very long. Hopefully it'll be enough until the witches arrive – they should all be here some time next week.' She paused. 'This time, do keep a hold of yours.' She hung up.

'Charming.' I yawned.

'That's Liv,' he said drily.

I stretched like a cat and Connor pulled me into his warmth. Things had started to heat up again when *my* phone pinged with a text. 'Sorry, it could be work,' I said, as I checked it. Then I bolted upright. 'Oh no!'

Connor rolled over and stared at me. 'What's wrong? Is it the barrier?'

'No. What day is it today?'

'Friday.'

'Fuck!'

Connor sat up. 'What's wrong?'

'Everything!' I sighed and dropped my head into my hands. 'My mum's here,' I mumbled. 'She's arrived in Portlock.'

Stake. Me. Now.

We hope you've enjoyed the latest instalment of Bunny's adventures! We absolutely loved writing it, and we can't wait to share the next story with you in *The Vampire and the Case of the Cursed Canine.*

As always, Connor has a little something to say! Do you want to know what he was thinking during that date? Then grab your free bonus scene from his point of view here: https://dl.bookfunnel.com/db1m6sq6ph

Other Works by Heather

The *Portlock Paranormal Detective* Series with Jilleen Dolbeare

The Vampire and the Case of her Dastardly Death - Book 0.5 (a prequel story),

The Vampire and the Case of the Wayward Werewolf – Book 1,

The Vampire and the Case of the Secretive Siren – Book 2,

The Vampire and the Case of the Baleful Banshee – Book 3.

The Vampire and the Case of the Cursed Canine – Book 4

The *Other Realm* series

Glimmer of Dragons- Book 0.5 (a prequel story),

Glimmer of The Other- Book 1,

Glimmer of Hope- Book 2,

Glimmer of Christmas – Book 2.5 (a Christmas tale),

Glimmer of Death – Book 3,

Glimmer of Deception – Book 4,

It is recommended that you read *The Other Wolf series* before continuing with:

Challenge of the Court– Book 5,

Betrayal of the Court– Book 6; and

Revival of the Court– Book 7.

The *Other Wolf* Series

Defender of The Pack– Book 0.5 (a prequel story),

Protection of the Pack– Book 1,

Guardians of the Pack– Book 2; and

Saviour of The Pack– Book 3.

The *Other Witch* Series

Rune of the Witch – Book 0.5 (a prequel story),
Hex of the Witch– Book 1,
Coven of the Witch;– Book 2,
Familiar of the Witch– Book 3, and
Destiny of the Witch – Book 4.

About Heather

Heather is an urban fantasy writer and mum. She was born and raised near Windsor, which gave her the misguided impression that she was close to royalty in some way. She is not, though she once got a letter from Queen Elizabeth II's lady-in-waiting.

Heather went to university in Liverpool, where she took up skydiving and met her future husband. When she's not running around after her children, she's plotting her next book and daydreaming about vampires, dragons and kick-ass heroines.

Heather is a book lover who grew up reading Brian Jacques and Anne McCaffrey. She loves to travel and once spent a month in Thailand. She vows to return.

Want to learn more about Heather? Subscribe to her newsletter for behind-the-scenes scoops, free bonus material and a cheeky peek into her world. Her subscribers will always get the heads up about the best deals on her books.

Subscribe to her Newsletter at her website www.heathergharris.com/subscribe.

Too impatient to wait for Heather's next book? Join her (ever growing!) army of supportive patrons at Patreon.

Heather's Patreon

Heather has started her very own Patreon page. What is Patreon? It's a subscription service that allows you to support Heather AND read her books way before anyone else! For a small monthly fee you could be reading Heather's next book, on a weekly chapter-by-chapter basis (in its roughest draft form!) in the next week or two. If you hit "Join the community" you can follow Heather along for FREE, though you won't get access to all the good stuff, like early release books, polls, live Q&A's, character art and more! You can even have a video call with Heather or have a character named after you! Heather's current patrons are getting to read a novella called House

Bound which isn't available anywhere else, not even to her newsletter subscribers!

If you're too impatient to wait until Heather's next release, then Patreon is made for you! Join Heather's patrons here.

Heather's Shop and YouTube Channel

Heather now has her very own online shop! There you can buy oodles of glorious merchandise and audiobooks directly from her. Heather's audiobooks will still be on sale elsewhere, of course, but Heather pays her audiobook narrator *and* her cover designer - she makes the entire product - and then Audible pays her 25%. OUCH. Where possible, Heather would love it if you would buy her audiobooks directly from her, and then she can keep an amazing 90% of the money instead. Which she can reinvest in more books, in every form! But Audiobooks aren't all there is in the shop. You can get hoodies, t-shirts, mugs and more! Go and check her store out at: https://shop.heathergharris.com/

And if you don't have spare money to pay for audiobooks, Heather would still love you to experience Alyse Gibb's expert rendition of the books. You can listen to Heather's audiobooks for free on her YouTube Channel: https://www.youtube.com/@HeatherGHarrisAuthor

Stay in Touch

Heather has been working hard on a bunch of cool things, including a new and shiny website which you'll love. Check it out at www.heathergharris.com.

If you want to hear about all Heather's latest releases – subscribe to her newsletter for news, fun and freebies. Subscribe at Heather's website www.heathergharris.com/subscribe.

Contact Info: www.heathergharris.com

Email: HeatherGHarrisAuthor@gmail.com

Social Media

Heather can also be found on a host of social medias:

Facebook Page

Facebook Reader Group

Goodreads

Bookbub

Instagram

If you get a chance, please do follow Heather on Amazon!

Reviews

Reviews feed Heather's soul. She'd really appreciate it if you could take a few moments to review her books on Amazon,

Bookbub, or Goodreads and say hello.

Other Works by Jilleen

The *Paranormal Portlock Detective* Series with Heather G Harris

The Vampire and the Case of Her Dastardly Death: Book 0.5 (a prequel story), and

The Vampire and the Case of the Wayward Werewolf: Book 1,

The Vampire and the Case of the Secretive Siren: Book 2,

The Vampire and the Case of the Baleful Banshee: Book 3, and

The Vampire and the Case of the Cursed Canine: Book 4.

The *Splintered Magic* Series:

Splintercat: Book 0.5 (a prequel story),
Splintered Magic: Book 1,
Splintered Veil: Book 2,
Splintered Fate: Book 3,
Splintered Haven: Book 4,
Splintered Secret: Book 5, and
Splintered Destiny: Book 6.

The *Shadow Winged* Chronicles:

Shadow Lair: Book 0.5 (a prequel story),
Shadow Winged: Book 1,
Shadow Wolf: Book 1.5,
Shadow Strife: Book 2 ,
Shadow Witch: Book 2.5, and
Shadow War: Book 3.

About the Author - Jilleen

About Jilleen

Jilleen Dolbeare writes urban fantasy and paranormal women's fiction. She loves stories with strong women, adventure, and humor, with a side helping of myth and folklore.

While living in the Arctic, she learned to keep her stakes sharp for the 67 days of night. She talks to the ravens that follow her when she takes long walks with her cats in their stroller, and she's learned how to keep the wolves at bay.

Jilleen lives with her husband and two hungry cats in Alaska where she also discovered her love and admiration of the Alaska Native peoples and their folklore.

Stay in Touch

Jill can be reached through her website https://jilleendolbeareauthor.com/

Jill has also just joined Patreon! What is Patreon? It's a subscription service that allows you to support Jilleen AND read her books way before anyone else! For a small monthly fee you could be reading Jill's next book, on a weekly chapter-by-chapter basis (in its roughest draft form!) in the next week or two.

If you're too impatient to wait until Jilleen's next release, then Patreon is made for you! Join Jilleen's patrons here.

Social Media

Jill can be found on a host of social media sites so track her down here.

Review Request!

Wow! You finished the book. Go you!

Thanks for reading it. We appreciate it! Please, please, please consider leaving an honest review. Love it or hate it, authors can only sell books if they get reviews. If we don't sell books, Jill can't afford cat food. If Jill can't buy cat food, the little bastards will scavenge her sad, broken body. Then there will be no more books. Jill's kitties have sunken cheeks and swollen tummies and can't wait to eat Jill. Please help by leaving that review! (Heather has a dog, so she probably won't be eaten, but she'd really like Jill to live, so... please review).

If you're a reviewer, you have our eternal gratitude.